For love and laughter, the

David F Burrows was born and raised in Suffolk. He lives there to this day with his wife Jenny. They have two grown up daughters and three grandchildren.

Having had a few short comedies published over the years David still looked on his writing as a relaxing fun hobby. Now that he is semi-retired he has had a lot more time to devote to his writing, resulting in the unique Fish Bone Alley Series of short stories.

To find out more about David and his work please visit his website at: **www.dfburrows.co.uk**

Fish Bone Alley

Series of short stories

Book 1

David F Burrows

Platen
Publishing

ISBN 978-1-9164050-0-4

Illustrations by Steve Royce Griffin
www.steveroycegriffin.co.uk

David F Burrows
www.dfburrows.co.uk

Published by Platen Publishing *an imprint of David F Burrows*

Contents

Fish Bone Alley

I am Detective Inspector Gerald Potter, known by the criminal fraternity as Jerry Pot. It is 1896 and a fine morning here in the slums of London. I am weaving my way towards the notorious Fish Bone Alley, where I am to meet Detective Sergeant Richard Head, while ignoring the stench, interminable din and endless 'pure' collectors scooping up buckets of steaming dung from the filthy cobbles.

I spy the Sergeant talking to a prostitute outside of Cheap Skates Emporium. Already there's several prostitutes hanging around, one's even hanging out of a third-storey window by her neck.

"Good morning, Sergeant," says I, stepping up.

"Morning, sir. I've just been talking to Flo here. That's her gran hanging about up there."

Flo smiles at me, displaying surprisingly white teeth, all four of them.

"You want anything me duck. I'm offering five minutes, then get five more for free."

"Not just now, thank you. I'm on duty.

"What about my Nan then, you buggers goin' to investigate her murder or what?"

"We are Scotland Yard; if it is murder we shall investigate, but if it is suicide we shall leave it to the plods."

Her eyes narrow, "It was murder alright! You come and see."

I check my fob-watch. Ten-thirty. "We are on an important case of stolen jewels and our chief won't be too happy if we deviate from our task just to investigate some dead old trollop."

Flo scowls at me, "She weren't just any ol' trollop, ya know! She's slept with aristocrats 'as my Nan."

"Come on then," relents I. "An hour or so won't matter much."

Flo leads the way, we keep on the pavement to avoid being flattened by the chaotic traffic, while risking being urinated on from above, until we reach the third terrace along where we enter and climb the stairs, stepping over drunks, drug addicts and homeless urchins. At the top of the landing there is a small crowd in front of the dead woman's bedsit, they move back as we come closer and we step into the room to find it has been ransacked.

"There she is!" yells Flo pointing to the window. "That's my Nan."

"The inspector can see that," grates Head as we step over the rope that's tied to an iron bedstead while the other end is, of course, noosed around the victim's neck. At the window we stick our heads out and look down at the victim. She is naked apart from a pair of woollen drawers. Her neck is well stretched, her face is twisted up from her death throws but apart from that she doesn't appear too bad, really.

"What is her name?" asks I of Flo.

"Mable Barns."

"How old is she?"

"I dunno. Fiftyish? Sixtyish?"

"I know," yells someone from the small crowd who have edged their way into the room for a better view.

"Come forward that person who yelled out," orders I.

An old crone hobbles in on her cane and snarls, "She's sixty-two. I know because I'm her muvva. And as her muvva, I claim everything she owns."

"Clear off you ol' cow," snaps Flo. "The only thing you ever gave birth to had four legs and grunted."

"Let's get them all out, Sergeant" orders I, and except for Flo we push the crowd out and Head slams the door shut.

"Right, Sergeant. Let's haul her up."

Leaning out the window we grab a sticky armpit each and start hauling the victim inside.

"She's nice and floppy, sir," comments Head. "Couldn't have been dead much more than an hour."

Suddenly Mable's drawers slip down her long legs, flip off her bony feet and float zig-zag down to the pavement below where an urchin leaps up and grabs them before anyone else can.

"Oi!" I yell. "Bring those up here. They are evidence."

"Piss off, copper," he yells back before sticking two fingers up and running off while sniffing at Mable's crotch.

Finally, we have Mable in the room laid out on her back on the bare floor boards and I loosen the rope around her neck, then to our horror her toothless mouth jerks open and there appears to be something lodged in her throat. I stick two fingers down her gaping orifice and extract a diamond ring. Holding it close to the light from the window I can see it is both stylish and expensive.

"It's a ring!" cries out Flo. "Can I 'ave it?"

"No. It is evidence," snaps I. "Now, tell me what you know."

"Um... About what?"

I wave an impatient arm around the room. "About this. The place is a mess. Someone or ones have been through the place searching, no doubt, for this ring." Mable's clothes lay torn and ripped by the bed and it is obvious she has been strip searched. "But, when they couldn't find the ring," I hold it up for a more dramatic effect, "they decided to send a 'don't cross us' message by hanging Mable out to dry. So, Flo, you better start talking."

She appears frightened and merely shrugs.

Head growls, "You better start talking Flo or it's down the yard for you."

"We don't need to go down the yard no more, Dick. We can use this place now Nan don't need it anymore."

"No. No," I snap. "What the Sergeant is saying is; start telling us what you know or you'll be arrested."

With a heavy sigh, she goes and sits down on the messed-up bed. "Alright. Alright. A pair of heavies stomped up the stairs an hour or so back. They were real bruisers. Nan was on her way to work and had just stepped out the room as I was coming up the stairs to meet her when the bruisers shoved me out the way and go for her. Nan tried to nip back inside but it was too late, they shoved her in the room, went in after her, and slammed the door behind them, then all hell breaks loose; Nan screams, there's lots of shouting, banging and thumping, lots of noise like things being thrown about and such. Then suddenly everything goes quiet for a bit, then there's these horrible screams echoing up the stairs and I figure the bruisers have just flung Nan out the window and she's landed on the pavement. I rush downstairs and outside where I see everyone's looking up, so I look up to see my Nan swinging about."

"What then?" asks Head.

"I rushed back in and up the stairs, but by the time I get there the bruisers had gone."

"Why didn't you send someone for the local plods?" asks I.

"I was goin' meself when I bumped into Dick. I mean Sergeant Head."

"But Mable's been hanging around for an hour or so," I remonstrate. "You should have left earlier."

"I had a couple of customers to see to. A girl 'as got to earn a living, Inspector. Life don't stop just because someone's been murdered, ya know."

"Obviously not," grates I. "Anyway, Sergeant, I spied a pair of uniformed plods coming up the alley when we were hauling Mable up, go and fetch them, we'll hand this over to them for now."

"Right away, sir," says he and leaves.

While he's gone I search the room for evidence, but find nothing of interest except for a photograph in a frame, I ask Flo, "Who are these five females in this photo?"

She points, "That's Nan, next to her is Ethel me ma, then it's me, I was about eight then, then that's me sister Beryl and next to her is Betty, she'd be about fifteen then and she's me ma's younger sister."

"When was this taken?"

"About twenty years back I reckon."

"I shall need the photo," says I, taking it from its frame. "I'll return it later."

"Make sure you do," she frowns. "It's precious." Suddenly she goes and gazes lovingly down at her gran and starts to sob, "I never knew my Nan had a belly-button," she laments. "Guess I never knew her at all, really."

Head returns with the plods. He introduces them as Sergeant Thomson and Constable Jones.

I tell them all I know, give them their orders and not to touch the body until they have informed forensics. I also inform them that I have the ring in my possession. I would have pocketed it but Flo witnessed my finding it. "We shall return once we have seen to other important business," says I.

Head and I head downstairs, out into the street and set off further down Fish Bone Alley.

"Now, Sergeant, did you get the photographs?"

"In this envelope, sir."

He hands me the envelope then swears as he steps into something squelchy. "Bloody horses!"

"Do not despair, Sergeant. We'll be rid of them in a few years or so. We'll all be on bicycles or riding around in horseless carriages. The air will be cleaner and the roads safer."

Hundreds of urchins are running about playing games, such as jump the piles of dollop, throw dollop at strangers, bat and dollop, or catch the dollop as it falls before anyone else gets it.

At last we're outside the Pawnbrokers. Proprietor: Bray Waunepcy, [I quickly solve the anagram in the name]. We enter the dark, smelly shop to a distinct sound of chopping. The place is crammed from floor to ceiling with all manner of rubbish. You can purchase anything from a chastity belt for horses to an expensive second-hand glass eye, cheaper if it's the wrong colour and even cheaper if it's cracked.

Waunepcy's behind his junked-up counter; a shrivelled up, rat-faced old fence with a stinking grey beard down to his stomach.

"Well, well," he drawls. "Inspector Jerry Pot and Sergeant Dick Head, no less. To what do I owe the honour?"

Head sweeps a load of junk and a headless cat off the counter and taking out the four-inch square photographs I begin showing them one by one to Waunepcy. "Fenced any of these?"

He studies the first one. "A diamond tiara. Nice."

I flick through the photographs, he shakes his head releasing dust and dead fleas from his beard.

"Diamond necklace," he salivates, "with matching earrings. Gold snuffbox." He goes through all the photos. "I ain't seen any of that gear, governor," squawks Waunepcy. "Honest I ain't. Nor 'ave I 'eard anything."

Strangely, I believe him. "Come on, Sergeant, let's go."

"Hang on a minute," demands Head. "Look at what's on that manikin, sir."

I follow his pointing finger and there in a junked-up corner is a headless manikin wearing Mable's drawers. "That was quick," says I. "Sergeant, bag those drawers."

"Um… Have you a bag, sir?"

"No. Waunepcy, have you got an old bag we can use?"

"She's upstairs having a kip. Help ya self."

Sometimes I despair of the human race, "Just stuff the drawers in your pocket, Sergeant, and let us get on."

"Oi! You going to pay for them goods?" demands Waunepcy.

"No. They are stolen items, think yourself lucky we don't arrest you."

Back out in the street I ask, "Sergeant, who at the palace gave you these photographs?"

"A tubby butler called Jeeves. He was waiting for me at the gates."

I scratch at the fleas beneath my hat, confusion reigns. "We should have had these a week ago when the jewels were first reported stolen so we knew exactly what we were searching for." Something is very wrong about all this. I extract the ring from my pocket. "One of the photos matched this ring, Sergeant. The question is; why on earth would it turn up in the gob of an old prostitute?"

"She stole it?" offers Head. "But from whom?"

"From someone she was hiding the jewels for; someone very important and very rich."

He shrugs. "What, like the Queen?"

"No!" I remonstrate. "She is beyond reproach. But that Edward, he's always short of readies. I reason we could be looking at an inside job. An insurance fiddle."

Head is aghast, "What! By the royals?"

"Quite possibly."

A lump of flying dollop suddenly knocks Head's bowler off. "Bloody kids," he swears, bending down to retrieve it, only he comes up also holding something disgusting. "Look, sir. A severed member!"

Gingerly I take the long grey object from him and hold it up to the light to peruse it. "It's just a rotten sausage. Someone must have dropped it."

An urchin jumps forward holding out a battered top-hat. "Got any eats, mister?"

"Good timing," says I and drops the slimy sausage into his hat.

"Cor, thanks mister, you're a real gent," beams the urchin before running off with his prize.

"You're too kind, sir," offers Head.

"It's my nature, Sergeant. Now, let's go to the palace and re-review the scene of the crime. But first I must stop off at home."

Presently, having left the cesspit of the slum behind, I enter my home while Head waits outside because he smells.

"You're home early, Detective Inspector?" quizzes my wife. "Anything wrong Detective Inspector?"

"I have come to pick something up," I tell her before going into the parlour and rummaging through the sideboard where I keep interesting articles and such. "Got it. Just what I need."

My wife sees me out. "What time do you want dinner, Detective Inspector?"

"What is it?"

"Beef balls in mash."

"Lovely. Say, dinner time."

Head and I catch a Hackney and shortly we're at the palace's servants' entrance, where a suited jobsworth shows us up to the stately room where the alleged crime took place. "According to the palace spokesman," I reiterate, "someone sneaked into the palace grounds, shinned up a drainpipe and onto the balcony, jemmied open the French doors, picked the safe and then made off with the jewels."

We go out onto the balcony and look down. "That's one heck of a climb, Sergeant," I muse.

"Yes, sir. Must have been a monkey. Or someone from a circus."

"Just one problem," I muse some more, "there isn't actually a drainpipe up to this balcony."

"Christ! How the hell did we miss that one?"

"Simple, this being about royalty we simply believed what we were told and didn't investigate properly."

We go back into the room where the jobsworth is waiting.

"Everything to your satisfaction, officers?" asks he snottily.

"No, it isn't," I counter, meeting his pompous stare with glowering menace. "Apparently, this Lady Apple-Pip, was staying in this room and was downstairs at the ball. When she finally came up she found the safe open and all her jewellery gone."

"That is correct," returned jobsworth. "But you know all this."

"True. Tell me, who exactly is this Lady Apple-Pip?"

"I cannot answer that."

I pace the room because my right leg's gone stiff. Taking out the article from inside my coat I wave it in his face. "I believe this Lady Apple-Pip is also known as Lady Marmalade, Lady Bird and several other ladies. In this article, it tells of several other similar robberies all over the country while listing the various insurance companies that have paid out accordingly. No one questions it because we are dealing with the aristocracy. Only, my investigations lead me to believe Lady Apple-Pip is not only not a lady, she is in-fact a high-class piece of pastry who hails from Fish Bone Alley and whose real name is Betty Barns!"

"Very clever," sneers jobsworth. "So, what now?"

"I shall expose myself and arrest her."

"You cannot. The establishment will crucify you rather than accept a royal exposure."

"Even so, I shall blow this case wide open and the press shall have a field day."

While clapping kid-gloved hands together the lady herself enters the room and glares at me. "Oh, so clever, Inspector. Shame you have no evidence."

I gawp at her. In truth, she is the most beautiful woman I have ever seen. And so hot her eyes could melt ice-cream, one kiss would burn your lips off and her heaving, barely covered bosom has such a deep cleavage you feel you could drop a round of bread into it and it would be toast in seconds.

I stroll over to her safe, which I noticed earlier wasn't fully closed, and swinging open the door reveals a pile of jewellery. "I dare say," I say daringly, "those jewels will match the photographs I have in my pocket. Am I correct?"

"So, what?" She laughs a scornful laugh. "I am untouchable. Ask Bertie if you don't believe me."

"Betty, I believe you about Bertie. For that is the essence of your scam, you deliberately select aristocrats that are cash poor and get them to collude with you, they get your services, plus a social disease, for free and you all make a tidy sum. Everyone's happy except for the insurance companies. As to you being untouchable, I'd say you've been more touched than Michelangelo's David."

"Perhaps. So, Inspector Potter, how did you come up with all this?"

I show her the ring. "Recognise this?"

"You know I do. Where did you find it?"

"Inside your mother's mouth just after I released the rope from her neck. The rope that a pair of thugs, no doubt employed by you, put there just before they tossed her out of the window."

She flops down onto a sofa and buries her head in her hands. "They weren't supposed to kill her," she sobs, "just scare her into handing over the ring."

"Tell me all, Betty," demands I unmoved by her tears as she gazes up wet eyed at me.

"Mum was supposed to hold on to the jewels for me. I mean, who on earth would think of looking for them in that dump. I paid her well, but when my men brought them back to me the ring was missing. I knew right away that mum had stolen it. Now she's dead because of it. Will you arrest me now you know everything?"

She looks so lovely in her sadness I am starting to wilt and contemplate giving her a big hug. "No, I cannot. Instead I will dictate a letter. You will write it on headed paper and it will be addressed to the insurance company you intended to defraud. Afterwards I and my rusty Sergeant shall take the letter and deliver it by hand while you pack your bags and leave my patch never to return. Agreed?"

She shrugs with indifference. "Agreed."

"Also, I want the names of Mable's killers and where I can find them. They shall not escape justice."

"Very well," she sighs. "I believe they have gone to hide out in the Gut. Bill Stringer and his brother Rob are the ones you want."

"Good," says I. "Just one more thing, Sergeant, give Betty her mother's drawers."

We leave to the sound of Betty weeping uncontrollably into Mable's drawers and catch a Hackney to the insurance company. We'll pick up the killers later.

"So," muses Head. "She gets away with it?"

"Of course. She's an associate of the prince. Never mind, Sergeant, we shall be able to collect the reward from the insurance company for returning the jewels. One hundred pounds no less. That's eighty percent for me and twenty percent for you."

"How much is that in money?"

"Five pounds."

"Cor, lovely. Thanks, gov. You're a gent."

"I know," says I. "I know."

Pickle Lane

Just to remind you, I am the famous Victorian detective, D.I. Gerald Potter, I am enjoying tea in bed, while dunking biscuits with my lovely wife, Betty. She's not so famous.

"Do you have to go in today, Detective Inspector?" she asks.

"Yes, there has been another brutal murder and I have to meet D.S. Head in Pickle Lane by ten."

"Do you require any more intercourse before you go, Detective Inspector?" she asks in hope.

I shake my head. "Twice in one night is enough, thank you my dear. Now I must get a move on or I shall be late."

After a good clear out, wash, shave and dress, and a hearty breakfast of something unrecognisable, I am ready to leave.

Betty sees me to the door. "What time will you be back, Detective Inspector?" she quizzes, kneeling down to fuss over my fly buttons because I hadn't done them up in order.

"Sometime later," I muse.

We say goodbye and off I set. It is a warm cloudy day and I enjoy the walk until I reach the stink and chaos of the slums where I am immediately accosted by a shrivelled up, toothless old hag with one eye who offers me a penny bag of horse dollop, "For ya roses, lovey."

Momentarily distracted I fail to see a shoeshine urchin trying to polish my shoes as I walk and I trip over him.

"That'll be a copper, copper," demands the urchin.

"Clear off," squawks the hag. "I saw 'im first."

I stand up and straighten up my bowler. "I am here to investigate another brutal murder," I grate. "Clear off the both of you before I arrest you."

The urchin runs off but the hag stands her ground. "I 'ave information about the murders," she offers. "For a quid or two."

"What is it?" demands I.

"Everyone who got murdered, isn't really dead."

Ignoring the psychotic psychopath, I walk on down Fish Bone Alley before turning into Pickle Lane, coming to a halt outside Bob Pickles' pickle shop. Head is waiting for me.

"Morning, sir," he says with a yawn.

"Morning Sergeant. You seem tired."

"Sorry, sir. I was drunk and unconscious all night and didn't get any sleep. My wife left me."

"Never mind, Sergeant. Console yourself that you will never have to gaze upon her ugly features, ever again."

"Actually, I was out celebrating the fact."

"Good," says I. "Let's get to it."

We enter the shop and are immediately assaulted by a powerful stench of vinegar. Jars of various pickled stuff are everywhere, while a short, greasy-haired woman behind the counter, stares cross-eyed at us.

I introduce myself and Head to her.

"You took your bloody time, you buggers," she snarls. "He's been reported dead for two days and he's starting to stink the place out."

I demand to be shown the corpse. Stepping around huge jars of God knows what on the floor we follow the smelly lump into the processing room. Several urchins are peeling rotten onions and poking them into jars, then adding vinegar half way up before topping the jar up with urine, it's cheaper. Mid-room the headless body of a big bellied man in a suit is laid out on its back.

"Do you know where his head is?" is the first question I ask.

"No, I don't," she grates. "I came down the other morning and found him like this. Headless!"

"Who is he?" asks Head.

"Why, my husband of course."

"How do you know that if he hasn't got a head?"

"Because he's wearing his best suit."

"Why is his penis hanging out of his trousers?" asks I.

"Oh, I took it out just to make sure it really was him," she smiles.

"Well you might have put it back!" I remonstrate.

She looks confused. "I hadn't thought of that."

Head and I bob down to peruse the body. "Severe trauma around the neck," I observe. "Other than that, he appears untouched."

"What do you make of his what-not?" asks Head.

"Um, it's very small and spotty," I muse.

"That's what I was thinking," agrees Head.

I go through the body's pockets and oddly find nothing at all. We stand up. "That's all we require for now," I tell the woman. "We may call back later."

She is incredulous, "That's it? What am I supposed to do with him now? He's ruining production."

"Do not fear, good lady. I have all in hand. Police photographers will arrive shortly."

"Do they want my picture?" she asks patting at her greasy hair.

"No, the body's. Then they will take it away to the morgue."

Back outside in the fresh smoggy air a party of gentry, hankies over mouths, stop in front of the shop.

"This is the place where the third headless murder has just taken place," instructs their guide taking off his red top hat and sweeping it around like a show man. "We shall go in, once these two gentlemen," he sneers, "move out of the way."

Head looks angry and ready to pounce at the man's rudeness. "Leave it, Sergeant," says I. "Let's move on."

Retracing our steps, we chat as we walk. "What was the first thing you noticed when we entered the shop?" I ask Head.

"It stank of vinegar, sir."

"What else?"

"That woman was holding a knife, which she quickly put down and then covered over with a cloth."

"Exactly! Because?"

"Um..., No idea, sir."

"She was about to cut her husband's member off. And I'll give you five guesses why."

"She wanted to see how sharp her knife was?"

"No."

"She likes cutting willies off?"

"No."

"For a souvenir?"

"No."

"To pickle it?"

"No."

"To eat it?"

"Definitely not. I'm thinking, Sergeant. That that member doesn't belong to her husband. It's someone else's."

"What? Was it stuck on then, sir?"

"No. No. What I mean is; the entire body doesn't belong to her husband," ponders I, recalling what the old hag had said earlier. "In fact, I do not believe it is her husband at all. And all will become clearer once we know more about her real husband's member."

Head looks confused. "Oh, I see," he says in confusion.

We come to a halt and face each other just as someone from a window above slings the contents of a potty out and a lump of something plops onto Head's bowler. "Dirty swine," he growls, taking off his hat and perusing the brownish lump now ensconced upon it.

Just then an urchin leaps forward holding out a bucket of pure. "Oi, copper that was for me."

"Just in time," says I, grabbing the waif by the collar so Head can wipe his hat clean on the brat's raggedy shirt. The urchin starts to whinge so I toss a penny into his bucket.

"Thanks, copper," he beams before skipping happily off.

"Now," says I, to Head. "Ask around the local prostitutes, see if any of them have had any doings with Bob Pickles. If they have, have them describe in detail what his member looks like. Have you a notebook and pencil?"

"Yes, sir."

"Good. Draw a picture from their description. While you are doing that, I shall be visiting the morgue to speak to the autopsy man. We'll meet back at the Skinners Arms in an hour or so."

Head wonders off while I wonder what I'm wondering about, but I have a good idea.

It isn't long before I am outside the local morgue. A lifeless building if ever I saw one. I go in and up to reception where for some reason the female receptionist is laid out naked and fast asleep on the counter. "Excuse me," I bellow poking her in the ribs. "I need some service here."

"Can I help you, sir?" says a grumpy voice from behind me.

I spin around to be faced by a tall skinny man in a bloodied white coat and with a face akin to a dead zombie. "You can, as your receptionist is not only unresponsive, she seems to be asleep on the job."

"That's because she's dead."

"You sure? She was soft and squidgy when I poked her just now, not all stiff and stuff."

"That's because she's rotten. Anyway, she isn't the receptionist, I am."

"Why isn't she on a trolley like all the others lined up in the corridor, if she's dead?"

"Because we've got a tail back. She's waiting for one to become vacant."

"Couldn't you at least cover her up for dignity's sake?"

"Short of blankets."

"Well do something, man! It's appalling leaving her out so that any Tom, Dick or Hairy can see her. What is the world coming to? No trolleys. No towels. People left out in corridors. Why I long for the future when no one will be denied their basic dignity and have to hang around in corridors where everyone can gawp at them."

"As you wish," he moans and stepping forward he shoves her off the counter so she lands with a thud behind it. "There you are, sir. Is that better?"

"Yes, it is. Now, I am Detective Inspector Gerald Potter."

He points a bloody finger at me. "I've heard of you. You're the brilliant detective known as Jerry Pot. What can I do for you?"

"I want to speak to whoever has been carrying out the autopsies on the headless murder victims."

"That'll be Fred Hackman. He is out on private business. He'll be back in an hour or so."

"What private business?"

"It's no secret. He takes posh parties out on gristle tours."

"Don't you mean whistle tours?"

"No, gristle. They are gristly tours all about the recent murders. That's why we've got such a tail back. What with that Sidcup Slasher. The Hackney Hacker."

"Yes. Yes," I groan. "Is this Fred Hackman a tall arrogant prat who sports a red top hat?"

"That's the one."

Everything clicks into place. I thank the bloody man and make my way outside into the putrid air wafting out from the locals' armpits and make my way towards the Skinners Arms.

Head is already in the snug and tucking into a bowl of stewed pigs' testicles. I go up to the bar and order a pie and a pint. Frequented mostly by pickle picklers, mass murderers, prostitutes, escaped lunatics and chickens, this place is the place to be if you don't want to be noticed. I take my beer over and sit across from Head; my pie should arrive in a few minutes. "How is the stew, Sergeant?"

"Very nice, sir. Suppose you've ordered one of those Sweeny Todd and Co. pies?"

"Yes," says I, licking my lips. "The best in London and full of meat with a strange, but delightful flavour. What did you manage to find out?"

He looks pleased with himself, and after a fart and a burp, he relates all. "Apparently, Bob Pickles was a regular with several of the girls. And get this; they all said he was so big they charged him double for the trouble."

"What trouble?"

"Well, sir. Once he'd been with them they had to rest up for a day with a tub of soothing lard just to get back to normal. If you know what I mean? Anyway, what did you find out, sir?"

"That is to be revealed, Sergeant. For now, let's enjoy our food and drink and then we shall be off to the only insurance broker in the area who will deal with the likes of those from around these parts."

One hour and two minutes later we are at the insurance brokers. Proprietor: Robby Doulin [I solve the easy anagram in his name in one point five seconds]. Once inside Doulin's office, I ask him how much he has paid out so far on the headless murder victims.

"Fifty quid to Maisy Chutney for 'her' husband. Seventy-five for Terry Tang's 'wife'. And now I've got that Pickles woman already on my back for a pony. This carries on I'll be in the poor house in no time."

"Do not pay her," I urge and explain to him exactly what's going on. He thanks me with hugs and kisses. "Trust me Mr Doulin. You shall get your money back, but I will expect a reward."

"How much?"

"Twenty percent from the first two, but only ten from the third."

"Agreed," he smiles.

We shake hands and Head and I head off for the morgue.

The zombie is there when we arrive and greets us amiably, "Ah, Detective Inspector. And this must be your sidekick, the famous, Detective Sergeant Dick Head? Fred's in the cutting room working on the new headless corpse."

We head down the corridor to a door with a sign on it saying: 'Keep Out. Work in Progress'. We go in anyway. Fred has the body on the slab and is sawing away at it while happily singing: 'I've got a friend in Jesus.' I flash my warrant card and shout out "Police!"

Fred looks up looking sick and dropping his saw makes a run for the back door, but Head heads him off and rugby tackles him to the ground, only Fred's back on his feet in a flash and as Head jumps up, Fred kicks him one in the genitals. Big mistake! Head butts him, knees him in the roundies and finally yanks out his truncheon and lays Fred out flat. Head cuffs him, we charge him, and then drag him off to the yard, we have to drag him because he can't walk after the kneeing he's received.

One hour later me and Head are in Chief Inspector Clump's office relating all over a welcoming glass of scotch.

"Hackman and the picklers set up the scam," says I. "Hackman used dead vagrants, as they often die because they eat dead rats and stuff, such are their lifestyles. He cuts off their heads so no one knows who they are. He then puts them where they could be found in and around their so called loved ones. Of course, they were pronounced dead because they didn't have a head and a death certificate was issued by a bent quack who wrote down whatever name anyone wanted to put down. The insurance money was duly claimed and everyone got a cut with Hackman adding a bonus to his earnings by capitalising on his murder tours. Case solved."

"But what happened to the heads?" quizzes Clump.

"Who knows," I shrug, while wishing I had not found that tooth in my pie earlier. "Perhaps they were incinerated."

"And the supposedly dead loved ones?"

"Hiding out in the Gut until it was safe to return. I've sent a party of plods to go and fish them out."

"Good work you men," beams Clump. "Take tomorrow off as a reward."

Head is overwhelmed by the Chief's generosity, but I am not. "It's our day off anyway, sir." I remind him.

"No such thing as a day off once you're in the force, Inspector," grins he grinningly.

Leaving the yard, me and Head, head off home.

"I really thought the chief was going to actually give us a day off," grumbles Head.

"No chance, Sergeant. However, console yourself with your share of the reward, which we shall be picking up in a day or two. Thirty-five pounds, no less. That's eight tenths for me and two tenths for you."

"Err... How much is that in money, sir?"

"That is two pounds ten shillings to you, Sergeant."

"Marvellous. Thank you, sir. You really are a gent."

"I know" says I. "I know."

Hervington House

D. S. Head and I are on a train heading north into Essex. We have
a second-class compartment all to ourselves. I am enjoying the
countryside whizzing by, while Head, sitting opposite me, is
engrossed in a book titled: *Colloquial Dictionary for the East Angles.*

Head suddenly lifts his head. "Can you help me, sir?" he asks,
confused.

I nod. "If I can. What is the trouble?"

"Well, sir. I looked up clod-hopper and it said see turd-hopper.
I looked up turd-hopper and it said refer to clod-hopper. Where
do I go from here?"

"Um… Look up hopper," I yawn, train journeys make me
sleepy.

Head flicks through the pages. "Ah, here it is. Hopper;
someone or something that hops around."

"Now look up clod and turd."

"Clod; a clump or lump of dirt. Turd; a clump or lump of poo."

"There is your answer, Sergeant. A hopper is someone or
something that hops around a clod or a turd."

"Ah... I see," he says with a smile and then appears confused again. "But why would you want to hop around a clod or a turd?"

"Because it is infinitely preferable than actually standing in it."

"Of, course it is," he sighs in enlightenment.

"Now then Sergeant. Look up bumpkin for me. Until this morning, I had never heard the word until C. I. Clump advised me to beware of bumpkins once we were in the countryside."

He flicks through. "Here it is, sir: Bumpkin; someone or something that has a relative with bumps or lumps, such as a mole, camel or mumps."

"Where exactly did you find this book?"

"In a book shop in Hackney."

"Then I fear, dear Sergeant, that you have been duped, and have purchased a piece of useless literature that is fit only for lighting fires and wiping bottoms. How much did you pay for it?"

"Tuppence."

"I rest my case."

"Give it a try, sir. It may improve."

"Very well. Just one more. Here is an easy one that even the most moronic moron would be able to answer correctly. Look up countryside."

He fans the pages and appearing quite pleased with himself, says, "Countryside; a secret place close to the inner thighs..."

"I think we will leave it there, Sergeant!" I cut in. "Kindly throw the book out of the window."

Head pushes down the window. A big mistake as smoke and soot flies into the compartment, whirls around and starts to choke me. Head shuts the window.

"I think, sir," he says eyeing me eyeingly. "I shall return the book and demand my money back."

"That is a good idea, Sergeant. Now, let us relax while keeping an eye out for this Man in the Tree Station. Once there, we shall alight and take a carriage to this Hervington House, where they will be putting us up in suitable quarters until we have solved the mystery of their missing painting."

"What if we don't solve it?"

"Then C. I. Clump will not be happy. Apparently, this Lord and Lady Hervington are acquaintances of his, so he will not want to lose his face. Hence the reason he has sent two of Scotland Yard's finest detectives."

We settle down again, Head perusing his book while I am deep in thought. I may not be seeing my darling Betty for some time and I know how much she doesn't like to be alone. But at least the postman and the milkman have promised to look in on her and make sure she is happy and satisfied.

We stop at Colchester Station where several people get on, and after a while an elderly, robust, red-faced gentleman enters our compartment and sits down beside Head. He is expensively dressed in country attire, complete with silk top hat and carrying a silver topped cane. He lights up a fancy pipe while eyeing me with suspicion.

"Where are you bound, sir?" he asks in a posh tone of voice.

"Man in the Tree Station and then on to Hervington House."

"There is no such place as Man in the Tree Station," says he. "But there is a Manningtree Station a couple of stops along. Hervington House is two miles from there."

"Thank you, sir," says I. "Do you know of this Hervington House?"

"Oh yes, everyone does around these parts."

"It is a stately home I believe?"

"More of a state I'm afraid."

"And Lord and Lady Hervington?"

He frowns. "Mad eccentrics. And beware sir, that Lady Hervington has strong desires."

"Of what kind?" asks I, frowning back.

He screws up his face. "Of the bedroom kind."

I screw up mine. "Is she an attractive woman?"

"Is a pig's arse attractive to anything except another pig?"

"Sergeant," says I calmly. "It may be that you will be called upon to go beyond the call of duty during this case."

Head lifts his head from the book. "As you know, sir. I am always ready for action."

"That is good," says our posh fellow. "Have you made out your will?"

Head shakes his head.

"Do you have liability insurance?"

Head shakes his head.

"Do you enjoy rigorous exercise?"

Head nods.

"Then, sir, you have my blessing."

Suddenly there is a blood curdling scream and Head is up in a flash, flinging open the door and leaping out into the corridor. Rising, I stick my head out of the door to see a young woman in a yellow dress charging towards us screaming: 'Murder! Murder!' She cannons into Head, who to my horror punches her one in the face so she goes down like a pole-axed pig.

"Sergeant," I yell. "You have just pole-axed a woman, by God."

"No, sir, I did all by myself," says he smugly as hauling her up to her dizzy feet, he grabs hold of her blond hair and to my horror rips it off her head!

"It's a man!" I gasp.

"No less," gasps he. "See, I have her wig in my hand."

I go up to the man dressed as a woman. She is coherent, though blood drips from her nose. "What mean you of this, madam-mister?"

"Murder," he croaks pointing back the way he-she had come.

Head lets go of him-her and he-she crumples to the floor. We hurry down the corridor coming to a compartment where the blinds are drawn with a sign saying: 'Private party, keep out!' Throwing open the door, Head and I go in anyway, and are met by the sight of a body in a suit laid out on his back while blood still seeps out of his chest.

Bobbing down we peruse the body. I slap its face. "Dead as a rock," says I.

"Murdered," says Head.

"Stabbed in the chest, Sergeant!"

Head sticks a finger in the wound. "Yes, sir, by a very thin blade I'd say."

Standing up I pull the train's stop cord, the brakes are slammed on, they screech, grate and make a terrible din as the train shudders and shakes to a halt. Head and I find ourselves thrown into a heap over the dead body. Screams and curses can be heard reverberating throughout the train but at last we get back on our feet, adjust our dress and are ready to continue. "Sergeant, go and cuff the man-woman and bring her-him here."

While he's gone I search around the compartment for evidence, perhaps the killer had dropped something?

Head returns, shoving the man-woman into the compartment just as the Ticket Inspector sticks his head in. "Who pulled that cord?" he demands.

"It was I," says I.

"That's a one pound fine!"

I flash my card. "Police. Now, go and get your driver, the guardsman and any other railway personnel and get them to ensure no one leaves the train. We have a murderer on board."

"That's all well and fine," says he, "but who is going to pay the stop train fine."

"Send the bill to Scotland Yard," snaps I. "Now, do as you are told or I'll have my Sergeant arrest you for construction."

"Don't you mean obstruction?"

"Sergeant arrest this man!"

The man looks horrified and quickly makes off. Head pushes the suspect down onto a seat and takes out his note book and pen as I start to question him-her.

"Sex?" demands I. "Male or female?"

The suspect shrugs as if he doesn't understand. Head whispers in my ear. "He is definitely a man, sir."

I stare down at the suspect. "Name?"

"Polski," he replies smearing the blood from his nose.

"Polski who?"

"Polski Polski."

I scratch my head beneath my bowler. "Do you know what he means, Sergeant?"

"I think he's trying to say he's Polish, sir."

"Polish!" gasps I. "Speak you ingwish?"

"Let me give him another punch, sir," Head kindly offers. "He obviously does speak ingwish, he shouted out murder, murder, clear enough."

The prisoner holds up his cuffed hands. "Alright, alright. I speak English."

"Real name?"

He drops his head to stare forlornly at the dead body. "I am Rupert Thurmantly," he whispers.

"Any relation to Sir Humphry Thurmantly, the eminent judge?"

"His grandson," he croaks.

All becomes clear. "So, Rupert, you are a male prostitute who dresses as a woman to hide your identity and you work the trains looking for customers?"

"Yes, sir," sighs he.

"And if your family should find out, they will not only disown you, they will probably have you incarcerated forever in a loony-bin to cover it up?"

He groans, "Something like that."

I sit down beside him. "Right, tell me what happened."

Suddenly an urchin sticks his grubby head into the carriage. "Can I go through the dead body's pockets, governor?" asks he.

"No, clear off," snaps Head.

"Can I keep this wig then?" he smiles holding it up.

Head snatches it off him and clips him a ringer around his ear and he runs off wailing and cursing.

"Proceed with your tale," says I to Rupert.

"Very well. I was booked to meet that man," he points at the body, "once the train pulled away from Colchester."

"For disgusting purposes, I presume?"

"Yes. Only, when I got to his compartment he was already dead."

"Do you know who he is?"

"Yes. He is Humpty Dumpty."

"Do you want another punch?" growls Head shaking a clenched fist at Rupert's face.

I hold up a restraining hand. "I fear, Sergeant, that is the only name the victim ever gave. Search his pockets and we may uncover who he is."

Head bobs down and goes through the man's pockets, as he pulls stuff out he hands them to me with a running commentary. "Snot-rag, complete with bogeys. A dirty picture of a goat. Toothpick with a bit of food stuck on it. Six sticky humbugs in a bag. A pen. Diary. Wallet. Cigars and lighter. Train ticket. A packet of sheaths, unused, thank God. A receipt." He peruses it. "Ten shillings for services rendered. No mention of from whom, but there is a signature?"

I show it to Rupert. "Is this your signature?"

"No," he gasps. "It's my grandad's."

"Like grandfather like grandson," I muse. "You shall not be off to the loony-bin after all."

The door is pushed right open and the ticket collector re-appears. "We're going to drive the train into a siding, sir, or we shall be crashed into by the ten-thirty."

I look at my fob watch. "It is ten-thirty-five. Good thing the train is late then, isn't it? Has anyone left the train?"

"Not that we have noticed."

"Good, well keep watch, please."

He nods and leaves, closing the door behind him. "Anything else, Sergeant?"

"An expensive fob-watch and a large carrot? Perhaps it was for his lunch?"

I shake my head. "The mind boggles," I grate.

The door opens again. It is the trolley man. "Tea, coffee, crisps with salt cellars, alcoholic beverages, buns, apples, etc. etc."

"I'll have a coffee and a bun," says Head.

"And me," says I. "Rupert, do you want anything?"

"I'd like a scotch, but I haven't got any money."

Opening the victim's wallet, I take out a pound note. "Do not worry, Rupert, he'll pay."

"Does he want anything?" asks the trolley man pointing at the body.

"Not just now, he's dead."

As we eat and drink the train moves off into a siding. Tea break over we resume our investigations. I go through the wallet. It reveals the usual stuff plus a business card: 'Walter Williams. Dealer in fine arts. Holland Park London'. I go through the diary and read the text for today. Booked tranny for ten-thirteen. Collect B M money.

"What's a tranny?" I ask Head.

He shrugs. "Um... A granny on a train?"

I ask Rupert.

He shakes his head. "Never heard the word before."

There is a knock on the door and the posh elderly gentleman appears. "How much longer before we leave? I have an important appointment at eleven in Ipswich."

"As soon as the ten-thirty goes by we shall continue our journey, sir."

He goes away and five minutes later the late ten-thirty thunders by. "Sergeant, go and inform the ticket collector to take the train to Manningtree Station and put it in a siding there."

He goes off while I ponder what B M money means. Of course, black mail money! The victim was blackmailing someone who is on this train and that someone murdered him. I resolve to question everyone on the train once we reach the station. The train begins to move. Head returns and ten minutes later we are in a siding at Manningtree, where everyone is marched off the train and escorted into the waiting room ready to be questioned. Two hours later, with the help of the local plods and having grilled everyone, including the railway staff, and taken their names and addresses, we let everyone go, including Rupert - once I've had a fatherly talk with him over the potential perils of his trade. The body is carted off to the local morgue to be autopsied and I officially hand the case over to the local plods.

Carrying our overnight bags Head and I head for the exit just as a pair of urchins leap forward.

"Take ya bags for a penny, mister," they cry grabbing at the handles.

Feeling kindly, I let them take mine, Head does the same and I hand them a sixpence from Walter's wallet, having kept most of his money towards 'expenses'.

Outside there are a few taxi carriages waiting for trade. We pick one with a driver who looks more alive than the others, I gaze up at him. "Did you see a pair of urchins come out of the station carrying a bag each?"

"Ah. Oi did," he yawns.

"Where did they go?"

He yawns some more. "Off somewhere."

"Off where?"

"Wherever 'em goes."

"But they took our bags!"

"Oi 'spect they did.' Spect you payed 'em an' all for the privilege?"

"I did."

"There ya go 'en. It be ya own fault. Now, where ya goin'?"

"Hervington House," says I, as Head and I climb up into the rear of the tatty carriage and take a seat.

"Giddy up Dobbin," orders the driver, only for the nag to collapse in a heap on the ground.

"Is it dead?" asks Head.

The driver cranes his neck around and winks at us. "No, 'e loikes a laugh does Dobbin. 'E'll be up in a mo, an' off like a thoroughbred once 'e's got 'is faculties back."

After an age, the nag finally gets up and sets off at about one mile an hour up a dusty lane.

"Can you not get it to go any faster?" demands I.

"Oi could," yawns the driver. "But 'e don't loike ta be pushed too hard."

"Tell me driver. Do you charge by mile or by time?"

He yawns some more. "'Pends wus most lucrative," he yawns.

"Say, half as much again?"

"You sure 'bout that?"

"I am."

"Be it on your 'ead then." Laughing he whacks the horse's rump with a long thin stick. The nag rears up, snorts and rockets forwards as if it's been threatened with castration.

Head and I cling on for grim death as the rickety carriage bounces and sways maniacally all over the place, but the worst of it is the thudding and jarring into deep potholes that sees our backsides and backs brutally assaulted. "One day," I yell out to Head. "We shall no longer have to suffer such dreadful roads! Potholes will be a thing of the past and it will be a pleasure to take one of those automobiles out for a quiet run in the countryside without risking the bloody wheels falling off!"

"Agreed, sir," he shouts back. "Ask him to slow down before the nag has a heart attack or we get our necks broken."

As if he had heard, the driver slows the nag down just as a huge Georgian stately home comes into view.

As we draw ever nearer to Hervington House we can see it is in a crumbling state of repair. Nor does it offer any kind of warm welcome as a paint peeling sign states: 'Hawkers. Trespassers. Vagrants and all other unwanted visitors, especially tax collectors, will be shot on sight'. The next sign by a dried up lake, states: 'Do not feed the ducks'.

At last we come to a stop on the drive beside stone steps leading up to the front entrance.

"'At'll be two bob," demands the driver.

Head and I climb wearily down and I pay the driver.

"Nuver two bob an' oi'll get ya bags back an' all."

I hand him the money with a warning. "Do not cheat us, my good fellow, or I shall have my Sergeant extract your teeth."

He touches his cap. "Oi live in terror of it," he smiles displaying a set of shiny toothless gums. "Don't 'e worry, oi'll be back."

He plods off and we climb the steps and pull on the bell chain. Several minutes and umpteen pulls later the door eventually opens, and a stiff upright, bald headed potbellied man in scruffy butler's livery stands before us.

Yawning he says, "Are you the detectives from London?"

"We are," I answer proudly.

"You'll class as lower-class, then," he yawns. "You'll need to go around back to the lower-class entrance. It is signed."

"I do not believe we shall fit in here Sergeant," says I as we trudge around to the back of the house.

"No sir."

Presently we arrive at a door with a sign above it, saying: 'Servants and lower class only'. We bang on the door for ten minutes or so until at last it opens and we are confronted by the same butler as before.

"Are you the detectives from London?" he asks.

"We are," replies I.

He stands aside. "You may enter. Do you have any baggage with you?"

"No. We had our bags stolen at the station."

"No. No. I meant baggage. Any wives, mistresses, brats or urchins? Animals excepted."

I shake my head, truly I am losing my patience.

"Follow me," orders he, setting off down a long bare corridor at the speed of a sloth. Presently he leads us into an office type room and tells us to sit by a large wood wormed table.

"Fill these in," he demands, handing each of us a sheet of paper and a pencil. I take out my pen.

"No pens!" he snaps.

"Why not?" demands I.

"Because we can't rub out your answers if we don't like what you've written."

"If you are intent on erasing anything you do not like, what is the point of us writing anything about anything?"

He glares down at me. "Look, I'm merely the hired help here. I don't make the rules. If you don't like it take it up with her Ladyship."

Head whispers in my ear, "These country folks are all mad, sir. Best to play along with them I reason."

"Agreed, Sergeant."

We set to filling in the forms; they are simple yes or no, short answers.

1. Have you had diarrhoea lately?

2. Do you suffer from hem-a-roads?

3. Do you or your family suffer from any of these? Please tick all that apply to you.

I stop writing, the questions go on for ever and scanning the bottom of the page I note they are all ridiculous questions about a man's libido, such as: "When did you last make love? Was it with a man, a woman or both? Was it free or did you pay for it?"

"Sergeant, cease completing this ridiculous questionnaire immediately." I tear up the form and scatter it over the desk. I address the butler, "My good man. We were prewarned by a gentleman on the train that her ladyship is a woman of a certain kind. Um… How may I put this?"

He buts in, "She is a sex maniac?"

"In short, yes." I stand up as does Head and we face the butler square on. "Inform your mistress that we refuse to complete her silly forms. We are policemen, here to solve a crime not to become the playthings of an aristocratic nymphomaniac. If she cannot accept that then we shall leave immediately. Is that clear to you?"

"Very well," he sneers. "Gentlemen, please follow me."

We crawl along behind him to a wafting aroma of something cooking and I realise I am famished having had nothing to eat since breakfast, except for a bun. "What is for dinner, butler?" I ask to his back.

"Slow cooked venison," he answers deadpan. "But that is only for the Hervingtons."

"What is for us, then?"

He comes to a halt and turns to face me. "Did you not bring sandwiches?"

"No, of course not. I was informed that all would be found."

"I will ask her ladyship," he yawns carrying on up the corridor.

Head whispers in my ear, "They yawn a lot out in the countryside."

"It is the air, Sergeant. Apparently, it is so pure it makes you sleepy, unlike the smoke and fumes of the towns and cities that are thick with toxic chemicals which help to keep us alert and awake."

"Then I think, sir, that the sooner the countryside has more of this toxic air the sooner the people in it will wake up."

"Agreed," says I. "Perhaps it will also raise their levels of intelligence?"

At last we reach what can only be the dining room; it is nearly bare, there is a refectory table that goes on forever, but with only ten chairs around it all bunched up to one end, as the other end appears to be covered with bird droppings. The walls are covered in faded wallpaper with a floral design that is peeling and hanging off in places and clearly showing brighter areas where paintings once hung. Upon the clean end of the table there is a large hand-bell and a pair of rusting candelabra. Tall dirty windows allow a semblance of the bright afternoon sun to filter through to expose the dusty interior. This house has obviously seen much better days.

"Take a seat," orders butler.

We sit down on embroidered high backed rickety chairs.

"Her ladyship will be here shortly. I am instructed to offer you refreshments for now. You will be served something for dinner around seven thirty once the Hervingtons have eaten. So, do you want tea, coffee or scotch?"

Desperate for a little pleasure, we opt for scotch.

Butler picks up the bell and clangs it violently causing a lump of plaster to fall from the ceiling and crash onto the rotting wooden floor.

Ten minutes later a near dead body enters carrying a wooden tray with a bottle of scotch on it, three tumblers, a pitcher of water, a large jam sponge, two chipped china plates decorated with pink castles and a cake knife with a dead fly on it. The waitress is at least ninety, very wobbly on her stick legs and has stiff white hair jutting out of her cap, while her face is such a mass of wrinkles it's difficult to tell whether she's a woman or a walnut.

"Thank you, Mother," says butler as she drops the tray onto the table. Watching her leave I wonder if she will make it back alive to wherever she had come from.

"We shall await her ladyship," butler informs us. "She will be here shortly once she has finished with the gardener."

"What's she doing with the gardener?" queries Head.

"What has that got to do with you?" demands butler.

"I was merely making conversation."

Butler puts on his snooty look. "Well don't!"

Heads jumps to his feet and I join him, "Listen here my good man," I grate. "If you speak to my Sergeant like that again I shall arrest you for perverting the course of justice."

Hands on hips, butler glares at me. "You are insane! When was I supposed to have perverted the course of justice?"

"Just now. When my Sergeant asked you a question about her ladyship and the gardener, which may be relevant to our investigations, you not only evaded the question you also made veiled threats to him."

"I did no such thing!"

"Your tone of voice left no doubt in my mind that you intended to become violent towards my Sergeant should he dare to ask you anything about anything."

He folds his arms. "Very well. Ask me anything you like and I give you my word that I will answer truthfully."

"What is her ladyship doing with the gardener?"

"Burying him."

Head and I are aghast. "Why?"

"Because he is dead. Even you must know that it is customary to bury dead people."

I am about to castigate him when a tall, attractive woman enters the room. She is buxom with dark, piled up hair flecked with grey, and wearing an embroidered cream gown that is a little tatty, while remaining both stylish and complimentary to her curvaceous figure.

"I am Lady Hervington, and I apologise for keeping you waiting, gentlemen," she smiles as she draws near. "We have just had a service for Jenkins our gardener. Sixty years he had tended to our gardens. The least we could do was honour his wishes and bury him in the grounds."

"That was kind of you my Lady," says I. "Was he buried beneath his favourite tree or something?"

"No, actually we laid him to rest in the family plot between Roger and Bobby."

"Ancestors of yours?"

"Not really. They were two of my favourite dogs."

She goes to sit and butler rushes forwards to pull out a chair for her. "Pray be seated gentlemen. Roberts, serve the refreshments. Then you may leave us."

"Yes, your Ladyship."

Roberts pours a generous measure of scotch into all three glasses and then cuts two huge wedges of cake onto each plate, passing one each to me and Head before waddling off.

"I am watching my figure," says her Ladyship. "Hence the reason I am not partaking of the cake."

I am wondering why the gentleman on the train gave us the impression that her Ladyship was a pig's arse when she is in fact eloquent, sophisticated and very desirable. I am also wondering if we are on a wild goose chase, the Hervingtons are obviously cash poor and the painting has probably been secretly sold and then a claim will be made on the insurance, when we fail to recover it. However, for now I am prepared to enjoy the moment and the company of this woman while hoping that Head will stop gawping at her as if he could eat her.

She gazes seductively into my eyes. "You must be Detective Inspector Gerald Potter. May I call you, Gerry?"

"I prefer a more formal address, my Lady, if you do not mind."

"I will let you call me Harriet," she coos.

"I must maintain the modus operandi."

"As you wish Inspector. What about you, Sergeant? Do you mind if I call you Dicky?"

"Not at all your Ladyship," replies Head with all the subtleness of a rampant ram. He is so enamoured with the woman his eyes are burning with lust.

"That is the formalities over with," she smiles. "Let us make a toast."

We stand up and raise our glasses.

"To a successful outcome over the stolen painting," says she. "And the complete satisfaction of all involved except for the thief."

"To success," calls out I.

"Complete satisfaction," calls out Head.

"Be seated gentlemen. Dicky, top up the glasses, please."

Like a panting lap dog, Head tops her glass up and then fills mine and his. Truly I have never seen him so smitten. He is already completely under her thumb.

"May I ask your Ladyship whether you have any idea who may have taken the painting?" says I, trying to distract Head from ogling the woman while steering the conversation onto the reason why we are here.

"Of course, I do. My useless husband stole it and has probably already gambled away the money. His gambling addiction has seen him sell off anything not nailed down."

"I am afraid, your Ladyship, that your husband is perfectly entitled to steal his own property and gamble it away should he so wish."

"I know that Inspector. However, he did not legally own that painting, I did. So, therefore he has stolen it from me. Correct?"

"If you can prove you own it, then yes, you are correct."

"I can prove it. As I can prove that I legally own all my jewellery. Jewellery that I keep under lock and key to ensure the useless old goat doesn't steal that as well. He may have sold off all that he owns to fund his addiction, but he is *not* going to sell off the little that I have left as well."

"Your husband sounds a right prat," puts in Head.

"Maintain your professional status, Sergeant," admonishes I. "Her Ladyship does not want to hear your flippant comments about his Lordship."

"Oh, but I do, Inspector. Well done Dicky, you summed my husband up in one word. What exactly is a prat?"

"It's a…"

"I will explain to her Ladyship, Sergeant," I cut in. "Madam, a prat is a twat."

"Really? Oh, I see… You are saying my husband is a vagina?"

I can see I am about to dig myself into a big hole. "I shall rephrase that, madam. A prat is an idiot, a fool, a stupid person."

"Of course, he is. Actually, I prefer the word twat. My husband, from this moment forward, shall be known as Lord Harrold 'The Twat' Hervington. I think it suits him admirably. Don't you gentlemen?"

Head and I nod in agreement, it is easier. "Madam, to continue," says I. "Have you reported the theft to the insurance company?"

"No."

"Why not?"

"Because, Harold 'The Twat' has made so many false claims over the years, no insurance company would touch us with a bean pole. The painting wasn't insured."

"Ah…" says I. "Then I will require a detailed description of the painting, when it disappeared and how much you believe its value to be."

Her ladyship picks up the bell and rings it. Five minutes later, Roberts appears.

"You rang, my Lady."

"Go to the drawing room, Roberts, and fetch the family's photograph album and try and get back here before it's dark."

"Yes, madam," he sighs and slopes off with all the enthusiasm of someone going to be shot. The man has three speeds, stop, reverse and slow ahead.

"The picture is a Rembrandt. Worth approximately three thousand pounds," informs her Ladyship. "I have a photograph of it in the album."

"That was sensible of you, madam," praises I. "It will be of invaluable help to us in finding your painting. Now, while we are waiting for Roberts. Have you ever heard of an art dealer by the name of Walter Williams?"

"Most certainly. He is the man my husband has sold all our other paintings to. No doubt, The Twat, has already sold my Rembrandt to him. How do you know of this Williams character?"

"Williams was murdered, today, on the very train that the Sergeant and I were on."

"Stabbed through the heart by a thin bladed weapon," puts in Head.

"Did you catch the killer?" asks her Ladyship.

"No, and for now, I have handed over the case to the local police," answers I. "But it may be that the murder is related to your stolen painting."

"How intriguing," she says, looking intrigued.

We pause to drink more scotch and stuff our cake, it is nice but would be better if it had some jam in it. At last, Roberts returns and sets the photo album down beside her Ladyship.

"Anything else, your Ladyship?"

"Top up the glasses, Roberts, then you may go," orders her Ladyship as she opens the album, spins it around and pushes it over to me.

There, in clear black and white is a picture of her picture taken from where it used to hang on the wall. Beside that is a close-up, and beside that is a picture of the elderly, well-dressed, gentleman on the train. "I know this man," says I stabbing a finger on his face "It is a Sir Richard Grayson. I interviewed him about the murder."

"He is also known as, Lord Hervington," gasps her Ladyship.

"The cane he has in his hand. Does it also double up as a sword stick?"

"Yes, it does. He carries it with him at all times for defence in case anyone he owes money to should attack him."

All becomes clear. "Head, we have our killer. I believe that this Walter Williams was blackmailing Lord Hervington; because he knew that the Rembrandt that he'd bought off his lordship was stolen, and his Lordship was to meet Williams on the train to pay him off. Only his Lordship murdered Williams instead with his swordstick!"

"Williams also had a swordstick?" queries Head.

"No. No. Only his Lordship had a swordstick."

"What did Williams have?" put in her Ladyship.

"Nothing!" Truly, sometimes I despair of people. "His Lordship stabbed Williams through the heart with his swordstick."

"But you just said this Williams fellow didn't have a swordstick" says her Ladyship. "So how could my husband have stabbed him with his own swordstick?"

"Let me put it another way. His Lordship drew out his own swordstick and then stabbed Williams with it. Now, let's move on. Where is your husband, your Ladyship?"

She yawns. "Probably at his club in Ipswich gambling away what little money he has left."

"When will he return home?"

"God knows. Once he's run out of money, I suppose."

"What is the name of this club?"

"The Gentleman's Retreat. It is just off Silent Street near to the docks."

"Have you a carriage that can take us to Ipswich?" asks I.

"Yes, but I don't have a horse to pull it."

"Why, what happened to it?"

"The Twat leaves it at Ipswich so he can ride home on it late at night when there's no other transport available. But we do have a couple of trusty bicycles."

I stand up, "Then, madam, they will have to suffice."

She clangs the bell and to our amazement, Roberts arrives in barely a minute.

"You rang, my Lady?"

"Fetch the bicycles, the detectives are off to Ipswich to arrest his Lordship."

"Very well, my Lady," says he and slopes off.

"Come on Sergeant," orders I. "We shall go with him, it will save time."

We follow Roberts out of the back of the house to a shed where he opens its creaky doors and we all go inside.

"Penny farthings!" I grate. "The most tortuous invention since the rack. I would rather walk."

Walking along I say to Head, "We'll walk to the station and catch the train to Ipswich."

"What if there isn't a train?"

"Then we'll take a cab."

He groans, "Do we have to, my backside's still aching from the last one."

"It's that or allow a murderer to escape. That's if he hasn't already fled the country."

We carry on in silence until at last we reach the station where we are informed that the next train is due in in one minute's time. The train arrives on time and we board, it pulls away and we settle down for the journey, but it isn't until we arrive at Colchester Station that we realise we are going the wrong way. We get off and cross the bridge to the other side and twenty minutes later are on our way to Ipswich. Once there we take a cab to Silent Street and the Gentleman's Retreat.

The club is inside a three-storey detached Georgian house. We climb the steps to the large, blue painted doors and I pull the bell. It is quickly opened by a bulldog in a suit complete with top hat. Head and I flash our cards.

"We are here to interview one of your members regarding a police matter," says I.

He looks down his broken nose at us, "Are you members?"

"No, we are policemen."

"If you're not members then you can't come in unless you have been invited to the club by another member."

Me and Head look at each other, both knowing what the other is thinking. "Look here my good man," warns I. "You are obstructing an Officer of the Law in the execution of his duties and are on the point of being arrested."

He slams the door in our faces, "That's it Sergeant," growls I. "Let us show that fool who he is dealing with."

"Best be careful, sir, he's a big bugger!"

"Did you bring protection with you?"

"Always," he returns and producing a packet of sheaths from his pocket he waves them in my face.

"No, no. Not that kind of protection, the kind that can subdue the criminal."

"Ah…," says he and opens his jacket where his revolver sits under his armpits. "I've also got on me," he grins "knuckle dusters, flick knife, short truncheon and a pot of pepper."

"What's the pepper for?" demands I.

"To throw in the buggers' faces, one whiff of it and they collapse on the floor choking and sneezing and can't see a thing."

I shake my head, "I can't see it ever catching on, but we'll try it anyway." I ring the bell again.

The door opens and Head hurls the pepper right into the face of someone other than the doorman, the man immediately goes into a seizure and, unable to see, he slaps his hands over his eyes and collapses back inside onto the tiled floor.

"Run like hell!" orders Head.

And we do, down the steps and off up the street like a pair of greyhounds. After a while we come to a stop beside a church and leaning back against the wall we catch our breath. Head peeps around the corner of the church to see if we've been followed.

Appearing unhappy he says, "I've just hurled pepper into Chief Inspector Clump's face!"

"Clump! What the hell is he doing here?"

"Perhaps he's a member?"

All becomes clear. "I doubt that. I sent Clump a telegraph from Manningtree Station informing him of the murder and the victim's name, and I'll wager Hervington sent Clump one also, because he stood behind me in the telegraph office and would have heard everything I said. Clump then hotfooted it down here to talk to his friend, Lord Hervington, before anyone put two and two together and arrested Hervington for William's murder. And Clump's going to make sure Hervington gets away with that murder. The old boys' network no less. Now do you understand all that, Sergeant?"

"Yes…," he says in a but tone. "But how the heck did Clump get here so fast if he was on foot?"

"Never mind," I sigh. "We must get back to Hervington House as quickly as possible before Clump recovers and beats us there. I am sure Lady Hervington will cover up for us and easily convince Clump that we hadn't left the house since our arrival. Come on Sergeant, let's go."

We grab a cab to the station where luckily, once again, we're on a train in minutes and off it half an hour later and into another cab ferrying us to Hervington House, but thankfully it's not the same yokel we had before. Twenty minutes later we are sat back at the table with Lady Hervington and explaining all.

"Do not worry, gentlemen," she coos. "I shall keep your little secret, providing you do something for me."

The look in her eyes tells me exactly what she wants and I am not too happy about it.

We are suddenly interrupted by Roberts entering while carrying our bags.

"Your bags have arrived," he states. "Would you like me to put them in your rooms?"

"Just one moment," says I, thinking they appear to look a little light the way he's so easily holding them, one in each hand. Standing up I go over and take hold of the bags, "They're empty," says I angrily. "All our clothes have been stolen. That damn cab driver! I paid him two-bob to return our bags. He has conned us."

"No, sir," puts in Roberts. "He has returned your bags as promised, even if they are empty."

I hate clever clog butlers and am on the point of losing it completely when her Ladyship, says, "Never mind Inspector, it will be a warm night so you can comfortably sleep in the nude."

"Can I as well?" grins Head.

"No," snaps I. "You and I will be up all night staking out the place in case his Lordship deigns to return."

"So long as you don't forget the little favour you will owe me for lying to old Clumpy once he gets here," smiles her Ladyship.

I smile back to placate her. In truth, I could easily find it in myself to satisfy her cravings, but I am married and a policeman on duty. I have a sense of honour, but obviously Head doesn't.

"I am ready for anything," he states, gazing evocatively at the woman's voluptuous bosom.

"That's the ticket, Dicky," she beams. "Let me show you to your room, right now!"

Head is up on his feet like a randy dog sniffing a bitch on heat. I am appalled, why it's only three in the afternoon! I am about to say something when her Ladyship gets in there first.

"Roberts go and run the Inspector a bath, he looks in need of a relax and a refresh."

Thirty minutes later I am ensconced in a huge iron bath that must hold enough water to fill a large pond, it's just a pity there's only enough water to cover my heels, and its stone cold. Five minutes later I am in my room laid out on a four-poster bed while wearing 'one of his Lordship's old white dressing gowns'. In minutes, I am fast asleep.

I am woken up by a rapping on the door as the handle is turned, but as I had locked it, the door can't be opened.

"Inspector, it's Harriet, I must see you immediately. I have something I must show you."

Against my better judgement I go and unlock the door and peep around it to preserve my dignity. "What is it?" asks I.

"Let me in and I'll show you," she whispers conspiratorially.

"Can't you show me here?"

"No, someone might see."

"Is it important?"

"Very!"

I stand aside to let her in, she closes the door and instantly pins me against the wall. "Madam!" I protest. "This isn't seemly. I am in my dressing gown, and you, I can see, are in yours. You must show me what you must and then leave so we can maintain our dignity."

"Very well," she sighs, breaking away from me she goes to the centre of the room. "Are you in to horticulture, Inspector?"

What an odd question, I ponder, especially under the circumstances. "Well, I do love my roses."

"Oh, good," she smiles and throws off her dressing gown to stand utterly naked before me. "What do you think of this for a well cultured bush?"

Sometimes you have to admit defeat and answer the call of duty.

Two hours later her Ladyship leaves and I crawl across the room to retrieve my dressing gown, haul myself up by way of the door knob, put on the gown and go to the bathroom, where I take another dip in the cold bath, and then hobble back to my room and get dressed, just as there is a knock on the door. "Who is it?"

"It is I," Heads voice calls back. "Clump and his Lordship have just arrived."

I open the door and Head steps in, "What time is it?" I ask, still feeling somewhat disorientated by Harriet's assault on my faculties.

"Seven o'clock, sir. Dinner will be served in thirty minutes according to Roberts, and Clump has demanded we attend."

"We best go then, Sergeant." As we take the stairs I say, "I trust we will keep what has happened with her Ladyship strictly between ourselves, Sergeant."

"Of course, sir. Mum's the word."

On entering the dining-room, we find Clump sat next to his Lordship and Harriet sat across from them. Clump's eyes look like they've been poked with sticks, they're that bloodshot, while the rest of his face looks like he's got mumps. He doesn't appear the least bit happy.

"Good evening, sir," says Head and I in unison.

"Why are you both walking so funny?" demands Clump.

"Are we, sir?"

"Don't answer a question with a question when speaking to me," growls Clump. "Now come and sit down, we have a lot to discuss."

We go and sit either side of Harriet where we are scowled at by his Lordship and glared at by Clump.

"Now," begins Clump. "I have solved the murder of the art dealer. After I received your telegram, Potter, I went to Williams' place of business and what do you think I found?"

"Her Ladyship's painting?"

"Exactly. And during my search of the premises do you know what else I found?"

"No idea, sir."

"I found that Williams was blackmailing all kinds of people for all kinds of reasons. He kept detailed records of his crimes hidden away in a secret drawer in a bureau. When I read the names of all those you interviewed at Man in the Tree I found six of them were on Williams' list of blackmail victims, and of course were all on the train."

"So, all we have to do, is find which one of those murdered Williams," puts in I, flicking a glance towards his Lordship who is staring at me while appearing to be very smug indeed.

Clump shakes his head. "Far too important people, Inspector. Besides which, Williams could have been killed by any of a hundred people, he was that prolific in his doings. No, the case is closed, a villain has been justly punished and we shall leave it at that."

"But…"

"No 'buts', Potter, that's an order. Her Ladyship's painting has been packaged and should arrive back here tomorrow."

"But there's still the matter of the thief," I quickly add.

"There was no thief," comes the smug retort. "His Lordship merely employed Williams to have the painting cleaned as a present for her Ladyship's birthday next month, only Williams kept it with the intention of having a forgery made which would be returned to Hervington House, and then Williams would have sold the original on the black market."

Rarely have I heard such rubbish, but unfortunately, I am stuck with it, and the worst of it is knowing that Lord Twat is going to get away with everything just because of who he knows and who he is.

The sound of a gong interrupts as Roberts comes in and announces, "Dinner is served."

Walnut face hobbles in carrying a large tureen of soup, most of which is slopping out of the lid onto the floor. She bangs it down onto the table, puffs and pants for a while, and then hobbles off.

Roberts sets down a basket full of rolls, and ignoring the mouse droppings, I grab a large crusty brown before anyone else gets it, I am that hungry. Roberts goes around serving the cream of something soup and after grace we all tuck in. A main course of venison pie with all the trimmings follows, washed down with copious amounts of red plonk. We finish off on tinned peaches and cream.

"That was delicious," praises Clump. "My compliments to the cook."

We all applaud walnut face and Roberts, and being gentlemen, Head and I help clear up while Clump and his Lordship go off to the drawing room for port and cigars. Head and I were not invited anyway. Once done in the kitchen we re-join her Ladyship at the table.

"I knew my twat of a husband would get away with it," moans her Ladyship. "He and Clump went to Eton together. The old school network, and all that."

"At least you shall have your painting back," says I.

"True. But it is small recompense to seeing the bugger hang for murder. Then I could have collected on his life policy and gone off to the Caribbean to live with all those fit young natives."

"You have insurance on your husband?" quizzes I.

"Of, course. I took out a policy on him years ago when we were more affluent. I have never missed a payment and should he croak it I stand to receive a pay out, in excess of two hundred thousand."

"Pounds or pence?" queries Head.

"Pounds."

"Marvellous," grins I, leaning conspiringly closer to her. "For a ten percent cut of that pay out, your Ladyship, me and my rusty Sergeant will, shall we say, ensure you get that insurance money."

"That's a bit steep," returns she, sucking air in through her teeth. "How about two percent plus unlimited sex."

"Five percent plus limited sex."

"Three percent and three quarters unlimited sex, plus I'll throw in a bit of bondage."

I scratch at my chin, it is a fair offer, the trouble is I have already been unfaithful to my darling Betty and I don't think I could stray again. But then I have an idea. "I will consult with my partner, if you don't mind my Lady."

"As you wish, Inspector," she smiles.

Head and I head over to a corner and put our heads together. "Are you in, Sergeant?"

"What would I have to do?"

"Help me get rid of his Lordship."

"How?"

"I haven't worked out a plan, as yet, but fear not, I soon will. Now, I am to receive a three percent cut from the insurance pay out, of which you shall receive one sixth of that, plus you shall receive all three quarters of the sex plus a bit of bondage. How does that strike you?"

"Um… How much is that in money?"

"Approximately a hundred pounds, no less."

"Wow! But does the three quarters sex, mean, I have to stop three quarters of the way through. I don't want to sound ungrateful, sir, but that sounds a bit cruel?"

"Fear not, Sergeant, you shall get complete satisfaction, trust me." Even if you can't walk afterwards, I muse to myself. "Anything else?"

"I take it we're not inviting the Chief to join us?"

"Absolutely not. And we must keep this to ourselves."

Re-joining her Ladyship, we tell her the deal is on. She is ecstatic, we shake hands and she rings the bell. Roberts comes in, "You rang my Lady."

"Come closer," she whispers. "We could be off to the Caribbean very shortly, my dear Roberts, but don't tell your mother just yet in case she gossips to the new gardener when they're in bed."

"At last!" he cries and skips off.

Head and I are aghast, she'll get us all hung, blabbing to the servants.

"Remain calm, gentlemen," she soothes. "You can trust Roberts to the grave. Plus, we've also been trying to get rid of my husband ever since he took up gambling and plunged us into poverty. We just never came up with a fool proof plan."

Just then, Clump and his Lordship walk in and his Lordship clangs the bell. Unusually spry, Roberts answers the call immediately. "You rang, my Lord?"

"Hitch 'my' horse up to the carriage, Chief Inspector Clump and I are off to my club. And hurry up, you lazy scallywag!"

"Will you be back tonight?" asks her Ladyship.

"No, so don't wait up."

"I never do."

Clump says to me, "Stay here tonight, Potter. Make your way back tomorrow and I will expect a report on my desk by lunch time."

"Very well, sir," returns I.

"And help yourself to anything you require," smirks his Lordship. "Especially my wife."

They swan off laughing and I can see the fury in her Ladyship's eyes. "Have no fear good Lady, he will get what's coming to him."

"Have you a plan, Inspector?"

"Not yet, but trust me, I soon will have."

We all retire to bed early. Head and her Ladyship are next door making a good deal of noise throughout the night, but it doesn't stop me working out a failproof plan to get rid of his Lordship.

Morning arrives, bright and sunny. After ablutions, I join Head and her Ladyship for breakfast.

"Did you sleep well, Inspector," asks her Ladyship.

"As well as could be expected," I reply, glancing at Head whose unkempt appearance is akin to someone who's been dragged into a thick bush several times.

Roberts enters and announces: "A policeman from Ipswich to see you my lady."

"Oh…, show him in please, Roberts."

In full uniform, a constable enters. "Apologies for the interruption, Lady Hervington, but I am afraid I have some bad news for you. You may wish to hear it in private."

"We are all friends here, Constable. Please carry on."

"Very well madam. I regret to inform you that Lord Hervington passed away last night at his club."

"Really?" she returns, unable to keep the joy from her tone. "What happened?"

"Apparently, he was playing cards and had a practically unbeatable hand, but someone beat him and as a result, his Lordship had a heart attack and pegged it, I mean died."

"Wonderful," smiles her Ladyship. "Where is he now?"

"At the morgue. Do you wish his body to be brought here once they've finished with it?"

"Oh no. They can keep him. Thank you, Constable."

"Thank you, madam. I also have a message from Chief Inspector Clump, for Detective Inspector Potter."

"I am he," announces I, realising my deal with her Ladyship has now been scuppered because that twat Hervington went and died before I could kill him.

"The Chief said to inform you that having stayed the night in Ipswich, he will be on the ten-thirty train back to London and will see you later."

"And that's all?"

"That is all, sir."

We thank him and Roberts shows him out. "So, my Lady," sighs I. "Obviously our deal is off."

"I'm afraid so, Inspector. Never mind at least the old git's off to hell and me and my loyal staff will soon be off to the Caribbean. You may have lost out on a share of the insurance money,

Inspector, but I am more than willing to honour the rest of the deal."

"Thank you," grates I. "I am afraid I do not have the time and my Sergeant obviously doesn't have the energy."

After breakfast, Head and I head off on foot down the dusty lane, carrying our empty bags, towards Manningtree Station. It has been a frustrating trip, profit wise and police work wise, but at least Head is happy, even if he can't walk properly.

The clip-clop of a horse coming up behind us causes us to stop and turn around to see Dobbin and the toothless cab driver come to a stop beside us.

"Mornin'," drawls the driver. "Need a cab, do ya?"

"I'd rather walk thank you," says I.

"'Ow about yon fella. 'E looks loik he ain't got a walk in 'im. Bin rompin' with 'er Ladyship I take's it."

"I could do with a lift, sir," pleads Head.

"Very well," I sigh, and we clamber up into the back of the carriage.

"Now then," says the driver. "Do you want ta plod or get ta the station quicker?"

"Plod will do," I groan, remembering the last trip we had with him and his demented nag. I also remember something else as Dobbin plods on. Our missing clothes. "Stop the carriage," I order.

"Wus up?" demands the driver.

I pull out my revolver and point it at the back of his head. "Kindly get down from there and take off my clothes, or I will shoot you."

"Thas a bit 'arsh," he grates.

"Off! Now!"

Reluctantly he clambers down onto the road and I climb into the driver's seat. "Get stripping. The jacket, shirt, trousers and the shoes, please, but you can keep that old floppy hat, it never did suit me."

He strips off down to his wee stained long-johns and hands me back my clothes. "What now?" he asks glaring up at me.

"I am requisitioning this carriage for urgent police business."

"What am I s'posed ta do 'en?"

"Walk. We'll leave your rig at the station." With that I take up the reins and click the horse on, it collapses in a heap just like it did before.

"Is it dead?" asks Head.

"No, Sergeant. He's just 'aving a laugh!"

Checkmate

We are in Clump's office. A bottle of scotch with three tumblers is set out on his desk. We are in for some real crap.

"What do you 'lads' know about Black Magic?" asks Clump as he pours the scotch.

"Not much, sir," says I truthfully.

"I like the cherry and coffee creams," smiles Head.

Clump glares at him and pushes over two, full to the brim tumblers. "Your feigning ignorance every time you think I am about to dump on you, Sergeant, is becoming somewhat tedious. I ask again. What do you know about Black Magic?"

"Do you mean Voodoo and such like?"

"Of course, I do!"

"Then not much, sir."

"Never mind. I am sure you will soon learn." He grins grinningly and holds out his tumbler. "Cheers."

We clink glasses. "Cheers," croak Head and I, before downing the scotch in one as it helps to deaden the senses from what we about to hear.

"Let us get down to the nitty gritty," smiles Clump as he refills our tumblers. "A body has been found washed up on the foreshore over Battersea way. Well, when I say a body, I mean a part of a body."

"How big a part?" asks I.

"Not a very big part," he returns cagily. "In fact, a small part, but big for its size."

Inwardly I yawn. Why doesn't he just get to the point? "What part of a body is it, sir?"

"A penis part."

I glance at Head, but he is staring down into his scotch as if it held some mystical answer to some unanswerable question.

"A part of a penis?" groans I.

"No, a whole one."

"What happened to the rest of the body?"

He shrugs, "No idea. It could be miles upstream or miles downstream. Perhaps crabs or fishes ate it."

"Perhaps," I sigh. "So, Chief, that is all you have? One severed penis. Would it be gross of me to suggest that the victim may have survived having his member cut off and there might not be a body?"

"Survived! I doubt it, Inspector. Would you want to survive if someone had cut off your penis?"

I shake my head, "Anything else to go on, sir? For instance, did it come in a bottle with a message?"

"Don't be a comedian, Inspector. It didn't come in a bottle, but it did come with a lot of clues. It is black. It is circumcised. It has a solid gold ring through the end of it. Meaning it is probably from a visiting African of some description."

"Why do you suspect this has anything to do with Black Magic, sir?"

"Because it is black. Anyway, it isn't my job to come up with conjecture but your job to go out and investigate."

Head adds his bit, "Not being funny, sir. Why waste time on investigating a dead man's dick when there's no body? It could take hours and hours and never get solved anyway."

"Because the Commissioner has told me to. Look 'lads', the son of an influential African King has gone missing from his rooms in Oxford, and the Commissioner is worried the penis might belong to him. That being the case we could have a diplomatic incident on our hands. So, it is important that you swiftly find out who the penis belongs to so we can hopefully rule out the King's son. Anyway," he goes on while producing a file from his drawer beneath his desk. "Here is the report on the case thus far. Take it away, study it and get yourselves going. Then start by viewing the body part down at the morgue. Any questions?"

Head puts his hand up, "Can I take a month's leave, sir?"

"No! Now, get off the both of you. And 'lads' good luck."

We down our scotch, pick up the report and leave.

"I don't believe this," says Head as we head back to our office to pick up our coats and stuff. "A bloody willy with no body. How the hell are we going to solve this one?"

"We shall take it one step at a time," says I, going into our office, "Let us read the report first."

We sit down at my untidy desk and I open the file. It contains information as to exactly where the object was found, a full report, along with close up photographs of the object. There is also a long white jewellery box that probably once held a necklace. The object was sent to the station in the box along with a letter. I read it out, "I found this gruesome piece of flesh washed up on the foreshore, see enclosed map, while I was bobbing down to pick up my dog's poo. I cannot become involved in this as I am a far too important person."

"What a load of rubbish," scoffs Head. "Who on earth would pick up their dog's poo when we've got millions of 'pure' collectors to do that?"

"Who indeed?" I ponder passing Head the note.

Having looked over everything in the file, Head says, "There's nothing much to go on, sir. It will be like looking for a flea in a Tibetan Yak's hairy coat."

"There are more clues here than first meets the eye, Sergeant. Let us go and view the object in question and then go down to the foreshore and see where it was supposed to have been washed up."

We don our bowlers, put on our coats and set off for the morgue. The morgue is attached to the end of the building and it takes us a few minutes to get there. On entering the sanitized, white tiled, operation room, we find the pathologist poking around a body on the mortuary slab. He is a tall skinny man who's wearing huge bottle-lensed glasses looped over jumbo sticking out ears. He has a beaky nose, wiry sticking up black hair and is muttering to himself. I have never seen him before.

"Good morning," says I.

Straightening up he sets his scalpel down by sticking it in the chest of the body he is working on and turns to face us. He has a vacant expression in his large saucer shaped eyes and stares blankly at us. But then he smiles like a madman and says, "Hello. Who are you?"

"D. I. Potter and D. S. Head. Who are you?"

"I am Dr Archibald Johnson. Temporarily standing in for Dr Smithson as he has had to rush down to Eastbourne because his mother's ill." He wipes his hands on his dirty bloody white coat and then stepping up close to us holds out his hand. "Pleased to meet such famous detectives," says he, grinning even more.

Reluctantly I shake his hand and am left with a sticky, sweaty feeling in my palm. Head also reluctantly shakes his hand.

"Now, Detectives, what can I do for you?"

"We wish to peruse your penis," says I.

"That's an odd request," he returns, grinning oddly while displaying a set of clean sharp teeth. "Shall I just drop my trousers or what?"

"The Inspector means the severed penis, not yours," snaps Head.

"What, the black one?"

"Do you have more than one?" I ask in horror.

"Not detached I don't," he grins even more. "I'll fetch it out for you."

Going over to number one of the three cold rooms he swings open the heavy door and goes inside, then he comes back pushing a body trolley with a white sheet spread over it. "Here it is," he grins throwing off the sheet to reveal a rather large black member with a gold ring through the nob end and an information ticket tied to that.

"That makes my eyes water," says Head shivering in horror. "It must have hurt like hell."

"Incredible," says I. "How long is it?"

"It is seven and one-half inches long and has a circumference of seven and one eighth of an inch," grins Johnson. "The gold ring is unmarked and weighs about two ounces."

I do wish he would stop grinning and staring with his saucer eyes, it is becoming very unnerving. Reluctant to touch the object I ask, "Can you turn it over for me?"

He promptly flaps it over as if it were a kipper.

"Thank you," says I.

"You're welcome," grins he. "Anything else, Inspector?"

"Not just now."

"Can I go ahead and do an autopsy on it now you've seen it?"

"What's the point of that?" puts in Head, aghast.

"Well you won't know until you cut into it!" comes the angry retort.

"Which would be a sacrilege," says I. "Why don't you just preserve it in a jar for now?"

"Well I need to do something with it. I can't have it taking up an entire trolley any longer. I'm short of trolleys."

"Why not put it on a tray, then," snaps Head.

"Regulations," comes the sneering retort that quickly turns into a grin. "All cadavers must be kept on separate trolleys for the duration until they have been autopsied. Then I can put bits on trays, pickle bits in jars or whatever. I can then stuff the insides I don't need back into the corpse and sew it up all ready for burial or cooking."

"Well you cannot autopsy this one until our investigations are complete," says I, pointing at the object." We might unearth someone who can identify it and they won't want to identify it if it is sliced into pieces."

"I see," he grins, rubbing at his stubbled chin. "Very well then!" he grates screwing up his face. He covers the object with the sheet and then angrily shoves the trolley back into the cold room and slams the door shut. Hands on hips he turns on us and demands bitchily, "Is that it?"

"For now," I retort, giving him the evil eye.

"Good. Then I can get on."

We leave him to go back to hacking at the body on the slab.

"He's as nutty as a nut," growls Head. "I should have given him a slap."

"In his defence, Sergeant, I would say you have to be nuts to work in a morgue. Plus, he seems to be on his own. What happened to the assistant mortician, Owen 'Limping' Lesley?"

"You're right, sir. Limping Lesley is always around. It's even been suggested that the man sleeps here over night."

"Perhaps he's on leave?"

Head shakes his head. "Limping never goes on holiday. The man lives only for the dead."

"Let us not worry about Limping for now," says I, as we go outside into a cloudy drizzly day and hail a Hackney.

"To Battersea foreshore," I order the driver as we climb into the back and settle down. "What five things did you deduce from seeing the evidence, Sergeant?"

"It was unusually large."

"Correct."

"It was black."

"Correct."

"It had a golden ring through it."

"Correct."

"It was circumcised."

"Correct."

"Um… That's it really."

"It could have been cut off shorter than its actual length. And why didn't whoever cut it off steal the ring? Weighing two ounces it must be worth a few quid."

"Which means?" ponders Head.

"Which means, Sergeant," ponders I, even more ponderingly. "Whoever committed the foul act didn't do so for financial gain."

"I see," says he thoughtfully. "A crime of passion, perhaps?"

"Perhaps," I wonder as I take out my notebook and jot down my observations. I am also wondering why the mud larks didn't get to the object before the dog poo picker-upper?

Presently we are dropped off at the embankment and take the stone steps down onto the foreshore. The rain has stopped but the sky is still full of the stuff. The foreshore is packed with soaked to the skin shivering mud larks fishing around for anything left behind by the receding tide. We trudge across the muddy flats to where our sketchy map tells us, roughly, the object was supposedly found and are quickly accosted by a small group of mud larks.

"Oi! Mister," snaps the tallest and meanest looking one. "You can't come pokin' 'round 'ere. This is our patch. So, piss off or pay up."

"How much do you want?" asks Head.

"Sixpence. That's a tuppence each."

"We are Police Officers," grates I. "Clear off before you receive a ringer around the lugs."

The brat straightens himself up, "Pay up or get splattered."

"Never," returns I with finality.

"Well that was a waste of time," moans Head, while still trying in vain to wipe rancid grey mud from his face with his handkerchief as we head back up the stone steps. "It would have been easier to pay them, sir."

"On reflection, Sergeant" I sigh. "It would have been."

Betty will be furious when she sees my coat is splattered with mud, as is my face, neck and hat, while my shoes feel as if half the mud from the Thames is stuck to them. Luckily it starts to rain heavily, at least it will wash some of the mud off.

"Where to now?" asks Head, his shoes flip-flopping on the pavement as we walk.

"I think we should go home, get cleaned up and take it easy for the rest of the day."

"But it's only about twelve, sir. We can't knock off this early."

"Agreed," agrees I. "Let us find a pub to kill some time and have a spot of lunch."

"A good idea," smiles he.

We go into the Neck Breakers Arms, a rough unfriendly sailor's pub that is packed with lunch time boozers. We go up to the bar where a massive bald man with prickly hairs sticking out of his grubby white vest glares at us through piercing dark eyes. "Did you just walk in here?" he demands.

"We did," I muse.

He sticks out a rippling with muscle arm that is covered with tattoos and points behind us.

"Are they your dirty footprints on my nice clean solid oak floor?"

Head and I look behind us to see that we have left a trail of sloppy mud prints from the entrance right up to the bar, "They are," confesses I. "If you have a mop and a bucket we shall swab the floor for you. We don't mind a bit of cleaning, even if we *are* Police Officers."

He leans a cauliflower ear nearer to us, "What was that?"

"I said we are Police Officers."

"Well don't bloody shout it out," he hisses fearfully. "Pretend you're a couple of toffs looking for a cheap doxy to warm you up a bit. Now me ol' mates," he roars, so the entire barroom can't fail to hear him. "What's ya poison?"

"Two pints of your best bitter, landlord," I roar back. "And I'll have a beef pie with all the trimmings."

"Bangers and mash for me," shouts Head.

"Take a seat, lads," beams the landlord. "I'll have a comely wench bring your beers right over. The grub'll be up in a bit."

"Thank you," thanks I. Head and I take a table and chairs in a quiet corner where we can survey the entire room.

"That was clever of you, sir," says Head. "But what if the landlord didn't give a shit and had shouted out that we're coppers?"

"It would have started a riot and we would have been massacred. The truth of the matter is he couldn't afford to start a riot. This place is infamous for handling smuggled goods from all over the world and the last thing the landlord needs is the place swarming with plods."

"I see," ponders Head as a comely wench in a thin pink dress limps over on her left leg and bangs two tankards of beer down onto the table.

"Compliments of the 'ouse, gentlemen." She smiles at Head, flicks back her curly mass of blond hair and pouts her ruby lips at him. What is it with him and the fairer sex? I have no idea, but certain women just seem to lust over him from the moment they see him.

She retreats while Head stares rampantly at her swaying rump.

"Let us review where we are at," says I, to take his mind off the obvious. "Which is nowhere."

Head takes a gulp of his beer, "Agreed, sir."

"That being the case, we must change nowhere into somewhere."

"Somewhere is better than anywhere, but then anywhere is better than nowhere," says Head. "The trouble is; who knows where anywhere is? Nowhere is nowhere. Somewhere is somewhere. But where is somewhere?"

"Who knows?"

"Someone must know if anyone does."

"Ah… But what if no one knows?"

"But what if everyone knows?"

"I see what you are saying, Sergeant. If someone in the know, knows someone who knows, then someone somewhere might know what everyone else knows. That being the case, we need to know who knows what about anything, everything and everyone."

"Agreed," nods Head while appearing utterly lost.

"Which brings us back to the beginning, Sergeant. Which is; we know nothing about nothing and might as well just drink our beer and hope it inspires us into lateral thinking."

"Exactly," says Head as the comely wench comes over with two plates of food and I notice she is now limping on her right leg.

"Bangers and mash?" she asks.

"That's me," says Head holding up his hand.

She gently puts his plate down and winks at him.

"Pie and veg'?"

"Obviously me," I sigh.

My plate is banged down so hard it slops the gravy over the edge.

"Any condiments?" demands she.

"Any tomato sauces?" asks Head.

She places her hands on her hips and smiles saucily at him. "No."

"Brown sauce?"

"No."

"Any sauces at all?"

"No."

"I won't have any then."

"We got salt, pepper, mustard and vinegar," says she.

"I'll have all of that," he grins.

She winks at him again and then flounces off limping on her left leg again.

"I noticed the woman limps on both legs but not at the same time" says I. "Any idea why?"

"Sympathy, sir," says he. "She plays the poor little thing so she can get what she wants."

"What does she want?"

"At least a good tip. Better still, a good man who will look after her, cherish her, give her babies, provide for her and never mess around with other women."

"Do you know such a man?"

"No, sir. Such a man doesn't exist."

Time to eat our meals.

"I have been thinking, Sergeant," says I, as I wipe my mouth with a napkin. "The gold ring in the evidence must have been done by a professional. It would be best if after lunch we seek out establishments that pierce ears and such. Someone might know something."

"A good idea, sir. But what if the penis floated downstream from miles away and as such was pierced and ringed at God knows where?"

"Admittedly it could have been done anywhere but we have to at least try. We'll start by visiting local places first and then move further afield."

"We could start at Piercer Pete's tattoo parlour in Fish Bone Alley."

"As good as anywhere I suppose," says I. "Do you know if he pierces penises?"

"No idea, sir. I don't think many places would go so far as to shove a needle through someone's todger."

"Todger! That's it, Sergeant. What a great alternative name for a penis. Never heard of it before but it is good, almost poetic. From now on the evidence will be known as Todger, which rhymes with Roger."

"Why not just call it Roger?"

"Brilliant. Roger Todger, but just Roger for short."

After three more pints we leave, the sun has decided to join us and as we walk along vapours float out from our sodden coats and at last we begin to dry out.

"I stink of the muddy shore," moans Head.

"Fear not, Sergeant. As everyone stinks of something or other no one will notice."

We walk on for over an hour until at last we arrive at Piercer Pete's. Pete is a short blubbery man covered in tattoos, he has rings through his ears, his nose and even his eyebrows. He is engrossed in tattooing a large picture of a galleon onto a man's back, in truth it is a work of art. Personally it is not for me, but I am fascinated to watch the man's skill at his craft.

"Can't say that this piercing lark appeals to me," says Head. "But I don't mind the odd tattoo."

"I am just thankful that females don't go in for tattoos and piercings, Sergeant. Could you imagine going down the high street and passing females with piercings in their lips and tattoos all over their bodies?"

"I have known a few women who had tattoos," smiles Head. "I must admit I found them rather intriguing."

Pete pauses from his work to dab a clean cloth over the galleon before sitting back and gazing up at us, "Now then, Sergeant Head, what can I do for you and your mate?"

"I am Detective Inspector Potter," returns I, taking out the picture of Roger and handing it to him. "We seek information on who may have been responsible for carrying out piercings such as these, so we may identify who Roger belonged to."

He takes hold of it and peruses it. "Roger, is it?" he muses. "Nothing to do with me, Inspector. I wouldn't go that far. Piecing a man's nob end could easily lead to nob rot which leads to a serious infection of your entire body. You'd have to have it cut off or you'd die." He hands me the photograph back complete with inky finger prints.

"Do you know anyone who would carry out such work?" asks I.

Pete shakes his head, "Nah. Least no one from around this area." He points a finger at me, "But I'll tell you something, your Roger is a sailor. Try looking down the docks for answers as to who he is."

"How do you know he's a sailor?"

"Sailors come to me all the time for a gold ring in their ears. They believe if they have a ring in their ear they won't drown. Your man had his put into his Roger instead of his ear because it was obviously his pride and joy."

We thank him and leave.

"Let us go home and get out of these stinking dirty clothes, Sergeant," says I, as a hackney pulls up to Head's whistling. "I am in dire need of a good soak."

"Me too," says Head as we climb into the cab and settle back in the seat. "Shall we meet up later?"

"Tomorrow morning will do. Come around mine at about eight and we shall go down to the docks and fish around."

"Shall I bring my fishing rods?"

"No. When I say fish around I mean search for evidence."

"Oh. I see," says he, sounding disappointed.

The cab drops Head off first and then takes me home as it starts to pour down again. Once dropped off I go around the back and step into the kitchen.

I yell out, "I am home."

"Good Lord, Detective Inspector," gasps Betty on seeing my bedraggled state. "Whatever have you been up to. You look as if you've been swimming around in the mud flats."

"As good as," I groan.

"Right. Well you can strip right off, Detective Inspector. I shall fetch your dressing gown, pour you a stiff drink and fill you a bath."

Betty helps me off with my coat and I strip down to my long johns. She hangs my coat up behind the kitchen door and then goes off upstairs. She comes back with my dressing gown and hustles me into the parlour where I sit in my favourite armchair by the roaring fire. Betty mixes me a scotch and water before going back into the kitchen to put large saucepans of water onto the hot plates. I settle back and relax.

We have an iron bath in the upstairs bathroom along with a new-fangled gas geyser which we have never used, due to the fact that if the geyser doesn't blow up the house and kill you the fumes from it will. I look forward to the days when gas and electric become safe enough for everyday use, until then Betty and I are content to keep to more traditional means of heating, lighting and cooking. But it is often hard work. Betty carries in the old tin bath from the outhouse and places it close to the fire. Over the next hour or so she is back and forth to the kitchen bringing in hot water and pouring it into the bath. At last it is ready. Betty rolls up her sleeves and swishes her hand around in the water.

"Just right, Detective Inspector," she smiles starting to undress. "Help me with my corset."

Standing up I throw off my gown, drop the long johns and help Betty to strip off. I get into the bath first and squash right back so Betty can squeeze in between my legs. We are seriously crammed together, but it is heaven feeling her lovely warm back against my still cold chest. We are just getting comfortable when there is a knock on the door.

"Ignore it," says I. But a face appears at the window, we hadn't drawn the curtains.

"It's the postie," says Betty, and forcing herself out of the bath she dons my dressing gown and goes to the front door.

"Afternoon, Betty," sounds the postie. "I see you're all ready for me."

"Oh... You really are a devil," she giggles.

"A parcel for you," says he.

"Thank you, Percy."

"Any tea going?"

"The Detective Inspector is home."

"Oh... He's early."

"That's what I thought."

"He hasn't got the sack, has he?"

"No. But I think he fell in the Thames."

"That's not good, Betty. I'd get him sanitized if I were you. Chuck some soda crystals into a bath of really hot water and give him a scrub with a stiff brush."

"Shut the bloody door!" I yell. "You're creating a draught."

"Alright. Don't get shirty," retorts the postie.

The door is shut and Betty returns carrying a small oblong parcel wrapped in brown paper.

"A parcel addressed to you, Detective Inspector," she says handing it over before shutting the curtains. "I wonder what's in it."

I peruse it. It has been posted locally. Stretching out I manage to put it on the sideboard. "I shall open it after our bath, Betty. Come on, get back in while the water's still warm."

We enjoy a very pleasant, if cramped, bath together without any further interruptions, which leads to us drying each other off followed by a quickie on the sofa. It is absolute bliss. Once dressed we carry the bath out back and tip the scummy water down the drain before hanging the bath back in the outhouse.

Betty gets on with preparing dinner while I sit back with another scotch and go through the daily paper. Nothing so far about Roger. Putting the paper down I pick up the parcel, tearing off the brown paper reveals an oblong black velvet jewellery type box in which you would expect to find a necklace. I open it up, inside it is lined with more black velvet, nestling on that velvet is another severed penis! Only this one is white and it hasn't got a ring through the end of it, nor is it anywhere near as big as Roger. There is also a message on a scrap of paper reading: 'It is your move.' I snap the lid down as Betty comes into the parlour.

"What's in that expensive looking box, Detective Inspector?" she quizzes, her eyes sparkling with excitement.

"Never you mind," I return, picking up on her thoughts as we are barely two weeks away from our wedding anniversary.

"Is it something a girl can wear around her neck?"

"Not really."

She holds out her left arm and wiggles her fingers, "Could a girl wear it on her wrist or her fingers?"

I shake my head.

She frowns and folds her arms, "Would a girl get a lot of pleasure from it?"

I am tempted to say not in its current state but opt for the safer answer, "She might."

"Ah... Is it one of those saucy French adult toys?"

"Perhaps."

She claps her hands together, "Oh... I can't wait to get my hands on it, Detective Inspector. Don't show it to me now or it will spoil the surprise."

It will be a surprise alright, I ponder and change the subject, "How long before dinner?"

"About an hour."

"I have to nip into the Yard," says I, getting up.

"What, right now, Detective Inspector?"

"I'll be quick," I wink. "I can't leave this in the house for you to go snooping around or it will really spoil the surprise. It will be safer kept at the Yard until the big day."

She comes over and gives me a kiss on the cheek, "Well don't be long. I've a lovely black pudding on the go."

"Marvellous," says I. I fetch my coat and slip the velvet box into my pocket and go out the back door. It has stopped raining and is somewhat brighter, but the night is fast drawing in. Taking my bicycle from the outhouse I set off for the Yard. Fifteen minutes later I am in Clump's office. He is sat back in his chair with his feet on his desk while puffing away on a fat cigar and swigging scotch.

"I did not expect to see you tonight, Inspector," he slurs. "What is it?"

"This," says I, putting the black box on his desk.

Swinging his legs down, the cigar smoking in his mouth, he opens the box, "Bloody hell! Another one."

"Sent to my home," I grate, taking a seat opposite him. "With a note inside it."

He pours me a scotch, it is the much better stuff then we usually get and I gladly receive it.

"What the bloody hell is going on?" he growls, as ash falls from his cigar to land in the box instead of on the floor as is usual.

"No idea, Chief. Whatever is going on it comes to something when you receive something like that delivered to your house."

"It wasn't delivered to my house, was it?" amazes he. Obviously, he is far more inebriated than usual.

"No, sir. It was sent to *my* house. Whoever sent it obviously knows I am on the case and is specifically taunting me."

He nods thoughtfully, "This is criminal, Inspector. Bloody criminal, and I want whoever is behind this strung up by their balls before the week is over. Do you understand me?"

"Perfectly, Chief. But I shall require as much extra help as is possible to solve this one in less than a week."

He downs his scotch in one and bangs the glass down, "And you shall have it, Inspector. This is the work of a madman, Inspector, and we must pull out all the stops if we are to prevent even more of these horrific crimes from happening. Now, have you managed to find out anything yet about the black penis?"

"We have, Chief. We know no one from around these parts would have pierced Roger Todger and put in a ring. We have also ascertained that Roger's owner could well be a sailor and not the missing African Prince."

"Sorry, Inspector. With all the hullabaloo going on, I forgot to tell you. The missing Prince has turned up safe and well, so forget about him. A sailor you say? What the hell has this got to do with a sailor? And who the hell is Roger Todger?"

"What it has to do with a sailor I have no idea. Roger Todger is the name we have given to the severed penis as we are fed up with saying penis."

"So am I," grunts Clump as he refills mine and his glasses. "I hate the word. What's wrong with dick, or chopper, or even prick? Having said that I like Rodger Todger, it sounds almost poetic." He tips the velvet box to one side so I can see into it. "What name shall we give this one, Inspector?"

"How about Harry Hampton, Chief?"

"Excellent. Well, Inspector. It is getting late and you have had a long day. I will take Harry Hampton down to the morgue while you get yourself home and see to that lovely wife of yours. Be here tomorrow for nine sharp. I shall call everyone into the briefing room and see if we can't hand over a lot of the donkey work to uniform so that you, and Sergeant Head, can concentrate on the more important aspects of this case."

"The more important aspects?"

"Someone is out to get you personally, Inspector. That much is obvious, and if that someone is ruthless and evil enough to cut off Roger and Harry he will take infinite pleasure in cutting you up or anyone else who is close to you. Get home and make sure your Betty is safe."

I down my scotch, thank him and leave.

As I cycle back home I turn over the events of the day. Nothing has really materialised but everything has turned decidedly dark. This is fast becoming a far more scary and dangerous case then I could have possibly imagined barely a few hours ago. Someone is playing a weird game of chess with me. A white box. A black Roger. A black box. A white Harry. 'It's your move?' The worst of it is; whoever is behind this not only knows where I live, they will also know that the most important person in my life is my beloved Betty. I cycle home so fast, the friction from my hard leather saddle is in danger of setting my backside on fire, while my mind races with thoughts that something terrible has already happened to Betty.

I breathe a sigh of relief on finding Betty innocently dishing up dinner on the kitchen table. She has obviously been on the sherry because she is giggly and her eyes are sparkling. An ocean of love crashes over me and I cannot stop myself from wrapping myself around her and crushing her to my body.

"Not now, Detective Inspector," she teases, pushing me away. "You need to eat first or you'll pass out from too much scotch and fatigue."

"You are right, as usual, my little raspberry. I shall wash my hands and sit up at the table like a good boy."

"And what do good boys get who sit up at the table nicely, without being pests?"

"They get extra oats for breakfast, dinner and tea. If they are really good they get their oats throughout the night as well."

I sit down and Betty puts my dinner down in front of me. Usually I love black pudding, but thoughts of Roger put me right off the meal before me.

"You've hardly touched your meal, Detective Inspector," says Betty after a while. "Is there something wrong? I hope you haven't picked up something nasty from the Thames?"

"I'm not really hungry my love. I ate too much for lunch."

Betty knows me better than I know myself. She starts to badger me, leaving me with no choice but to tell her about the scary turn of events regarding Roger and Harry.

"I think it best, Betty, that you go and stay over at your mothers until the case is solved."

"I think you are right," she sighs. "If I stay here you'll only worry, Detective Inspector, and if you worry you won't be thinking clearly. I shall go to mother's tomorrow."

"Good. That is a weight off my mind."

Suddenly my appetite returns and I tuck into my meal. We laugh and tease each other playfully over dinner and while we clear up. By nine o'clock we go up for an early night.

The briefing room is packed the following morning as Head and I take seats near the front. Roger and Harry's pictures have been blown up and pinned onto the blackboard. On the table in front of them, Clump has laid out all the evidence we have so far and is pacing up and down in deep thought. Suddenly he turns to face his audience, "Right. Quieten down," he orders waving his pointer stick around. "For those of you who do not know what has been going on regarding the investigations into the severed penises' case, I will enlighten you."

Clump rattles on for twenty minutes and manages to cover everything that has gone amiss since Roger first materialised. By now Clump is ready to set out his plan of action.

"I want uniform," he booms out, "to get out there and find me two bodies that match up with Roger and Harry. Check out every bloody morgue, every hospital and particularly every bloody medical school that buys bodies to hack up. Some of you can get yourselves down the docks and find out if any ship is missing any crew members. We have good reason to believe Roger and Harry may be visiting sailors. Get out there and rattle a few cages, do it hard, one of our officers could be in mortal danger from the madman behind these atrocities. I want that man found. One more thing before you get to it. 'Limping' Lesley, that short fellow with the wooden leg, who works in our morgue has gone missing. If anyone knows where he is or has any information about him report it to the Desk Sergeant. Now, piss off the lot of you."

Clump has given Head and I carte blanche to continue our investigations in any way we see fit. We head down to the morgue where we find a grinning Johnson hacking away at a middle-aged woman's body.

"Murdered last night," he grins straightening up and facing us scalpel in hand. "Strangled. Some old tart from the slums."

"The Ripper?" asks Head.

Johnson pushes his glasses back up his beak nose, "Not his M. O."

"What's an M. O.?"

"Short for Modus Operandi," says I.

"I'll look it up later in my dictionary," says Head.

"Anyway," demands Johnson. "What do you want?"

"We want to see Harry," demands I.

Johnson waves his scalpel around in obvious temper, Harry! Harry! Who the hell is Harry?"

"Harry is the name we have given to the new severed penis you received last night."

He laughs manically, "You've given a dick a name? Are you mad?"

Not as mad as you are, says I to myself.

"Shut up with the insults," demands Head, angrily. "Just go and fetch Harry, or I will."

"What, now? Can't you see how busy I am?"

"It is an order," snaps I. "Not a request."

"Very well," he snaps back. Stabbing his scalpel in the body's chest he stomps over to cold room door number one and swings it open. Pulling out a trolley he shoves it in front of us and lifts the sheet off to expose Harry but then just as quickly covers Harry up again.

Head grabs a corner of the sheet and rips it from Johnson's hand, "Do you mind if we take a moment or two to inspect the evidence?"

"What's to inspect?" comes the angry reply. "It's a severed dick. It hardly warrants a fleeting glance, let alone an inspection."

I am becoming very angry with this rude, not right in the head, idiot, "I suggest you shut up, Dr Archibald Johnson, and allow us to do our job without having to put up with your grossly offensive comments."

"As you wish," he sulks before turning more agreeable. "How may I help you, Inspector?"

"Can you turn Harry over, please?"

He flips Harry over and back, over and back, as if he's battering a piece of fish, while his eyes blaze in fury.

There is something very wrong with the man, "Did you once work in a fish and chip shop?" asks I, as calmly as possible.

He stares vacantly into my eyes and I find his bottle lenses and saucer eyes very disconcerting. However, I will not be intimidated by the man. "I am finding your utter lack of professionalism very galling, Doctor. May I ask where you trained to be able to achieve your qualifications to enable you to carry out a pathologist's work?"

He glares at me, "What's it got to do with you?"

"Just answer the Inspector's question," demands Head, slipping his right hand under his coat and wrapping it around the handle of his revolver.

Ignoring us, Johnson goes back to hacking away at the woman's body, only now he works with furious intent, slashing and stabbing manically.

"Stop!" yells I. "Stop or I shall arrest you!"

He turns on me while waving his blood-soaked scalpel around, "Go away. I'm too busy to see you right now"

Head draws out his revolver and points it at Johnson, "Cease or I will shoot you."

"I'll gut you like a fish before you can fart out a bullet," comes the teeth-bared snarl.

There follows a load bang and the smell of cordite, followed by a scream as Johnson drops the scalpel, grabs at his left ear where Head has just shot a hole in it, and falls to the floor.

"Good shot, Sergeant," says I.

"I was aiming for his forehead, sir."

"You shot my ear," blubbers Johnson. "What did you do that for?"

Before Head can answer a pair of plods burst in the room, truncheons drawn and ready to face anything they might find.

"What's amiss Inspector Potter?" puzzles Sergeant Eastman.

"The Doctor isn't well, Sergeant Eastman. Kindly take him for medical treatment and then lock him in a cell. I shall come and sort him out shortly."

"Very good, Inspector," says he.

Johnson is promptly dragged away screaming and cursing while dripping blood everywhere, but as we are in a mortuary the blood blends in well with the surroundings.

"What the hell was that all about?" says Head.

I shrug, "God knows. Perhaps the man has been over working and has slipped into fatigue. He *has* been working without an assistant."

"I think he's mad," scoffs Head. "Mad as a cat with its tail on fire."

"How mad *is* a cat when its tail on fire?"

"Bloody spitting mad."

"How would you know such a thing unless you have seen a cat with its tail on fire?"

"I set light to a few when I was a kid. Especially on fireworks' night."

"Enough said, Sergeant. Let us put the bodies away. Then we shall go and talk to Johnson."

Picking up a pair of forceps I wheel Harry over to cold room one. Finding Roger, I pick him up with the forceps and place him on a tray. I place Harry beside him, making sure they do not touch each other as it wouldn't be right. I push out the two empty trolleys to see Head roll the woman's body off from the marble slab onto a trolley before pushing her into cold room one. We then look in cold room two. It is empty. We go into cold room three where we find four sheets covering over four bodies. We lift the nearest sheet up. We are faced with a middle-aged gentleman's body dressed in a tweed suit and wearing a deer stalker hat. He still has his shoes on and there is no identification label to say who he is.

"His throat's been cut," grimaces Head.

I go through the man's jacket pockets and eventually pull out a wallet. Inside I find the man's name and address. Doctor Archibald Johnson. Fifteen Meadow Gardens, Oxford. This being the real Dr Johnson, who the hell is the Johnson down in the cells?

Head lifts another sheet up, "Look at this, sir. It's Limping Lesley."

I peer under the sheet. It's Limping Lesley all right. He is dressed in his usual white jacket and trousers; his fly buttons are open and his penis has been cut off. His throat has also been cut.

"I believe we have just found Harry's owner," says I.

Head exhales dramatically, "I hardly dare look to see who's beneath the other two sheets."

"Nor I," agrees I. "But I suspect one of them is black."

Head raises another sheet to reveal an obvious vagrant who's showing all the signs of having died of a heart attack. I lift the last sheet and there is our black sailor with his throat cut and his Roger missing.

"All the time our killer has been right under our noses, sir", grates Head.

"While playing us for fools, Sergeant. But what is it all about? Why has that madman committed such evil crimes and why has he targeted me specifically?"

"He's probably someone you once arrested, sir. Someone who's just got out of prison and has tracked you down with the intention of murdering you."

"But only after he has tormented me. The trouble is I cannot recall ever seeing the man before in my life. Unless it was so far back that I have forgotten his face."

"Perhaps you never saw his face."

"What are you saying?"

"Perhaps he wore a mask when you arrested him."

"I would have taken it off him the second I arrested him."

"Perhaps he was so covered in hair, say like a werewolf, you couldn't really see his face."

"I would have had him shaved for his photographs."

"Well, I reason the only reason must be he has changed a hell of a lot since you last clapped eyes on him."

"I agree," agrees I. "Let us go and interview him and find out exactly who he is."

"Can I give him a good kicking for good measure?"

"Only if he doesn't tell us what we want to know."

Before we leave I have one more task to complete. I carry the tray with Roger and Harry on over to cold room three. Using the forceps, I place Harry back on Limping's body and Roger back on our mystery sailor. We shut the cold room doors and head off back into the Yard proper. As we walk up a corridor we are horrified to find Sergeant Eastman and his Constable lying around having sustained injuries to their heads. Eastman is sat upright against the wall groaning, while his Constable is face down on the floor not groaning.

"They've been done good and proper," cries Head. "The bastard must have overpowered them and clubbed them with their own truncheons."

"Look after them, Sergeant," says I. "I have to chase after our madman."

I am out of the station in seconds and out on the main road, there is no sign of the madman. I scan everywhere; up street, down street. Nothing. Betty! What if he is going after Betty and she hasn't left the house yet to go to her mother's. I hail a cab. "Drive like crazy," I order the driver. "I have a madman to catch."

He whips the horse into a fast trot and we speed along the road, the trouble is he is going the wrong way. I yell out to him, "Turn around." He turns around, I give him my address and within ten minutes we pull up outside my house. I pay the driver extra to go back to the Yard and inform the Desk Sergeant that Inspector Potter has gone home while in pursuit of the madman. I go up to the front door and let myself in. All is deathly quiet, so quiet I can't even hear the mice squeaking in the larder. Venturing into the kitchen I find a note on the table written in a hand I do not recognise: 'If you want to see your Betty alive again go to 10 Pickle Lane. Come alone'.

Back outside I realise the mistake I'd made by sending the cab away as now there doesn't appear to be a cab in sight. Hurrying around back I fetch my bicycle and ride like the wind just as two cabs come around the corner. Too late, nothing can stop me and I am outside Number Ten Pickle Lane within twenty minutes. I dismount, my focus is entirely on the property before me; a former pickle shop, now out of business and appearing derelict.

An urchin jumps forward, "Anything I can do for you, guv'?"

I am not thinking, "Take this," says I, handing him my bicycle.

And of course, he does, and runs off with it as fast as his bony legs will take him.

There is no time to chase him. The door opens to a bell tinkling. I go in. The place is festooned with cobwebs and dust. It is dark and smells of rancid vinegar. Weaving my way around a rotting wooden counter I make my way warily through to the back room. Once the scene of pickling enterprise, it is now derelict, damp and unwelcoming. At the back of the bare room sits Betty tied to a rickety chair in front of a table. Standing behind her is the madman, his right-hand gripping Betty by the hair, forcing her head right back while his left hand holds a scalpel against her throat. On the table sits a chess board with all the pieces set out ready to play.

The madman, blood still dripping from the hole in his ear, grins at me, "Take your revolver out with your left hand and place it on the table. No tricks or your lovely wife will get her throat cut."

I do as I am told.

"Now, step right back," he orders.

I step right back and he reaches across the table, picks up the revolver and points it at me, at the same time he slips the scalpel into a jacket pocket which looks suspiciously like one of my jackets. "Take a chair, Inspector. Relax. Would you like a cup of tea?"

"No thank you," replies I. As calmly as is possible I sit down opposite him and Betty. "I just want to know what this is all about."

A flash of anger screws up his face, "About? About? You know what this is all about!"

I shake my head in confusion, "I have no idea. Perhaps you can enlighten me?"

"You stole my life. You must remember. You stole my life and sent me off to an asylum for fifteen stinking years."

"I have no idea what you are on about. Mr, whoever you really are."

"I'm really me, Cecil Armitage. Once the shining star in the chess world until you went and beat me. I was fifteen and hadn't lost a game since I was ten years old until you came along. You cheated me and bullied me, just so you could beat me."

"I have never played chess in my life. Nor have I heard of a Cecil Armitage. You have the wrong man, sir."

He lets go of Betty's hair, her head levels as her terrified eyes stare beseechingly into mine.

Armitage glares at me in apparent astonishment. He levels the revolver, "You lie. It *is* you. You are Gerald Potter the chess player, aren't you?"

"I am Gerald Potter, but I am not a chess player. But I have a cousin who was a chess player, he is also called Gerald Potter. He is a couple of years older than me and we look very much alike, except I am of a kindlier nature while he is a liar, a bully and a cheat. He is also taller than me."

His cheeks begin to twitch, his nose also twitches like a bunny rabbit's, "I do remember you being taller, but then I was shorter." He suddenly takes off his glasses and I can see he has one brown eye while the other is blue. "Recognise me now without my glasses on?"

"No. In truth, sir, I have never seen you before in my life."

"We'll see about that!" One handed he grabs the back of Betty's chair and drags it to one side before replacing it with another, then he sits down while keeping the revolver pointed at my face. "Let's play. We'll soon see if you're lying."

I hardly dare to ask, "What are the stakes?"

He laughs manically, "You'll love this. You win and I get to kill you, but Betty goes free. You lose and I still get to kill you and then I get to have Betty all for myself in revenge for what you did to my sister."

"What sister? And what did I do to her?"

"Ah... Good try, Inspector," grins he, wagging a finger in admonishment. "You know what you did to her, you-you-you, filthy cretin."

"I honestly have no idea what you are talking about. Perhaps you can enlighten me?"

His mouth twists up in temper, "You seduced her! You took her drawers off and did it to her and then you dumped her because she was pregnant!"

"I am afraid, sir, I did no such thing because I still have no idea what you are talking about."

"I had to strangle her because of what you did," he snarls. "Oh... The shame you brought to our family. I had to kill her and they locked me away for it."

"I see," says I, soothingly as all becomes clear. "My wicked cousin has committed terrible injustices against you, Cecil. May I call you Cecil?"

He gives a suspicious nod.

"And you have the right to seek revenge. But why did you go about seeking that revenge in the way you have? Why didn't you just kill me and be done with it?"

"You had to suffer. I suffered for years in that shitty nut house while planning my revenge. When I got out I spent weeks tracking you down," he grins. "Then I saw your face on the front of a newspaper, telling the world what a hero you were. So brave, so clever, criminals beware! After that it was easy learning all about you. Where you lived and everything else about you I needed to know. I already had a rough idea of how I was going to go about my revenge, when by chance I bumped into Dr Johnson while I was hanging around outside Scotland Yard. He asked directions to the mortuary. Of course, I knew where it was as I had familiarised myself where everywhere was. I went there with him and quickly dispatched him. Then I had to dispatch that wooden-legged assistant. I set myself up as Dr Johnson and took it from there."

"Why the severed penises in the post?"

"To confuse you and torment you. I was looking forward to the day when I would play you at chess, beat you and then kill you. Then I would have anonymously informed the police where your body was, and you would have ended up on the slab. Then I could do an autopsy on you and chop you to bits, while taking the greatest pleasure in slicing off the dirty dick that fornicated with my sister. The wonderful thing about all this is, despite a few setbacks, I can still see my plan through to the bitter end."

"Where does the black sailor come into this?"

"Oh… Him," says he with indifference. "He came staggering down Pickle Lane drunk as a lord late one night. I invited him in, he was so drunk he stumbled in, got his thing out and peed all over the place. I was so incensed I slit his throat. The next morning, I borrowed a costermonger's cart and conveyed the body to the morgue."

"You pushed a body through the streets on a hand cart? Surely someone must have challenged you to ask what you were about?"

"They did. I just told them 'suspected cholera' and they'd get right out of my way. Now, enough of this. Let's play. You can go first."

"Is this game the same as draughts?"

"No! Draughts is for idiots. Chess is for clever people. Stop trying to trick me into believing you are a fool when I know you are a really clever Detective."

"I still can't play chess."

He screams out, "Play!"

I play but have no real idea what I am doing and muddle my way through. I am quickly beaten in a few classic moves.

"You're useless," snaps Cecil. "Again."

We play again, and again I am thrashed in a few classic moves.

Cecil points the revolver at Betty, who still appears utterly terrified, "Can she play?"

"I don't know," says I. "Betty, can you play chess?"

"No. But I can play draughts quite well."

Cecil is up on his feet and looking furious, "We're not going to play fucking draughts! If anyone mentions fucking draughts again! I'll fucking kill them!"

"How about you give me a few chess lessons instead," says I. "Perhaps then I might give you a run for your money."

He laughs and is instantly calm, "You can't learn the ancient game in a few lessons, Inspector. But hey-ho, why not?"

Cecil begins to teach me with obvious relish and within no time at all he has put the revolver down. He has become so absorbed in teaching me, all else is thrown out the window. After a while we take a break. Cecil has the rusty old oven in the kitchen going and puts on a kettle to make tea.

I call out to him, "Can I untie Betty?"

He comes back in and hands me the scalpel, "Of course. Tea or coffee, Betty?"

"Um... Coffee, please," says she, her voice trembling.

Cecil goes back into the kitchen and Betty whispers, "Why don't you shoot him, Detective Inspector?"

"Because he is *that* dangerous if I miss we are dead. He easily overpowered two policemen earlier, Betty. He was unarmed while they had truncheons drawn. He has already slaughtered three people that we know of since he arrived here from the loony bin. He is placated, for now, let us keep him that way."

"I've wet myself," cries Betty.

"It is a wonder that is all you have done," smiles I. "You are my brave little girl. Just keep smiling at Cecil and we'll be out of here soon." I am wondering where the hell Head has got to. I would have thought he'd have followed up on the message the cab driver would have delivered to the Yard, gone to my house and read the letter on the table.

Betty and I chat away as if it is an everyday occasion to be entertained by a raving madman. Cecil returns and places a plate of cakes and biscuits down before fetching in a pot of coffee and a pot of tea along with cups, milk in a jug and sugar in a bowl. All the crockery is chipped and well used but is clean.

"Betty, you can be mother," says Cecil.

"Oh... Thank you, Cecil," smiles Betty wanly. She pours the milk in the cups; her hand is shaking so much half the milk slops onto the table.

"I'll do it!" snaps Cecil, snatching the jug from Betty. He pours the milk, pours the tea and then the coffee. "Help yourself to cakes and biscuits, But, don't take all the Garibaldis."

There are only two Garibaldis anyway and I am more than happy to leave them to Cecil.

We are half way through our second cuppers when, silently and stealthily, Head, revolver drawn, comes into the room via the kitchen and puts the point of his weapon to the back of Cecil's head. At the same time two plods come in the room from the front entrance and point rifles at Cecil who is staring up at them in amazement. I can see a blood bath about to happen if I don't handle the situation the right way.

I stand up, "Gentlemen. You are just in time for tea. Please put down your weapons and find somewhere to sit."

Head's eyebrows go up to the ceiling as he gives me the questioning eye. But he knows me well enough to trust my judgement and puts his revolver back into its holster. The plods drop their rifles. There aren't enough chairs for everyone to sit, but the plods are happy to stand. Cecil makes more tea and before long everything is going along wonderfully. One of the plods mentions that he loves playing chess and I am ordered by Cecil to give up my seat and allow the plod to play. They play a cracking game and are well matched, but eventually Cecil triumphs. He is ecstatic, so much so he allows himself to be arrested and taken outside to be placed inside the Paddy Wagon to be carted off to the Yard.

"Are you coming with us?" asks Head as he climbs up to take the reins.

"We shall walk. Thank you, Sergeant."

And we do, returning the wave from Cecil as he pokes a hand through the bars to wave us good bye.

"Will he hang?" asks Betty, tears welling up in her eyes.

I put an arm over her shoulders, "No. He will be incarcerated for life in an asylum. Let us hope there will be other chess-playing nutters in there for him to compete against."

"You are an excellent liar, Detective Inspector," says Betty. "You even had me believing you."

"Forgive me, Betty. I saw no other option but to lie through my teeth."

"A cousin who just happened to be your double? You can't play chess? I thought you were a champion player before you met me?"

"I was. But I couldn't afford to let Cecil know. He would have killed us both."

"I could say, Detective Inspector, those were the scariest games of chess I have ever seen. God knows which one of you was the real winner."

"It was check mate for Cecil, and check mate for me."

"Did you seduce his sister?" she asks on a more serious note.

"No. Honestly. In fact, I did not even know she existed."

On passing by Bray Waunepcy's pawn shop, I spy my bicycle chained up outside with a price tag of two pounds on it.

"Wait here, my love," says I. "I shall be but a moment."

Waunepcy is behind his counter when I go in. He gazes up at me through watery eyes and sighs in frustration.

"Keys," demands I, holding out a hand.

"I've only just bought that bleedin' bike."

"If you buy stolen goods, Waunepcy, you can expect trouble."

He shuffles behind me as I go outside and unlock the chain on the bicycle.

"That brat who sold it me said you give it him," snaps he.

"No, you have got that wrong. I did not *give* it him, I *gave* it to him."

"So, you admit you give it him?"

"No, I didn't *give it him*, I gave it to him."

"Then he sold it me."

"No. He sold it *to* me."

"When did he sell it to you?"

"He didn't sell it to me. He stole it *from* me."

"You just said you give it to him. Now you're sayin' 'He stole it from me.'"

"I never said he said he stole it from you! It was my bicycle in the first place and I know exactly who stole from me."

"Whatever!" snaps Waunepcy, throwing his arms up in despair as dust and dead fleas fall out of his scruffy beard. "All I know is, I've just paid out two-bob for that bleedin' bike."

Betty joins in the affray, "Two-bob! Why, you mean old Scrooge. Fancy cheating a poor starving little urchin like that. You should be ashamed of yourself."

"Well I isn't. So, there."

"No," says I. "You isn't, should be you aren't."

"Keep the bloody thing, Jerry Pot! And I hope you get hemarods ridin' it!" With that he goes back into his shop, slamming the door behind him.

"Can we go home now?" sighs Betty. "I've had enough stress for one day, Detective Inspector."

I climb onto the saddle and gesture for Betty to get on the crossbar. She smiles at me, clambers up and sits side-saddle. Betty wraps an arm around my waist and we set off for home.

"This is nice," she coos just before a ball of horse dollop hits her smack in the face.

The Fox Hole Inn

We are on a train heading towards the fishing town of Lowestoft on the Suffolk coast. We are sharing a carriage with a woman and a boy who sit opposite us. She is a po-faced young woman in a cheap fur coat and matching hat, sat beside her is a porky boy in a black overcoat and black cap with an embroidered castle upon it.

Outside it is blizzarding snow; fanning past our window like millions of cotton balls. It is dark beyond the falling snow, dark yet grey, visibility is down to a few yards, the wind howls and it is very cold, but inside we are snug and warm thanks to the steam pipes that run beneath our seats, keeping our bottoms well warm.

Head is engrossed in his latest read: *The Oxford Dictionary*. He is keen to improve his poor spelling, while I am happy to relax and read my paper beneath the weak light from the lamps behind my head. Gazing over my paper I watch in disgust as the porky boy shoves a stumpy fat digit up his turned-up nose and begins to root around like a piglet in a trough.

"Dirty little swine," says Head putting his book aside. "Look, sir, that brat is extracting his finger, inspecting what's on it and then wiping it on his mother's coat!"

I cannot let this pass, "Madam. Your son is wiping grumbles onto your coat."

She reacts instantly by leaping to her feet and slapping the brat across the right side of his head and then his left, knocking his cap off in the process. The brat jumps to his feet, flings open the sliding carriage door and flees up the corridor crying; 'Mother! Mother!'

"That taught the little shit," says the woman retaking her seat and brushing down her coat.

I am astounded, "It certainly did, madam. But don't you think you should go after him and comfort him?"

She sneers at me, "Whatever for?"

"He is your son!"

"No, he isn't. I have never seen the little monster before in my life before tonight."

She goes back to staring po-faced at the seaside picture on the wall behind me. I look at Head and he looks at me, we are astounded by the woman's actions, but not half as much as when we see another woman suddenly filling the doorway with her huge hippopotamus bulk.

"Which one of you hit my little Willy?" she demands, scanning beady eyes encased in muscled fat around the compartment.

Head doesn't hesitate, "She did," he points.

Unable to squeeze into the compartment face on the hippo turns sideways and squashes her way in before going for Po-face like a demented bear, growling and snorting she gives Po-face a right and a left that should have felled an ox, but Po-face isn't about to crumble beneath the brutal assault and swings her black sequined bag with such ferocity at Hippo's face the big woman is momentarily stunned, enough for Po-face to jump to her feet and follow up the handbag swipe with a mean head-butt. Hippo woman falls backwards as Head and I shunt to each end of the seat before we are flattened beneath a ton of blubber. Po-face is on her again, yanking at her dark locks and slapping her face. Hippo woman has had enough and shoving Po-face away from her she makes a break for the door. Big mistake, she succeeds in only wedging herself in the frame. Po-face seizes her opportunity and starts punching the Hippo in the kidneys, right left, right left. Hippo woman screams and farts out in tempo while desperately trying to push herself out of the door.

I fold up my paper, it's time we intervened. Head and I jump up and grab Po-face by an arm each and wrestle her back, she kicks, spits and snarls while screaming out expletives unbecoming of the so-called gentle sex. It is like trying to hold on to a demented banshee, her strength is phenomenal.

"Cuff her," I yell.

One handed, Head pulls out a pair of handcuffs from his coat pocket and clamps them on her left wrist and we haul her back and clamp the other end of the cuffs onto the barred overhead metal luggage rack. She is held, but continues to fight, trying to claw at us with her free hand while trying to kick either of us in the gentleman's area and screaming out such vile abuse there is nothing else for it. I take out my short truncheon from inside my coat. "Madam," I demand. "We are Police Officers. Cease or I shall be forced to crack your skull."

"Try it!" she hisses.

So, I do, giving her a light tap on her skull over her fur hat enough to stun her into silence. She stares up at me in shock.

"Madam, if you so much as move an inch I shall give your skull an even harder tap with my truncheon and then arrest you. Do you understand me?"

She nods as tears start to fall from one eye that has already swollen to epic proportions from Hippo's punch, while the other eye is surrounded by the imprint of Hippo's knuckles.

"Help me. Help me," begs Hippo woman.

I glance at Head; we have been partners for so long we often think the same way. Taking off our bowlers we step back to the window and then charge forward and slam our bodies into Hippo's back, only to bounce back having not moved her an inch.

"Again, sir," says Head.

"Again, Sergeant, but with more force."

We back right up to the window, take a deep breath and charge. Hippo wails out in agony as we slam into her, but she hasn't been moved so much as an eighth of an inch.

"Bloody hell," pants Head.

"Immovable," I gasp.

"Stab her in the arse!" shouts out Po-face. "Shove ya truncheon up her ring. That'll get the old sow moving."

I tap her on the head again with my truncheon and she swiftly shifts as far back as she can while rubbing at her skull.

"What now, sir?"

"God knows, Sergeant. Perhaps the railway men can take out the door frame."

Suddenly the Hippo woman goes into a real panic, "No! No! Anything but that. God help me."

There is a rustling sound coming from beneath her crinoline dress, a bump appears near the bottom of her hem between her legs, the hem is lifted and an urchin's grubby face appears.

"I'll get her out, mister, for a sixpence," grins he grinningly.

"Done," agrees I and fishing out a sixpence from my trouser pocket I hand it over to the skinny hand that briefly appears, the head disappears back under the dress and I hold my breath.

Hippo woman suddenly screams blue murder as her body goes into violent contortions before popping out of the frame like a Champagne cork, she is free and cannons across the corridor to slam into the opposite side before wheeling to her right and storming away like a stampeding elephant, leaving behind her the urchin, who's sat cross-legged while perusing his sixpence held up in one hand along with a blood tipped, evil looking hatpin in the other. It is a miracle he wasn't trampled to death.

"Anything else, mister?" grins the urchin getting to his feet.

"Not just now, thank you."

Before you can blink, he's grabbed Po-face's bag, shot out into the corridor and disappeared. I slide the door shut to keep out the draft and Head and I retake our seats.

"What about me?" demands Po-face. "What about my handbag?"

"Your handbag is lost, madam," returns I. "And you will remain cuffed until we reach the next station."

"I'll have your guts for this," she snarls. "My uncle is a very important man who will see you booted out from whatever miserable little Police Force you represent."

"We are Scotland Yard's finest, madam."

She laughs, "Brilliant. My Uncle Arthur works for Scotland Yard."

"Arthur who?"

"Arthur Clump," she smirks. "Have you heard of him?"

Head whispers in my ear, "You couldn't make it up, sir."

"No, indeed not," sighs I. "Sergeant, uncuff the woman."

Head goes to uncuff her just as the door opens again, it is the ticket collector.

"Tickets please. Oi, oi. What's going on here then?"

"Nothing that concerns you," says I.

"Are you alright, madam?" says he.

"Piss off," says she.

"Charming," sulks he.

"Just check our tickets and go," demands I.

Head releases the woman, but she cannot produce a ticket as it was in her stolen handbag. Head and I produce our tickets, which are duly punched and returned to us before the ticket collector turns on Po-face, "You will be thrown off the train at the next stop unless you can come up with the fare."

"All my money was in my bag," she pleads.

I root around in my trouser pocket, "How much is the fare?"

"Two and six will do," he smiles.

I hand it over and he hands Po-face a ticket and leaves.

I shut the door but it is almost immediately opened again. It is the trolley man.

"Tea, coffee, alcoholic drinks, cakes, biscuits, sick bags and toilet rolls."

"Scotch and water," says I.

"Me to," says Head.

"And me," says Po-face. "I'll have a cake as well."

"Very well, madam," says he scratching his backside then sniffing his fingers. He pours the drinks and hands them over with a current bun on a plate for Po-face. I pay for everything, sit down and sigh with relief. Perhaps now we can continue in peace, only Po-face will have none of it.

"I had close on two pounds in that bag," she accuses. "If I go home broke my old man will go mad and so will Uncle Arthur once he hears how you let that sewer brat steal my bag. That's if I tell him of course."

"Black mail is a criminal offence, madam," I retort.

"So is assault with a deadly truncheon," she snaps back while rubbing her skull. "You should feel the lumps on my head."

Head whispers in my ear, "She's got us by the roundies, sir. She could cause us a heap of trouble."

He is right of course. I pay up but refuse to give the vile woman more than a pound note, which she reluctantly accepts. I am about to order her to go find another compartment when the train starts to slow as it approaches a station with a snow-covered sign that announces 'ham'.

Po-face gets to her feet, "Here's my stop."

Thank God, I sigh inwardly.

She flounces out the door, turns and says, "Nice doing business with you gentlemen." Shuts the door and disappears.

Two minutes later she is outside on the platform, the snow whistling around her head. She waves at us as the train pulls away, just as the urchin, still holding her bag, goes up to her and takes her hand. They both stick two fingers up at us before they melt into the grey fog.

"We've been had," says Head.

"Indeed, we have," ponders I. "But, obviously she knows Clump, so we must except we've got away lightly."

"Unless she heard us talking earlier, sir. When we were discussing our current assignment, we mentioned Clump several times."

"But not his first name," I counter.

"Perhaps she just guessed."

"Or perhaps she knows Clump via another route?" I rack my brains. The woman seemed familiar to me. I have known her from somewhere, plus she had a distinct London accent and wasn't a country type from these parts. It comes to me. "I know of her, Sergeant. Clump hauled her into the Yard some years ago. She was arrested for pickpocketing gentry while they waited for their connections." I click my fingers. "She was known as Fanny 'The Feeler' Frampton, pickpocket extraordinaire. They said she could feel around inside a man's pockets without them being remotely aware they were being felt up. Only realising something was amiss on discovering their wallets were missing."

"The cow!" snaps Head, going through his pockets. "She's snaffled my wallet and my watch."

"We have been truly shafted, Sergeant." I go through my own pockets, nothing is missing, but then she never had the opportunity to fleece me.

"That's that then," says Head flopping back into his seat. "I haven't a penny on me."

"Fear not, Sergeant. I shall fund us for the remainder of the trip. Let us hope we complete our mission sooner than later and are soon back home in the bosoms of our families."

"Only I haven't got any bosoms or family to get back into," moans he.

I sit back and ponder our mission once again. Clump, under orders from the Commissioner, has sent us to this Lowestoft place en route to the stately home of the Earl of East Suffolk to investigate the disappearance of his only son: Lord Sydney Melham. Sydney disappeared from the family seat three weeks previously. The local plods have so far failed to find even the tiniest clue as to Sydney's whereabouts and his parents are frantic, especially as Sydney is due to wed the industrial heiress Miss Angela Foley. Miss Foley wants to be accepted within the aristocracy while as usual the aristocracy wants her money because they haven't got any of their own. We are to alight at Lowestoft where we will be picked up by carriage and conveyed to Melham House and take it from there.

The ticket collector suddenly sticks his head in again. "Just to warn you, gentlemen, the snow has drifted so heavily on the track ahead it is almost certain we will not be able to continue beyond Darsham Station until the morning."

"Where have we just left?" asks I.

"Saxmundham. But we cannot go back there and must stay the night at Darsham."

"If we have to spend the night on the train without heating we shall freeze to death," points out Head.

"We shall supply thick blankets and hot drinks throughout the night, sir. However, should you wish to do so you may alight at Darsham and seek overnight accommodation in the village. I will keep you informed about what is happening."

"How many other passengers are still on the train?" asks I.

"Just two more. A rather large Lady with her Son."

"Is he a piggy porky boy?"

"That's the one. Now if you require anything to eat, order now or it may not be available later on."

We thank him and he leaves.

"This is a pain, sir."

"A bloody nuisance, Sergeant. But who can argue with nature. I am thinking it would be best to seek accommodation somewhere else rather than remain on the train should it not be able to continue on to Lowestoft. A proper bed, a good meal and a few bevvies by a roaring fire is infinitely preferable to the limited choice from the trolley man eaten in a cold compartment with only a blanket to keep you warm. Plus, we could be stranded here for days and Clump will have no choice but to pay our reasonable expenses, even if they are unreasonable."

The train chuffs on but is slowing down by the minute until we are met by a wall of snow at the end of Darsham Station.

The ticket collector appears. "Change of plan, gentlemen. It would be best for you to find accommodation in the village as we may be here for days. There is a good inn just a couple of hundred yards from the station that caters for travellers. It is called The Fox Hole Inn."

We thank him, take our bags down from the rack and head down the corridor to an exit door and step down onto the platform. The wind bites at our faces, the snow whips into our eyes causing us to blink incessantly as our feet sink into ankle deep snow.

We go through the station, no one asks for our tickets as the place is deserted, everyone has obviously gone home, there isn't even a single urchin about. The Station Master steps out shivering from his office to welcome us. We ask for directions to the inn and pointing he tells us to 'follow that lane' and we can't miss it. There are no cabs so we plod on by foot, the snow is much deeper out front and comes half way up our shins. A desperate sounding voice sounds behind us. It is the Hippo woman.

"This is all very scary," she cries struggling to catch up with us while dragging Porky boy behind her who still has a finger up his nose. "May we come with you?"

"Please do, madam," says I.

Luckily, she only has one bag with her which I take from her. She picks up Porky and carries him as Head leads the way and we follow in single file. Visibility is so low we can barely see a hand in front of our faces. Our inadequate shoes only add to the struggle. Talking is impossible and we battle on in silence, until at last, flickering yellow lights peep out through snow flecked small latticed windows encased in a timber framed thatched building with a sign that says, Hole (the rest of the inscription being covered in snow).

We trudge up to the entrance, an oak planked door within a porch. Head clicks up the latch and opens the door, but the wind suddenly picks up strength and whips the door from Head's grasp. It flies open inwards and slams with a resounding bang that is followed by a terrified chorus of screams that punch our eardrums and make us jump out of our skins, even Porky boy's finger shoots out from his nose. We step inside the barroom to be met by a hulking great brute with a shaven head, bare forearms of steel and a face like a well battered bulldog. He is holding a shotgun shoulder height that is pointing straight at us.

"Shut the bloody door and put your hands up!" demands he.

Head and I drop our bags and raise our hands as Hippo puts her weight behind the door and shuts it while still holding on to her Willy.

"Now bolt it," demands the hulk, raising himself up to his full height so his head is barely an inch below the oak beams.

Hippo bolts the door.

"Keep them hands up. Who are you and where are you from?" He points the gun at Hippo. "You first fatty."

"I am Mrs Jessica Hammond and this is my son William. We are from Lowestoft. And I am not fat, I am merely of larger proportions."

"Fat is fat," he snarls and points the gun at me. "You next."

"I am Detective Inspector Gerald Potter from Scotland Yard and this is my colleague, Detective Sergeant Richard Head, also from Scotland Yard."

He moves closer to me and stares into my eyes, "You say you are coppers? Show me your identification, but no tricks or I'll blow your head off."

I reach inside my inner coat pocket, take out my wallet, extract my warrant card and hand it over.

He peruses it, hands it back, lowers his gun and declares to the dozen or so people behind him, "He's a copper alright."

A cheer goes up, hands are clapped together, everyone is on their feet and smiling with obvious relief. Whatever is amiss it is serious.

"I am the landlord," says the landlord holding out a ham-fisted hand. "Bill Bennet. Welcome gentlemen, lady and boy. Come over to the bar for brandies on the house."

Picking up our bags we all go up to the rustic bar, behind it is a comely, dark haired wench showing more bosom than a Jersey cow. Beside her, is a golden haired young woman showing no bosom. At the bar, there are six men who look like labouring locals. Over in one corner, isolated from the friendly chatter at the bar, sits a young, very attractive brunette of obvious high class. She sits opposite a hard-faced middle-aged man in a black suit, short cropped black hair and two days' dark stubble around his cheeks. Beside him sits a ramrod straight shrew of a woman with sharp eyes and a beaky nose. All three appear apprehensive and confrontational.

As the brandies are poured I glance around the room. It is of a good size with several round tables, chairs and stools. There is a welcoming roaring log fire in the inglenook fire place and the smell of beer, cigars and pipes all add to the ambience.

"God has sent you to us," cries the young woman behind the bar as she raises her arms to the ceiling. "He has heard our plea. You have been sent to free us all from the evils of this world."

"My daughter, Sarah," says Bill. "Take no notice. She is frightened and prone to religious ranting and raving."

"I'm Martha Bennet," announces the older woman as she offers her hand across the bar. "The landlady."

We shake hands. Head shakes her hand and before we know it we are being approached by the labourers who are keen to shake hands with everyone, including Porky boy, only to immediately rub the palms of their hands down their trousers to get rid of the transferred nose secretions. Everyone is very friendly except for the trio in the corner, who remain stock still in their seats while staring over at us. The air is filled with friendly banter but everyone, except the landlord has at least a trace of fear in their eyes.

"What is amiss here, Bill?"

"Murder, Inspector," says he as the room goes deathly quiet. "Bloody and brutal. Here in this very place. We have a body upstairs."

"A dead one?" asks I.

"Yes, I believe so."

Martha puts a line-up of small brandies on the counter, I pick one up and chuck it down, so does Head, the labourers and even Mrs Hammond, Porky boy reaches for one only to receive a slap on his hand by his mother.

"Show me the body," demands I.

"Follow me," says Bill.

"Stay here, Sergeant," orders I.

"Will do, sir," says he.

I follow the landlord up the twisting creaking stairs, at the top there are six numbered rooms leading off from the hallway. Bill goes up to room number three and opens the door. We step inside, there laid face down on the floor is a splayed out naked body with a knife stuck in its back. The body has short black hair and a pair of testicles, so I assume it is a man. It is also young.

"Found him like this around five, two hours ago. He didn't come down for his dinner, so Martha came up to see what was keeping him. She screamed the place down. I rushed upstairs, as did a couple of the locals. Then I ordered everyone back downstairs and took out my shotgun intent on keeping everyone in the bar where I could see them. Then I sent James Parker out to get the Constable."

"Who is James Parker?"

"The local vicar."

"Pray continue."

James went out but never came back, nor did the Constable turn up. I thought about going out myself, but no one would let me leave they were that scared. Since then, except to go and pee, no one has left the room. Until you turned up we thought we may be stuck here for days before anyone came to our rescue. Oh… I do know he was still alive at three because he was downstairs by the fire reading his book. Then he went upstairs."

"Therefore, he was murdered sometime between three and five o'clock," says I "This is a damnable crime. To knife a man in the back when he is naked and then just leave him like that is appalling. Anyone could have found him. Who is he and why was he here?"

"He is a Mr Alwin Jones. He arrived a week ago and booked in for an undisclosed period. Said he just needed to escape to get his thoughts together."

"Escape from what exactly?"

"He didn't say. Seemed pleasant enough, and despite his Welsh name he spoke with a distinctly upper-class English accent. Obviously, a gentleman, very polite and forthcoming."

"Did he have any visitors while he was here?"

Bill shakes his head, "No, no one. Kept himself to himself mostly. Went out for walks a lot and liked to go to the church and chat to James. Other than that, he'd read a lot by the fire and smoke the odd cigar over a few glasses of red wine. Liked his food and retired early, usually around ten."

"Anything odd about him?"

"No."

"Did he have any correspondence in or out?"

"No."

"I shall look around." I look around and go through his clothes in the wardrobe and rummage through his pockets and find a wallet. His possessions are expensive, a tailored tweed suit of the finest quality. Shirts, cardigans, hats, etc. are all best quality. Even his leather suitcase reeks of quality. But everything is a little jaded, a bit tatty and has seen better days. Stepping away from the wardrobe I open the wallet, it contains a few pounds but nothing to confirm his identity or where he is from, I put it in my pocket, for now. Over on the dressing table there is a framed photograph along with the usual dressing table stuff. The photograph depicts obviously upper-class family members sat out in front of a stately home with the inevitable array of gundogs sat around their feet, behind the family stand various servants and I am thinking I am looking at a picture taken at the home of the missing aristocrat, Lord Melham. I go through the dressing table drawers, mostly underwear and socks. I inspect the iron framed bed, the candlewick bedspread is in disarray, the sheet lies beside the bed crumpled up and heavily creased, as if someone, or ones, had been rolling around on the floor in it. I know this because Betty and I do it all the time. Well not all the time, but quite often. Were there sexual shenanigans going on here which may well have led up to the victim being murdered? The question is, who was in bed with the victim and was it they who killed him? I inspect the body and can see nothing wrong with it except for the knife stuck in its back. I jot down notes in my book and then suggest to Bill that we wrap the body in the bedspread, take it downstairs and out back where we can lay it in the snow so it will freeze and remain fresh for a later autopsy. We roll it in the bedspread, and Bill, as strong as an ox, slings the young man over his shoulder and carries him down the twisty stairs, only to trip on the last step and fling the body forward so it flies into the bar, bounces back and then hits the floor where it unrolls in all its naked glory for all to see. Everyone screams, Martha faints, Sarah falls to her knees and begins to pray and even the tight-lipped trio in the corner appear horrified as they rise to their feet and edge their way closer for a clearer view. Head is quick to act and covers the body up again. "Have you any string?" he asks Bill.

"Loads. What type?"

"Any bloody type!"

String is duly fetched and Head ties it around the blanket and we lift it up.

Sarah is on her feet and coming out from behind the bar, she begins to pray, "God, we pray you take this poor sinner into your heart and absolve him of his sins. We also pray that the thing sticking out of the blanket is a finger and not an unmentionable. God forgive my gawping."

"Quick, shove this over it," urges Bill, handing head a pewter tankard. With the tankard suitably placed we carry the body out back into a biting wind and dump it in the soft snow where it sinks down a foot. We cover it over with more snow and hurry back into the bar because it's bloody freezing. Bill lines the brandies up again and we down them with relish. Time to give everyone some reassurance.

"We are all stuck here together for the duration. We have a murdered person and the murderer could still be amongst us. My Sergeant and I shall try and unmask the villain. We will begin by interviewing everyone one at a time, in the snug. In the morning, we shall see if we can find out what happened to the Vicar. I urge you all to relax as much as is possible but warn you to remain down here until we tell you that you may leave or go to your rooms. Mr Bennet, once my Sergeant and I are ensconced in the snug, please send in the locals first. One by one."

"Will do, Inspector. But, a word of warning, you may find them hard to understand as they have broad country accents."

"We shall overcome," smiles I grimly.

Head and I venture into the warm snug and close the door behind us. It is a small, heavily beamed room with a few tables and chairs. A pleasing fire crackles in the grate, flickering oil lamps light the room. We take off our coats and hang them over chairs to dry by the fire.

"Best to remove our revolvers, Sergeant," says I. "We do not want to intimate anyone."

"Or even intimidate anyone," says Head.

"Exactly. Intimation can lead to all kinds of trouble."

"As does intimidation," adds Head.

"We share the same ideals, Sergeant. That is why we have survived for so long."

We settle down behind a table facing the door just as it is opened and the landlady steps in carrying a tray with two pints of bitter on it. She sets them down on the table while affording us a fine scenic view of her deep valley, it is a delightfully short respite from the task in hand, but it is a good thing it is only short, the way Head's eyes are popping out of his head he is in dire danger of trying to hike down that very valley.

"I have the first interviewee ready, Inspector. Are you ready for him?"

"Yes, thank you, Martha," says I.

"Come in Sam," calls Martha. "This is young Sam Barker, Inspector," she announces as an old man with a white fuzzy beard comes into the room, removes his floppy hat and stands to attention. Martha leaves and shuts the door behind her.

"Take a seat, Sam," says I with a friendly wave of my hand.

He sits down and fiddles nervously with his hat.

"Now, Sam," begins I. "What do you do for a living?"

"I be a 'owman. 'Ork I on thee 'arm."

Head is taking notes, he whispers in my ear, "What's he saying, sir?"

"He is a cowman, working on the farm."

"Ah," smiles Head and jots it down.

I continue, "When you heard the scream, Sam. Where were you and what were you doing?"

"I by thee fire 'anking me ol' 'ock off an' cleanin' out thee cheesy stuff."

"What do I put down for that?" groans Head.

"The mind boggles. Just put sat by the fire warming himself. Now, Sam. What did you do next."

"I up and bugger off ta see wus goon on."

"And what was going on?"

"Murder be goon on as what. 'At ol' boy stuck ta death with ims googlies out."

"Thank you, Sam. One last question. Before Martha screamed to alert the bar that something terrible had happened, did you hear or see anything that may have been connected to the murder? Anything at all? Did anyone come down the stairs or disappear upstairs between three and five o'clock? Act suspicious in any way or do or say anything you thought odd?"

He scratches at his dusty beard and then his hair before shaking his head, "Don't know nuffin, 'cept that ol' bloke in thee black come sit down side that ol' beaky bird an' start whisperin' in 'er lug."

"Did you hear what they were talking about?"

"Nope, 'cause them wus whisperin'"

"Can you remember roughly what time this was?"

"Be 'bout fourish."

"Thank you, Sam. That will be all for now."

Sam leaves and is replaced by his double. I ask him to sit down and he does while fiddling with his floppy hat and staring bleary eyed at me.

"Name?" asks I.

"I be ol' Sam Barker."

"Any relation to young Sam Barker?"

"I be ims dad."

"Occupation?"

"Wus 'at?"

"What do you do for a living?"

"I be a 'owman."

"A cowman?"

"Nope. A 'owman."

I rack my brains, "A sow man?"

"Nope. A 'owman."

I go through the alphabet in my head. Got it, "A hoe man?"

"As roight. I 'ow thee fields round about."

"Where were you and what were you doing when Martha screamed out?"

"I wus a boozin' the landlady's gal."

"In what way were you abusing the landlady's daughter?"

"Jus' a boozin' wiv 'er."

"You mean drinking with her?"

"As what I said!" he returns frowning at me as if I am hard of hearing. "I wus boozin' beer an' she wus boozin' wutter."

"Just water?"

"As roight. 'Er don't drink no beer, it be 'gainst thee scriptures."

"Before the scream, did you hear or see anything untoward from three o'clock onwards? Did anyone act suspiciously, or say anything odd? Did you see the man in black come down the stairs at about four o'clock?"

He scratches at his beard and then his scalp, "Nope. 'Earing's alroight but can't see much past a yard."

"Thank you, Sam. You may go."

"This is a waste of time, sir," says Head watching Sam leave.

"Probably. But we already know that the man in black wasn't in the bar prior to four o'clock. So where was he and what was he doing?"

"Killing the victim?" ponders Head.

"Perhaps."

The third local comes in, he is a short, well-muscled dark haired hatless man with a thick black beard, bushy moustache and sharp eyes.

"Name?"

"Jim Brightman."

"Occupation?"

"Whitesmith."

"What is a whitesmith?"

"Same as a blacksmith."

"Why then don't you call yourself a blacksmith?"

"'Cause I aren't black, I's white."

"Do you forge metal and shoe horses?"

"I do."

"Therefore, you are a blacksmith."

"No, I aren't. I be a whitesmith. Look you here, ol' boy, I can't stand anything that's called what it in't. They say blackberry. I say purpleberry. They say, I'm off ta pick blackberries. I say, I'm off ta pick purpleberries. Now, see you here, them blackberries look black, but when you pick 'em your fingers go purple 'cause they's really purple not black. Same as I's white not black."

I give in and move on, "Where were you and what were you doing when you heard Martha scream?"

"I were playin' dominoes with ol' Jack by thee bar."

I ask him the usual questions to no avail and send him off.

The next one enters, he is tall and skinny with thick bushy sideburns and vacant eyes.

"Name?"

"I do."

"Do what?"

"'Ave a name."

"What is it?"

"Jack Fletcher is who I be."

"Occupation?"

"I do."

"Do what?"

"'Ave a occupation."

"What is it?" Truly I am losing my patience.

"I muck about."

"You muck about? Where do you muck about?"

"Wherever I's needed. Me lady says, 'Jack go muck them stables out' an' tha's what I do."

I give up and allow him to go back to his dominoes or whatever it is he is doing.

It is eight-thirty, time to take a break. Martha brings us in more beer with a large pork pie, cheese with pickled onions and sits down for a chat. It is obvious she did not see or hear anything between three and five o'clock being too busy in the kitchen. I ask her about finding the body and if she saw or heard anything then. Nothing, she was so terrified she couldn't think and has no idea why anyone would want to kill the nice Mr Jones.

"What about the trio out in the bar?" I quiz between mouthfuls of her excellent pie. "Why and when did they arrive?"

"Ah…Well, Inspector. Mr Ivan Shields, the dark haired shifty one, arrived five days ago and booked in for one week. He said he was on business, but the only kind of business he seemed interested in was nosing around and asking questions."

"Questions about what?"

"Mr Jones mostly. Why was he here and who had he been seen with? I told him, quite bluntly, that I had no idea and that I do not pry into my guests' personal life or spread idle gossip."

"How did he react to your reply?"

"He merely smiled and went out."

"What about the two females? They and this Shields are obviously together in whatever capacity they are together."

"Perhaps they're in a threesome," butts in Head while shoving a large pickled onion into his mouth.

"I doubt that, Sergeant," returns I.

"I agree, Inspector," says Martha. "It is obvious that Shields and that Spencer woman both work for Miss Saunders. But in what capacity?"

I believe I already know the answer to that question but will keep it under my hat for now. "All will be revealed, Martha. But for now, just go about your business as usual. Can you send in the last two labourers and then your daughter?"

She gets to her feet, "Bill will have to come in with Sarah when it's her turn, she will not stay in a room with just men present in case it gives the wrong impression."

"I understand. Thank you, Martha. The pie is delicious."

"One other thing," says she in afterthought. "All three approached Mr Jones on several occasions and always when he was well away from anyone else. However, it didn't seem as if he wanted to speak to any of them much, and often he'd just ignore them. Miss Saunders appeared somewhat perplexed by this and once she stomped off to her room and didn't come back until lunch time."

"Was that today or yesterday?"

"Today. At about nine-thirty, just after breakfast."

"Thank you, Martha."

"Funny old do, sir," comments Head after a burp or two. "What's it all about?"

"Unrequited love, I believe, Sergeant. Unrequited love."

We finish off the food and swallow half our beer as the next labourer comes in. He tells us he is Jack Fletcher's brother Joe and that he 'digs 'oles' for a living. He is the local grave digger.

A Bob Smith comes in next, but his accent is so strong neither Head nor I can understand a word he says. We call in Bill to see if he can translate, only to be told that Bob can only converse in a tongue known as butcher man's language. And that having been a butcher since he was six and never having gone to school, the Queen's English is foreign to him. Lovely as the labourers are, Bill has had enough of them for now, so I tell him they are as innocent as the falling snow, and he can let them go home if they think they can safely make it through the snow. He says, "They'll be going even if I have to throw them out as they're drinking the place dry while contributing nothing towards anything."

Bill goes off to fetch his daughter and Head ponders over this so called, butcher man's language. "So, sir, everything that Bob said was said in reverse. For instance; if I said, 'Dlo nam, woh era ouy? I'd really be saying; Old man, how are you? But then some words are the same either way. For instance; Dad. Mum. Nun. Did. Noon."

"You are not really getting to grips with this, Sergeant and I shall end this silly conversation with one word, Tit! Let us get on, please," I snap, realising I am becoming rather tired.

Bill and Sarah come in and sit down opposite us. I interview Bill first, hoping it will relax Sarah enough to stop her fretful fidgeting and twisting up her hair while staring up at the ceiling in search of divine intervention. Bill confirms everything Martha had said. He also confirms that Shields came downstairs just about four o'clock. Shields of course is our prime suspect and I suddenly realise no one is watching him. Bad weather or not he could still disappear.

"Sergeant," says I, whispering in his ear. "Go into the bar and keep an eye on that Shields fellow. Be casual about it as well. We don't want to panic him and scare him into doing something untoward."

"I'll appear casual if I'm having a quiet beer and a chat with the landlady," says he in hope.

"Just don't get drunk," I hiss, knowing how lightweight he can be at times. "And tuck your revolver in your trousers and pull your cardigan over it. And let us hope you don't need to use it."

He raises his eyebrows, "I'll be careful."

"Did you catch any of that, Bill?" asks I as Head leaves the room.

"Some of it," comes the worried reply as he leans forward to get close so Sarah doesn't hear. "Shouldn't you arrest Shields for safety's sake? What if he stabs someone else?"

"We don't know if the man is guilty of anything, Bill. Until then he is as free as everyone." I chat further with Bill and then turn my attention to Sarah. "Sarah, when you were drinking with old Sam did you notice anything untoward?"

She gazes vacantly into my eyes, "Yes, he had hair sticking out from his ears and his nose. God bless him."

"Did you notice what other people were doing at the time?"

"Um... Young Sam was doing disgusting things over by the fire. But then he often does. But then we are all God's creatures and must strive to be good and forgive people's disgusting habits, especially if they have small brains."

"That is very kind of you."

She smiles, "Not really. It is just being a good Christian." Her arms suddenly reach up. "Forgive me Lord for I am a sinner. I am begotten with self-importance and the arrogance of my youth. Plus, I wish I could get away with doing disgusting things in public like young Sam does."

"Did you have any contact with Mr Jones?"

"I cleaned his room, but only if the door was kept open. He often spoke to me, but never said anything naughty. I liked him. God liked him because the Reverend was always talking to him as if they were kindred spirits."

"Did the Vicar ever go up to Mr Jones' room?"

She looks away from my gaze, "Once or twice to give spiritual guidance." Her arms shoot up again. "God bless the Reverend Parker even though he has ginger hair."

"Thank you, Sarah. That will be all for now."

"Don't you want to hear about the sinful dreams I have?" she asks wide eyed. "They are not the kind of dreams a good Christian girl should be having."

"Perhaps later," I smile. "You may go, Sarah."

They leave and Head returns, as usual he is slightly inebriated, he flops down into his chair, burps a few times and announces, "I'm weddy, sir."

We call in Ivan Shields and I do not hold back on him.

"Is Ivan Shields your real name?"

He glares at me and is obviously not the least bit intimidated by me or Head.

"Why wouldn't it be?" he retorts.

"Is it, or isn't it?"

"It is,"

"And you are a Private Detective working for Miss Rebecca Saunders, whose real name is Angela Foley?"

Shields sits right back in his chair and nods in submission, "Very good, Inspector. However, there is no way you could have come out with what you have just said unless you were already on our trail. Who sent you?"

I tell him all and he tells me all. So now we know all what we need to know about each other. The problem is neither of us knows who killed Alwin Jones; more commonly known as Lord Sydney Melham.

Martha brings in a bottle of scotch and three glasses and then leaves. I fill the glasses, one for Shields, Head and me. As we drink I ponder over what Shields has told me so far. Melham disappeared because he did not want to marry Miss Foley. Miss Foley was livid and hired Shields to track down her fiancé as she was determined to force him to marry her as she was hell bent on becoming Lady Sydney Melham. Shields chased shadows for two weeks until by chance a ticket seller at a place called Beccles remembered the face in the photograph that Shields shewed to him. The Station Master also remembered that Melham had bought a one-way ticket to Ipswich. Shields, being good at what he does, didn't go straight to Ipswich, instead he stopped at every station along the way showing his photographs around. Low and behold the Station Master at Darsham informed him that the man in the photograph was staying at the Fox Hole Inn.

"Did Melham give any reason why he wouldn't marry Miss Foley?" says I with a yawn.

"His only excuse was that he was too young to marry and didn't love Angela anyway."

"Wha's love gotta to do with it?" slurs Head wobbling around in his chair.

"Just take the notes, Sergeant," snaps I.

Shields says, "When I passed by Melham's door on my way downstairs I thought I heard Melham talking to someone. I tried to spy through his key hole but the key was in it. I then tried the door but it was locked. I came down and kept an eye on the stairs to see if anyone came down but no one did. Martha then went upstairs and let out that terrible scream."

"Do you think Martha may have killed him?"

He shakes his head, "Definitely not."

"Anything else you remember?"

"No. Well, the Vicar came into the bar via the back door just after I had come downstairs. He was rubbing his hands and moaning about the cold, but this is it, he didn't appear cold. His face was flushed and his ears weren't red from the cold and he seemed a little flustered."

Interesting thinks I. I allow Shields to leave and call in Miss Foley who promptly bursts into tears. I interview her for ten minutes or so and learn nothing. The indomitable Miss Spencer comes in. She sits bolt upright and glares at Head.

"Your Sergeant is drunk!" she admonishes while her hard eyes run themselves all over Head. "Drunk and incapable. Is this normal behaviour for members of her Majesty's Police Force, Inspector?"

"Yes," I answer truthfully.

"Why, it's disgusting behaviour."

"I know," agrees I. "But it has been a long trying day."

"That is no excuse." She goes for Head, "You are a disgrace to your uniform, Sergeant. You should be stripped of your rank and denigrated to a toilet cleaner. What do you say to that?"

Head gathers himself together and sits right up, "Madam, I could never clean toilets because every time I peer down that bowl and there is a log still hanging around I would think of you and throw up."

She is obviously about to have another go when I warn her, "Madam if you do not shut up and just answer my questions I shall be forced to shut you up. Do you understand me?"

"I was only saying," she sulks.

"Well don't. It is now past eleven o'clock and everyone needs their bed. So please let us get on with this."

I question the woman for a while but to no avail, she obviously knows nothing at all about anything at all except how to stick her nose into everyone else's business. At last we call it a night. Bill shows me and Head to a small single room each. I unpack, fall back on the bed and am asleep before I can say Bobby Bunny loves carrots.

I awake shivering to a weak sunlight trying to filter through the small frosted up window while still dressed in my clothes from the night before. Deciding to freshen up I cover the two feet to the wash stand on stiff legs only to find there is ice on top of the water in the water jug. Just then there is a knock on the door and Martha calls out, "I have hot water for you, Inspector. Are you up at last?"

I open the door, we exchange pleasantries and I take the welcoming bucket of hot water into the room.

"When you have finished," she smiles. "Empty the dirty water back into the bucket and I shall fetch it later. Breakfast will be served in thirty minutes or so."

She closes the door and I strip off to my birthday suit. It is bloody freezing, my willy shrivels up to the size of a gherkin, but I am in dire need of a good all over wash. No doubt there are baths to be had, but in this cold the quicker you're back in your clothes the better. After a frantic shivering scrub around with the flannel provided, I don my bottom half and go for a shave. There is a knock on the door.

"You up, sir?" calls out Head.

I let him in and he sits down on the bed and watches me slide the cutthroat razer around my chops. I am shaking so much from the cold I'm in danger of slitting my own throat.

"What time is it, Sergeant?"

"Nearly nine, sir. Breakfast won't be long."

"Good I am famished. Did you sleep well?"

"I did until I got up for a pee and couldn't find the potty. I lit a candle and opened this cupboard door thinking the pot might be in there and fell down a hole. I fell down to my stomach and just managed to stop myself going down further by pushing out me elbows. The bloody candle burnt my nose and then went out, but I managed to haul myself up again."

I turn around to face him, "What hole?"

"Apparently, it's called a priest hole, according to Martha. We looked at it together when she brought me up a bucket of hot water a little while ago."

"Let me finish my shave and we shall go and look at it," says I intrigued.

Five minutes later we are peering down a very narrow hole in a small cupboard in Head's room. Having lit an oil lamp, I venture down the hole by way of a wooden ladder, it is a tight squeeze. The hole takes me down to the ground floor and at the bottom there is a metal ring handle on a three-foot-high door. Turning the handle reveals the outhouse at the back of the house where logs and coals are stored for burning, I bob down and shuffle my way in. Pushing open the door that leads to outside reveals that the lavatory block is joined on to the log store. Anyone who went out for a pee could have come into the log store and gone up into the bedrooms via the priest hole, providing of course they knew it was there. I shut the door and take myself back into the priest hole. "I'm coming up," I call out to Head. It is just as hard climbing back up as it was going down but at last I am back standing in Head's room and looking down.

"Martha, said," says Head brushing the dirt from my jacket that I'd picked from my endeavours. "That they keep quiet about the hole to stop guests going on about it. She said the cupboard door is normally always locked and she has no idea why it wasn't locked. Or who else had a key to unlock it in the first place, as the keys for this door and the one at the bottom of the hole are kept in a dressing table drawer in her bedroom. She went to check on them and found that the spare set were gone."

"Having had just one suspect, Sergeant," muses I. "We now have multiple suspects. Anyone could have used that hole to climb up here, go over to Melham's room and stab him."

"Does that mean we have to interview everyone again?" groans Head.

"No, I don't think so. I am thinking that we need to question Sarah Bennet some more. And then go and see if we can find out what happened to the Vicar. After breakfast of course."

A full English is served. It is delicious and very welcoming. Small talk goes around the room while it is obvious everyone is avoiding the subject of murder. Porky boy now has mittens on his hands to obviously stop him from picking his nose during breakfast. Once breakfast is over I take Bill and Martha aside. I ask them who else knew about the priest hole and where to find the keys. They inform me that no one apart from the locals would know about the priest hole and only immediate family knows where the keys are kept. Unless someone told them, I ponder. I ask them to call Sarah into the kitchen.

"Sarah," begins I. "You are not in trouble. I just need you to answer a few more questions."

She nods, "Is it about the keys to the priest hole?"

"It is. You gave the spare set of keys to someone, didn't you?"

"I have to clear tables," says she trying to walk away but being blocked by Bill.

"Answer the Inspector's question, Sarah," demands he. "Remember God is watching you."

She drops her gaze to the floor, "He said that I'd be doing God's work if I got the keys for him. He said there could be lonely spirits still trapped down the hole. Spirits of lost souls who died down there while trying to hide from that Queen Elizabeth's soldiers. He said he had to give them Holy Communion. He said I must not tell anyone or God will be angry with me."

She starts to cry and Martha hugs her.

"We are talking about the Reverend James Parker are we not, Sarah?"

She nods and then buries her head in Martha's ample bosom, and by the look in Head's eyes he would also like to bury his head there and not surface for a week or more.

"Let us get kitted up, Sergeant," orders I. "We have a clergyman to track down."

"Shall I come with you?" asks Bill.

I shake my head, "We could be wrong, Bill. That being the case you had best remain here and keep an eye on the trio just in case they decide to leave."

"Well they won't get far, Inspector. The village is totally cut off according to the Postman. He'd struggled for an hour to barely cover half a mile to deliver yesterday's mail to us this morning."

"Even so," says I. "Now, Bill, can you give us directions to the vicarage?"

A short while later, Head and I head outside into the bitter cold. As we walk away from the inn I look up the side to see where we had laid Melham's body the night before. It isn't where we had left it.

"Bloody urchins," grates Head pointing to several small footprints in the snow coming and going up the side of the inn. "They've stolen Lord Melham's body."

"They have dragged it away, Sergeant," says I. "Look, there are the tracks. We must follow them."

We set off down the way Bill told us to go, the urchin's footprints are going the same way. A few cottages line the way, each have long icicles hanging precariously from their roofs, thick smoke belches out from every chimney and it is easy to imagine everyone huddled around their roaring fires. Ahead there is a thick blueish mist that cuts visibility down to twenty yards or so and frosted air lays stagnant barely feet above our heads. As we walk and turn a bend the sound of laughter catches our ears as half a dozen urchins holding ice balls come out of nowhere to block our way. They are wrapped in all sorts of old blankets and rags with rags tied around their feet, anything to keep warm. We are instantly threatened by the tallest one.

"Two bob to pass through, mister. Or you'll get belted."

"Piss off," snarls Head, which was a big mistake as ice balls are released with furious speed and precision to crack on our bowlers, punch us in the guts and bounce off our bodies. Covering up as best we can we retreat several feet to gather ourselves together.

"Let's shoot a couple of the little shits," suggests Head.

"That's a bit drastic," counters I. "Let's charge them with truncheons drawn."

"I think my way is best, sir."

"But it's a bit bad shooting kids, even if they are merely urchins."

"They'd shoot you. Have no fear of that."

"The day will come, Sergeant, when street urchins will have disappeared and people will need have no fear of walking the streets and getting accosted by such little thugs."

"Well until that day, sir, may I suggest we carry on treating them as thugs and shoot the buggers."

"To kill or to injure?"

"Alright," he relents. "To injure only. But in the never regions so they can't breed anymore of their ilk."

Revolvers and truncheons drawn we charge but the little monsters scatter so fast they have disappeared in seconds, and I can't be bothered to chase after them. Putting our weapons away we continue, only to come up against four more urchins who all appear to be dressed in sections of the candlewick bedspread that had once been wrapped around Melham's body.

"Penny for the snowman," comes the urchins' chorus. "That's a penny from each of ya."

The snowman is of course Lord Melham, he is frozen solid and stood up against a small tree by the side of the lane. He is wearing a floppy hat that looks suspiciously like old Sam's, a pair of pince-nez with no lenses in them and a raggedy scarf around his neck. Thankfully they have wrapped a load of holly around his private area. His face is a terrible sight, almost like an egg-shaped block of ice with a ghost peering out from inside.

"What now, sir?" says Head sounding as horrified as I feel.

"We could barter with them," suggests I.

"Or shoot them," he snarls.

"You payin' up or what?" demands the shortest brat. "Or you'll be for it."

I recognise him from the train, he is the one who stabbed Hippo woman in the buttocks. "None of these urchins are local, Sergeant. They were on the train and have been exported from London."

"So, we are dealing with the worst of the worst," sighs he.

"Exactly," sighs I.

"Best pay them then," sighs he.

Reluctantly I fish out a half-crown and throw it to shorty who grabs it mid-air, peruses it and then shoves it in his pocket. Before you can say another word, they've run off to wherever they run off to. Head and I continue, we'll pick up Lord Melham on the way back.

Presently the Norman church comes into hazy view, a few yards to the side of that is the Georgian vicarage. We go up to the front door and knock loudly using the gargoyle door knocker. No answer.

"Perhaps he's run for it," suggests Head.

"Perhaps," I muse, but then I am certain I can hear music coming from somewhere inside. Someone is playing a bad rendition of Chopin. We go around back to find the planked gate is locked. Head climbs over, drops to the other side and opens the gate, as he does so there is a growling sound coming from behind him.

"There is a gigantic wolfhound standing behind you, Sergeant. Do not move or I fear it may eat you."

"Bollocks," swears he.

"Exactly, Sergeant. One false move and I fear you will lose them. Just edge your way to one side so I can get a good shot at it," says I, taking out my revolver.

"Good doggy," soothes Head. "Uncle Dicky has a nice treat in his pocket for you if you're a good boy."

"What is it?" asks I.

"Nothing," returns he. "But he doesn't know that."

"They are intelligent animals, Sergeant. He will know if you are lying to him."

"Listen to me nice doggy, Uncle Dicky will find you a nice big bone if you back off and let me pass."

The thing moves back and starts wagging its tail. Head turns around and offers the brute his right hand and to our amazement he begins licking Head's hand as if he's his master.

"You have a new friend," says I, going in through the gate.

We trail around the back of the house following the sound of music. The backdoor opens when we turn the handle and we step into a spacious kitchen. The dog, still wagging its tail, follows us in. We creep silently up a long wide hall towards the drawing room, where on entering we find a piano being played by a red headed man who has his back turned to us. This must be the Vicar. As if he has sensed our being there he stops playing and spins around on his stool to face us. He is young for a Vicar, perhaps in his late twenties, clean shaven with bright eyes and a kindly face.

"I suspect you are policemen," says he. "I wondered how long it would be before you came for me."

There is a roaring fire in the grate but the room is still quite chilly and the dog trots over to be beside the fire and lays down.

"James Parker," announces I. "I have reason to believe you are responsible for the murder of Lord Sydney Melham."

"Do you gentlemen fancy a cup of tea?"

"We would welcome it," says I.

"Right," says he, slapping his thighs and standing up to reveal his full height is just over six feet.

We follow him into the kitchen and take a seat at a long pine table. Parker puts the kettle onto the stove and then busies himself placing a small jug of milk on the table along with a sugar bowl, cups and saucers plus a plate of biscuits. "Smoke if you wish, gentlemen."

We decline, but he takes a pipe out of his jacket pocket, tamps it down and then strikes a match and begins to suck on the pipe until it comes to life. He studies us while drawing on his pipe, there is a look of curiosity in his gaze, a look of how did you know?

We remain patient and allow Parker his moment of contemplation until at last the kettle boils and Parker whirls around to fill a large brown teapot. The pot is placed on the table and he sits down opposite us. The dog pads into the kitchen and sits beside Head where it nuzzles its big shaggy head on his lap.

Parker puts aside his pipe and then stirs the pot with a large spoon. Picking up a strainer he fills all three cups and passes us each a cup.

"Help yourselves to biscuits," says he.

We do so, I go for a chocolate cream but Head reaches it first and I have to settle for a plain old digestive.

"Are you ready to talk now, Vicar?" says I.

He nods, a smile crosses his mouth. It is a smile of regret and sadness. "Sydney and I have been friends since we were at Cambridge together. We became more than friends. In fact, we became lovers."

I can sense Head stiffening up at this revelation, but he says nothing.

"We knew what we were doing was wrong," continues Parker. "Only we could not help ourselves. However, we fought against it until at last our studies came to an end and we parted. We would write to each other now and again but did not ever arrange to meet up again. I eventually took up Holy Orders and Sydney became heavily involved in helping his Father run the estate. They were in financial difficulties, for ever robbing Peter to pay Paul. In one letter he told me that they were now in so much debt his Father informed him that they would have to start selling off land, unless…"

"Sydney married Miss Angela Foley," I interject.

"Exactly. Sydney told me he would be complying with his Father's wishes and had asked Miss Foley for her hand in marriage, to which she readily agreed." He pauses to drink some of his tea. We do the same and Head takes another biscuit and sneakily gives it to the dog.

"How did you feel about the forth coming nuptials?" asks I.

"In truth, I was horrified. When we parted, Sydney and I agreed that we must never tell anyone about what went between us, we also knew we could never marry as life with a woman would be an utter sham. I must admit I was also very jealous. You see I still loved him and will always love him. I wrote to him again and implored him to break off his relationship with Miss Foley. He wrote back and accused me of emotionally blackmailing him and told me in no uncertain terms that our relationship, even by correspondence, was at an end. In a furious state of mind, I wrote back and foolishly threatened him with exposure unless he called the wedding off. In truth Inspector, could you imagine what that woman's life would be like living with a man who does not feel for women in *that* way."

Unable to contain himself any longer, Head sticks his oar in, "He may have got used to being with a woman once he'd tried her out. Worse things happen at sea you know and you should have let them be."

"Why don't you take the dog for a walk, Sergeant?" says I.

"His name is Belcher," offers Parker.

With a disgruntled grunt, Head gets to his feet and heads out into the garden with the dog lapping at his heals. I drink my tea and pour myself another cup. With Head out of the way I can help myself to all the nicest biscuits.

"Pray continue, Vicar."

"Yes, where was I?"

"You threatened Sydney with exposure."

"Oh, yes. I ordered Sydney to come and see me, here at the Vicarage, so we might resolve the issue. I didn't actually believe he would come. Then it was reported that he had disappeared and I feared for his life. What if he had taken his own life all because of me? I was in despair, until two weeks after he had disappeared he turned up at my door. We hadn't seen each other for five years but fell into each other's arms as if it had been yesterday. He booked into the inn and at first everything was fine. But it was dangerous for us meeting here with too many people coming and going. I also feared someone would become suspicious. I was brought up in the village and knew of the priest hole, so I hatched a plan that would enable us to see each other in absolute secrecy. I persuaded Sarah to let me have the spare set of keys and to keep it our secret."

"Surely she questioned your motives?"

"Not at all. Sarah believes everything I tell her because I am a man of God." Guilt swamps his eyes and he gazes momentarily down at his hands that are folded around his cup. "Everything was going well. I believe I had convinced Sydney to end his relationship with Miss Foley, but then I never dreamed she and her entourage would turn up to unconvince him. By the time that awful Shields man and that harridan of a woman, Miss Spencer, had pecked and pecked at Sydney's emotions he was ready to concede defeat and accept, what he believed, was his fate. We met up once more in his room at the inn. We made love and it was the most wonderful experience we had ever had. And then he simply got out of bed and announced he was leaving to go back to Melham House with Miss Foley. We argued. It turned bitter and he ordered me out and never to invade his life again under pain of death. He said that that Shields man would kill me if Sydney asked him to. I went into a rage, I wasn't thinking and picking up his letter knife, as Sydney went to open the door to throw me out, I plunged the knife into his back. It was a crime of passion. I wasn't thinking. I had lost my senses. I was in a temporary state of madness."

"Your story is very plausible, Vicar," cuts in I. "Except for the end of it. You went there that last time fully intending to murder your lover. You plead a crime of passion which is recognised in France but not over here. However, it can still invoke such sympathy within a jury that a lesser sentence may be given to the criminal. I may well have felt the same except for the fact that the knife in Sydney's back had probably never opened a single letter but had certainly been used to cut up meat and such. Behind you on the work surface sits a wooden block that has a collection of butcher's knives, one of which is missing, and I will bet good money that missing knife is the one still stuck in Sydney's back." That's if those bloody urchins haven't pinched it I grate to myself. "Which proves to me that you went to Sydney's room intent on premeditated murder. If you couldn't have him no one could. And that is the truth of the matter." I get to my feet just as Head comes back in. "Reverend James Parker I am arresting you for the murder of one Lord Sydney Melham," I read him his rights and order Head to cuff him.

"May I get my overcoat on first?" asks Parker. "It is freezing out there. The keys belonging to the inn are also in one of the coat's pockets."

"Do so," says I.

"Shall I go with him, sir?" offers Head.

"No, leave him be."

Parker goes to fetch his coat, Head feeds the dog more biscuits and I wait for the inevitable. It comes a few seconds later, a single shot from a revolver.

"Bloody hell!" yells Head and is off down the hallway as fast as his legs will carry him.

I follow him down. Sat back in a chair in the drawing room sits Parker having put a bullet through his brain. Head turns on me, "I knew I should have gone with him! He has escaped the gallows, sir, and in doing so has no doubt freed Sydney from having to be vilified and exposed for what he was."

"It has also freed a lot more people from having to suffer because of those men's relationship."

"There will still be an inquest," grates Head. "Everything will come out anyway."

I shake my head, "The establishment will somehow smooth everything over and cover it up. By next week it will be yesterday's news. Now, Sergeant, let us get on, we have a lot to do."

I decide to seek out the local Constable first and inform him that the Vicar has shot himself because of depression and could he attend to the matter. The Constable is a very capable man who takes charge without asking too many questions and does what I ask of him. We agree to meet up later and I leave him in charge at the Vicarage. Head finds a suitable conveyance in the garden in which to transport Sydney's body back to the inn. But it's a sod trying to keep the rigid body from falling off the wheelbarrow as we struggle to push it over the snow.

"You wouldn't think a frozen body could be so bloody awkward to move about," moans Head taking his turn to push the wheelbarrow. "It weighs a bloody ton."

"Perhaps we could somehow harness Belcher up to assist us," suggests I. The dog won't leave Head's side and he has fallen in love with it to the extent that he wishes to adopt the thing.

"He might hurt himself," pants Head as the wheelbarrow gets stuck in the snow and he has to exert himself even further to free it. "Feel free to help, sir."

"It isn't my turn," complains I. "You didn't help me when the wheel got stuck in that rut."

"I was comforting, Belcher. After all he has just lost his master."

Looking at the dog it is obvious he has forgotten the Vicar already and Head is now everything to him.

At last we make it to the inn. Leaving the body in the barrow we park it around back inside the log store to ensure the urchins don't see it and run off with it again.

Martha welcomes us back and pours us both brandies. Belcher quickly plonks himself by the fire where Porky boy and his mother have also ensconced themselves. Within seconds Belcher is being fussed over by Porky boy while having to suffer grumbles being embedded into his shaggy coat, which he doesn't seem to mind in the least. I call a general meeting.

Fifteen minutes later everyone is gathered in the bar except for Porky boy who has been sent out to play with Belcher in the snow. I spin my audience such a convincing tale as to what has been going on I almost believe it myself. I tell them that Sydney had once lent Parker a lot of money when they were at Cambridge together and had never worried that much about getting his money back. However, as his wedding drew nearer and nearer he desperately needed that money. Parker, being in debt because of gambling, couldn't afford to pay the money back and decided to murder Sydney rather than face trial and incarceration in Her Majesty's prison. Parker murdered Sydney because of money. Of course, Miss Foley and her entourage all knew my tale was a load of old bunkum, but everyone else swallowed it whole, I think. Sarah was distraught at having been so cruelly used by 'That lying bastard Vicar', she promptly renounced her faith and said she was taking up knitting instead.

Later, after lunch and a load more brandy, Head and I gather all of Sydney's things together and pack them into his suitcase. Including his wallet. I take out the few pounds that was in the wallet and hand it over to Bill in settlement of Sydney's bill. There is nothing else to do except assist the Constable in moving Parker's body to somewhere safe, namely the Vicarage's cellar, until it can be transported to the local morgue along with Sydney's body. We help the Constable clean up the mess left behind from Parker's suicide and then head back to the inn to sit it out until the trains are rerunning and we can return to London. I take time to write to the Earl of East Suffolk to inform him of his son's terrible demise. Head hands Belcher over to Porky boy as they have become inseparable. Porky boy's mother promises he can keep the hound providing he stops picking his nose. Which he does, but promptly takes up picking the dog's nose instead.

Three days later and after a belt of rain had swept over and melted the snow enough for the trains to run again we are on our way back to London. I had settled the bill with the inn and reluctantly waved the Bennet's and everyone else goodbye, while promising to return for a holiday one day. Head was miserable having had to give up Belcher while still being incensed at having had his wallet stolen. For myself I was aggrieved that I hadn't made a penny out of the trip and was in fact out of pocket. Clump would never agree to paying out for six bottles of brandy on expenses. But all was about to change.

As the train stops at Saxmundham Station who should board but none other than Fanny 'The Feeler' Frampton. Head and I shoot out into the corridor, grab the woman just as she'd turned to close the train door, and march her into an empty compartment.

"Let go of me you bloody shit-bags!" she curses, kicking and spitting.

"Sergeant," orders I. "Empty her bag."

While I hold Fanny in an arm lock, Head empties her bag. It contains five pounds in notes, a solid gold compact, a silver fountain pen, three expensive pocket watches, two even more expensive fob watches, two bracelets and various other items, all of value. We take the lot, including the gold necklace from around her neck and the pearl handled derringer stuck in a garter beneath her embroidered dress.

The train chugs out of the station and all is well except for Fanny.

"I'll cut your nuts off for this," she spits. "My Johnny will slit ya throats and feed ya blood to his pigs."

She is putting up such a wild cat fight despite being in an arm lock there is only one thing for it. Head pulls the window right down. "You wouldn't dare," she screams as between us we lift her off her feet and wrestle her towards the window. "You just try it, you bastards!"

So, we do, and Fanny is shoved out the window with such force she virtually flies up in the air before hurtling towards the railway bank, where she hits the snowy ground and tumbles over several times before coming to a halt in a 'cleared from the track' pile of snow nearly six feet high. Sticking our heads even further out of the window we just manage to see her getting to her feet and shaking her fist at us before we disappear around a bend.

"A good haul, sir," smiles Head.

"Profit indeed for all we have been through," smiles I.

"Fifty, fifty, sir," smiles he. "That's half for me and half for you."

I can see Head is becoming too clever for my own good. "Fifty, fifty," agrees I. "Half and half."

"Marvellous," he grins as we head back to our own compartment only to find our bags have disappeared. "Bloody urchins!"

Tannery Street

I am in bed with Betty. It is a Saturday and I have the entire weekend off for our wedding anniversary. We could have planned something special for the day but opted instead to spend all day in bed. Plus, it is as windy as hell outside.

"Do you want any more, Detective Inspector?" says Betty.

"Not just yet my little sugar plum. But a cup of tea and a biscuit would be nice."

"I think it's your turn, Detective Inspector."

"Is it? Are you sure?"

"Of course, I'm sure. You only make the morning tea on special occasions or when I'm ill."

I know when I am beaten. Swinging my legs out of bed I slip on my dressing gown just as there's a resounding knock on the door.

"Who on earth's that?" groans Betty. "If it's that blinking encyclopaedia salesman again chuck the potty contents over his head."

"We don't use a potty anymore."

"Well drop a plant pot on him or something."

I go and open the window and stick my head out. Looking down I find Head looking back up at me while holding onto his bowler to stop the wind from blowing it away.

"Sorry, sir," says he. "There's been another one. Clump sent a plod around to order me up and at it and to fetch you as well."

"But it is our anniversary, Sergeant. The Chief promised me he'd handle everything himself and wouldn't allow anything to interrupt us unless the Queen herself had been murdered."

"The plod also said that Clump said you'd be angry, sir. He also told me to tell you that Clump said he'd make it up to you by... um... What was it? Oh yes, by giving you a day off to go to the loo. Or something like that."

"A bloody day off in lieu," tuts I. "Hang on, I shall come down and let you in."

"It's not fair, Detective Inspector," sulks Betty, pulling the covers up to her neck. "I thought we were going to break all records this anniversary. Now we'll have to wait another year before we can try again."

I shut the window and kiss her on the forehead, "What can I do my love? It is my job."

"Well sometimes I wish you were a fishmonger or something."

"I shall put the kettle on," I sigh as I make my way downstairs. Betty doesn't ask for much and she was really looking forward to today. And now it's been ruined because some nutter decided to kill themselves. I ponder accidently falling down the stairs and feigning a twisted ankle but it is not in my nature. Clump wouldn't believe it anyway, so there's no point.

I open the door and let Head in. With him comes a fierce gust of wind that whirls dust all over the hallway. He rubs at his eyes, "Bloody wind!"

"Hot, dry and windy," says I shoving the door shut. "Nothing worse for starting and spreading fires."

"Indeed not, sir," sulks he, following me into the kitchen.

Now I have both Betty and Head sulking, I muse as I put the kettle on.

Head sits down at the table, he appears somewhat miserable and I fear it has more to do with loneliness than anything else. He needs a good woman.

"Sorry again about this, sir. I reminded the Chief only yesterday it was yours and Betty's special day today."

"Worry not, Sergeant. It is not your fault. Now, I shall get washed, shaved and dressed while you make the tea. Betty will have one as well." I get the biscuit tin out and set it down on the table. "Help yourself, Sergeant."

"I've had no breakfast, sir. I *had* planned a leisurely late breakfast down the Kings Arms as I was supposed to be having the day off in conjunction with you. So, I wonder if we can pop into Oily's place as we've got to go right past it?"

"The latest death being where exactly?"

"Tannery Street."

"Tannery Street! That's too near to the Gut for my liking, Sergeant. We shall require at least three armed plods if we are to enter that shithole."

"Not according to the plod's message from the Chief. Apparently, the Chief insists that everyone's so terrified about what's been going on, the slum bags will be only too pleased to see any police presence, however small, rather than no police presence at all. And we will be perfectly safe, at this present time, to go to such a dangerous area without suitable back up."

"It seems to me, Sergeant, the Chief had an answer ready for any and every argument we may have put forward for suitable back up. When what he really means is, there aren't enough plods to go around, because of so many 'suspected' suicides all happening virtually at once while being spread out right across London and even beyond," sighs I. "I best go and get ready."

Back upstairs I find Betty has put her nighty and dressing gown on. Her hair has been tidied up a bit but her disappointment hasn't. "Where's my tea, Detective Inspector?"

"The Sergeant is making it. I have to get ready."

With a huff she pushes past me and stomps off downstairs to join Head. I go into the bathroom, strip off and wash all over in cold water. With my trousers back on I nip downstairs and grab some hot water from the kettle and then it's back up for a shave. When I go back down I find Betty and Head chatting away amicably. I quickly swallow a cupper, slip on my holster and revolver, don my jacket and bowler hat and am ready to go.

Betty sees us to the door and gives me a big kiss on the lips, but she doesn't give Head one.

"When will you be back, Detective Inspector?" implores Betty. "I was thinking of cooking something special for tonight."

"No need. I shall be taking you out for dinner."

That cheers her up, "Oh. How lovely." I receive another smacker and then Head and I head off.

We hail a Hackney but the driver will only agree to take us within three streets of Tannery Street as he was mugged the last time he went down there.

"Stripped to me bloody undies, governor," groans he as we trot along. "Took all my clothes and then pushed me off me driver's seat before running off with me 'orse an' rig. The bastards."

"It is a dangerous area," says I.

"Cost me an arm an' a leg to get set up again."

He goes on and on throughout the journey and I am relieved when we finally come to a halt.

"This is far as I'll go, governor."

Head and I alight and I give the driver a half-crown for his troubles, which, at last makes him smile.

"Miserable old git," says Head as we set off for Tannery Street.

The wind is being funnelled down the narrow streets straight into our faces and we ram our bowlers hard onto our heads to stop them from being blown away. There seems to be a lot less chancers and urchins about than usual but there are still plenty to bother us. Ignoring them all we march on with purpose in our stride until we hit a group of prostitutes who are already out accosting potential clients. They appear to be all ages, from the far too young to the far too old. One old hag blatantly blocks our way and offers herself for a farthing. She looks so rough a corpse would probably get more business than her.

"Clear off before you drop down dead," snaps Head.

"I've got a lot of go still left in me, sonny boy," comes the waspish retort.

"Well use it to get back to the morgue while there's still time."

Suddenly the wind blows the old girl's bonnet and wig off. They are whipped away down the street chased by a dozen or so urchins. The hag has no chance of retrieving either as covering her patchy grey-haired head she hobbles off as fast as her tottering gait will take her.

"Poor old cow," says Head in a rare showing of sympathy. "She'll be dead before morning, but at least if she gets herself down to the mortuary now it'll save someone having to take her there."

Oily's place looms up before us and we go in and order a full English with coffee. The breakfasts are quickly delivered and eaten. Thirty minutes or so later we set off again and arrive at Tannery Street ten minutes after that.

Tannery Street isn't much different than any other of the streets, alleyways and lanes in the slum areas. Dilapidated three to four-storey terraced houses, homemade shacks where some building or other had long since fell into ruin, there's a few shops to boast about but plenty of sleazy pubs not to boast about, and as ever there's an oversupply of costermongers selling their wares upon the rough potholed street of broken bricks and left-over cobbles from more affluent times. The area reeks of neglect, overcrowding, poor sanitation and desperation, but is still home to many thousands.

We spy the latest 'victim' face down on the dirty street, arms and legs splayed out and dressed in a black dress and matching bonnet. She is bootless, either she wasn't wearing any footwear when she jumped or she had her footwear stolen after death. Beneath her, splattered out like a wheel-flattened toad, lies an urchin.

A plod stands guard beside the bodies while a small watching crowd stands quietly by. I see the fear in the crowd's eyes as we draw near, it isn't fear of us but fear of the unknown.

I introduce myself and Head to the plod, but I have to repeat myself as he seems to be hard of hearing.

"Constable Roberts, Inspector," says he. "Here are the bodies."

"We can see that," grates Head. "Why aren't they covered up?"

"What was that? I can't hear you properly because of the howling wind."

Head repeats himself.

"We did cover them up, Sergeant. But the wind blew the cover away and an urchin run off with it and now no one else will lend us another."

"You should have put bricks on the cover," says I.

"It wasn't a thick cover, Inspector. Just an old sheet."

Head and I bob down to inspect the bodies. We turn the woman over, she is completely dead, her neck has been broken and her face now has the imprint of a cobble stone or two. The urchin is even more dead, but at least he looks happy about it. He will go down as an accident.

We stand up and I ask Roberts, "Where did she jump from?"

"Oh… Well she humped all over the place. She'd hump anyone anywhere I suppose, like they all do."

"Jump man! Jump!" bellows I.

Roberts begins to jump up and down on the spot, much to the crowd's amusement.

"Stop!" yells Head, grabbing Roberts by his shoulders. "Where did the victim *jump* from?"

"Oh… You mean jump from?" He points up the terrace. "Three floors up. Room number 4c. Constable Jones is up there with one of those boffin types. I think his name is Dr Smelly."

The man is driving me mad, "It is Shelley, not Smelly!" I yell. "Get your hearing tested."

"Thank you, Inspector. It could do with a rest."

"Come on, Sergeant," sighs I.

We climb depressingly bare wooden stairs that creak and crack beneath our feet, the place has a pungent odour of unwashed bodies, decay and little four-legged pests. We reach the landing on floor three where there are four doors numbered in sequence from

1c to 4c. There is a plod stood to attention outside the open door of 4c. We introduce ourselves and exchange pleasantries and are pleased to find that this Constable Jones is not only not hard of hearing he is also a likeable fellow with a sharp brain. He informs us the suicide was known as a Miss Gloria Ann Barber, Glo' for short. The photographers left an hour earlier and he and Roberts had been waiting around for a detective to turn up for over two hours.

Stepping into the room we find Dr Shelley dusting for finger prints around a chest of drawers. Finger prints are a relatively new science that isn't recognised by the courts in trials at present, but one day I believe it may well have some value in hunting down criminals and helping to put them away. On a double bed lie a pair of prostitutes, each one has a length of rope tied to their ankles with the other end tied to the bottom of the iron bedstead. By the open window there is the back of a short rotund, bald man, who turns around to fix cruel piggy eyes upon us.

Shelley turns away from the chest of drawers to face us, "Ah... Inspector Potter. How are you?"

"Well, sir," says I. "You have met Sergeant Head before, I believe?"

"Indeed, I have. Good day to you, Sergeant."

"And to you, sir," returns Head with a smile.

"I'm Ned Bucket," announces Baldy aggressively. "I own the place."

I do not like his attitude. "I suppose you also own these two women?" grates I, pointing at the women.

"What makes you think that?"

"You have tied them to the bed!"

"No, he didn't," cries the blond haired one. "We did it ourselves in case we've caught the sickness from Glo'."

"I keep telling them there is no sickness," says Shelley. "But I am afraid they do not believe me."

"Whatever it is," growls Baldy Bucket. "It ain't good for business."

"And what is your business, Mr Bucket?" demands I.

"I provide respectable young escorts for respectable lonely gentlemen."

"You mean you're a pimp," puts in Head.

"Upper class dealer in the pleasures of the flesh to be more accurate," smirks Baldy.

"I think pimp is a more appropriate word for your trade, sir," grates I. "Now, tell us what you know about the bodies in the street below."

Baldy takes out a small cigar from his pocket and makes a show of taking his time to light it with a match. "I was actually coming up the street at the time when I saw Gloria up at the window. She was sitting with her legs dangling out and looking really strange."

"What time was this?"

"Just after seven this morning."

I check my pocket watch. Nine thirty. "Please continue."

"I shouted up to her. Oi! What are you up to, you stupid old prat?" And with that she spread out her arms and shouted out 'I can fly', leant forward and launched herself out of the window. She flapped her arms a bit and then crashed to the ground."

"Did you see anyone behind her? Someone who may have pushed her?"

He shakes his head and blows smoke out through his nostrils.

"What was the urchin up to?"

"Oh.... Him. He was standing in the road with his arms held out. I heard him shout, 'Go for it Misses. I'll save ya for a penny or two.' Course, it broke her fall a bit but it didn't save her or the brat."

I turn to the two women, "Names?"

"I'm Chloe," says the blond one.

"And I'm Shirley," says the dark haired one.

"Where were you Chloe when Gloria fell to her death?"

"I was in bed with Shirl', Shirl' was snoring like a pig an' woke me up. I see Glo' get up and go over to the window an' pull it up. She seemed strange, not with it like, but then we'd all had a hard night."

"From where did Gloria get up?"

"The bed."

"All three of you were in the one bed?"

"That's right. We always share this bed. It's a bit squashed, but it's better than most of the lice ridden, piss stained, mice infected, skiddy crap mattresses most people have to sleep on."

"I dare say," says I. "Did Gloria say anything before she jumped?"

"She was mumbling, but I couldn't understand what she was saying."

"What happened next?"

"She swung her legs out the window and just sat there. That's when I got up. I thought 'she's got the sickness'. I went to pull her back in but she just called out 'I can fly'. Course she didn't fly, she just fell to the ground."

I turn to Shirley, "And you slept through it all?"

"Like a baby."

I thank them and turn to the Doctor. "Anything different about this one, Doctor?"

"Not that I can see. They get up, go to the window convinced they can fly and commit suicide."

"The body wagon's here," shouts Baldy, flicking his cigar out the window.

I go and inform Constable Jones not to allow the wagon to leave before I tell them they may go. He sets off down stairs and I go back to the Doctor.

"I shall carry out a post-mortem on Gloria," says Shelley. "It will undoubtedly turn up traces of drugs of some description…"

"No, it won't," cuts in Chloe.

"Why so?" asks Shelley.

"Because, Glo' never touched any kind of drugs. She didn't even drink. She just saved her pennies for other pleasures."

"Which were?" asks I.

"The theatre. Funfairs. She loved shows and showmen."

Dr Shelley whispers in my ear, "If she's right, Inspector, and I don't find any trace of drugs in Gloria to back up my theory that this is all about an unknown hallucinating drug, then where will we be?"

"Buggered," says I. "We have half the Police Force in London and beyond searching for drug sellers selling something new, something so powerful it sees women flying out of windows and men standing in front of trains and such shouting out 'Stop' in the absolute belief that whatever is coming straight at them will just come to a sudden halt. It is madness."

"And so far, we have nothing to really go on," puts in Head. "Even the snouts haven't heard anything about anything."

"It's a bastard, all this business," moans Baldy Bucket, lighting up another cigar and pointing it at the women. "How the hell am I supposed to get you couple of tarts out on the street when you've tied yourselves to the bleedin' bed?"

"Why not get your customers up here instead?" says Head.

"That's not a bad idea," ponders Baldy. "I could charge extra for two in a bed plus bondage."

"And why not lay on tea and cakes as well," adds Chloe. "It would make it all homely."

"Yeah, it would," agrees Baldy. "Maybe we could incorporate a bar as well and charge even more."

"You'd need a liquor licence," says Head.

"What to sell stolen booze?"

"It will never happen," cuts in I. "No one is going to come up here in case they don't go down again."

"Well I've got to do something! If I can't get my tarts back out there sellin' their bits we'll all starve."

"Looking at your gut, sir, I would say a little starvation will be good for you," says I.

"I don't need to listen to your insults, Copper."

"Then don't. I have had enough of your presence here, Mr Bucket. Clear off before I arrest you."

"What for?"

"Perverting the course of our investigations."

"That's bollocks."

"I know but I am a Policeman, and you are a pimple."

"Don't you mean, you are a pimp?"

"The Inspector has never pimped in his life," snaps Head. "I'd just piss off if I was you before you get a smack."

"I ain't finished yet," snarls Baldy pointing his cigar at the two women again. "Just you be ready to walk them streets again tonight or you'll be really sorry."

"Get lost," orders Head, and Baldy does, slamming the door on his way out.

"Let us go through Gloria's possessions, Sergeant," says I.

There is a chest of drawers in which Gloria's things, we're informed by Chloe, are in the bottom drawer. It reveals surprisingly clean underwear, a few treasured possessions and a good supply of sheaths. The battered wardrobe contains a couple of Gloria's dresses, a corset and bustle, a coat, three hats, a fake fur boa, an umbrella and two pairs of well-worn shoes. It doesn't amount to much but is more than most women who ply their trade in the slums would normally own.

"Glo' were a better class than most," says Chloe. "She had principles. She wouldn't shag just any old git. They had to be clean an' not smell much. An' she couldn't stand a farter."

"Nothing worse than a farter," puts in Shirly. "Doin' it to ya and goin' trump-trump-trump with every thrust then burpin' in ya face."

Chloe grimaces, "Had one sick on me once."

"Enough, ladies," says I. "Now, where did Gloria normally ply her trade?"

"She just flogged her ol' twat around here like the rest of us," shrugs Chloe.

"Did anything unusual happen to her over the past few days?"

"She went to the theatre last Friday with a posh Tom," says Chloe. "Got picked up in a carriage, no less."

"Very hoity-toity," sneers Shirley.

"Did you catch the man's name?"

"Um…. It were an odd name. Weren't it Chloe?"

"Yeah. Called himself Mr Who."

"I think we shall leave it there, Ladies. If you think of anything else get a message to Scotland Yard and address it to me, Detective Inspector Potter."

"We will," says Chloe. "What shall we do with Gloria's stuff?"

"Give it to her family."

"She didn't 'ave no family."

"Then share it out between you both once we have gone."

"Thanks, Inspector," smiles Chloe.

"I am finished here," announces Dr Shelley.

"We also," says I.

We leave the women to it, they have already untied their ropes and are noisily fighting over Gloria's possessions before we've gone down even one flight of stairs.

Outside we find the bodies have been loaded up and are ready to go. I ask Constable Jones if he has anything else to report.

"Nothing worth pursuing, Inspector. No one knows anything. They're just worried they could be next to catch the sickness."

It is time to leave. The Doctor gets a lift with the wagon and the two Constables go off to get something to eat. Head and I decide to walk for a while as we have a serious wind build up from our greasy breakfasts, while nature's wind has dropped off, turning the air quite humid.

"Have you ever thought about flying, sir?" says Head as we walk along.

"I went up in a balloon, once. I must say I was enjoying the experience until it caught fire and plummeted back to earth."

"You're lucky you didn't get killed!"

"Luckily, Sergeant, we were only about twenty feet up in the air at the time."

"I think flying is best left to the birds, sir. It'll never take off, trust me."

"Very droll, Sergeant. Very droll. I think that one day there will be hundreds, if not, thousands of flying machines up in the sky even during our lifetimes, and your little joke will be obsolete."

"What's the oldest joke in the world, sir?"

"I have no idea. Enlighten me."

"What did Adam say when Eve gave him the apple?"

"No idea."

"Core, lovely," laughs Head.

"I don't get it, Sergeant."

"Core, as in apple core. Not as in cor blimey, cor."

I chuckle even though I still don't get it. We walk on until we find a cab to take us to the Yard. Once there we go to our office to write out our reports and go over the previous suicide cases.

Having put up a board with the names and photographs of the twenty-three known suicides, alongside any relevant information, we add Gloria Ann Barber to the list to make it twenty-four. Fourteen of these were prostitutes, all female, the remainder were all men who lived, one way or another, off the women's earnings. All the women, except one, attempted to fly out of a window that was two storeys or more up. All except two died instantly.

"Let us discuss the two women who survived long enough for someone to hear them say something, Sergeant," says I. "Mary Wheeler jumped out of a window barely three feet from the ground, but unfortunately she then got run over by a pony and trap. But, she was heard to say before she died, 'I flew. I flew'. So, the woman actually believed she had flown and we can assume that that is exactly how the other suicides felt."

"Except for survivor number two," says Head pointing to one of the photographs. "Maisie Thorn survived her fall for close on one hour, but apparently, she didn't once mention her short flight at all. All she kept saying was, 'Just my bleedin' luck'. Well she was getting married to a man who was quite affluent and fancied she'd be able to move away from the slum and shut up shop for good. Except for her new husband, of course.

"Once the honeymoon is over, Sergeant, most women shut up shop anyway and only open on special occasions, like birthdays and Christmas."

"But not in your case, sir," smiles Head. "You and Betty are eternal honeymooners. You're a *very* lucky boy, sir."

"I know I am, Sergeant. But then we have been trying for a child for ten years and nothing has happened. So, in that respect we are not so lucky. Anyway, let us continue. What consistencies and inconsistencies do we have about the female suicides?"

"They were all lower-class prostitutes and slum dwellers. But not all came from the same slum."

"Exactly. There is a difference of twenty miles from the two who were furthest away from each other. While two of them lived together and died together. What else?"

"Everyone had traces of one type or another drug in their systems. But so far no new type of drug has been discovered."

"And not one of the suicides was known to have done anything out of the ordinary in the days leading up to their taking up flying."

"On the surface, no. But, something must have set them off. Something must have got to them so they didn't give a damn and happily jumped to their deaths."

"Let us move on to the men, Sergeant. Ten men who all believed they had the power to stop a bolting horse, which is a definite possibility as it happens all the time. But, only a maniac would even remotely believe he could stop a moving train by simply holding up a hand and commanding it to stop."

"Even when the drivers did their best to bring the train to a stop our maniacs where so close there wasn't a hope in hell."

"Leaving the suicides quickly turned into a mangled mess of guts, blood and meaty bits."

"Only one survived being run over by a horse and carriage long enough to say anything, namely a chorus of expletives."

"We are nowhere with all of this, Sergeant. It is more confusing than the contents of a woman's handbag."

"I wouldn't go that far, sir. Most women know exactly what's in their handbags even if most of it is rubbish."

"There has to be a common denominator that links all the suicides together."

"What does that mean?"

"No idea, Sergeant, but it will sound good in my report. I still believe the most likely cause is down to hallucinating drugs that have a delayed action. You take it now and react to its full implications some hours later."

"Most of them committed suicide during the night. Does that have any significance?"

"Possibly," I shrug. "I suggest we wait until we have the autopsy report on Gloria to see if she was clear of drugs. That being so we'll have to rethink our entire strategy. Meanwhile, I suppose we had better report to Clump."

"Do we have to? Can't we just sneak off home instead? After all we are supposed to be off today."

"It's all hands to the pumps, Sergeant. We have a backlog of crimes to deal with along with an exceptional increase in suicides. Sneaking off anywhere under the circumstances would be viewed as a dereliction of duty. You know what he is like."

"I suppose so," grates Head. "To be honest, sir, once the chips are down there's no one as dedicated to the job as Clump is."

"Exactly. So, let us go and report to him."

We take ourselves to Clump's office, only he is nowhere to be seen. Bumping into an Inspector Granger on the way back to our office, I ask, "Have you seen Clumpy?"

"He's gone on a fishing trip. Back on Tuesday."

"The cheeky bugger," grates Head.

"The slippery eel," moans I.

"He said you two wouldn't be happy to hear he's sneaked off, so he's left you both a little something in his 'whisky drawer' as a sorry."

"He'll be sorry alright," moans Head as we head back to Clump's office.

Once there I open the 'whisky drawer' and find a bottle of Champagne with a message tied to it: 'Best wishes to Mr and Mrs Potter on their anniversary. Regards, Chief and Mrs Clump'. There are also two tickets to the Starlight Theatre for tonight for me and Betty.

"Things are brightening up, Sergeant," smiles I.

Head continues to moan, "Well I wish they would for me. If my personal life gets any darker I think I'll quit the force and go coalmining just to let some light in."

"What you need, Sergeant, is the love of a good woman behind you."

"I had one once but I made the awful mistake of marrying her."

"I have often noticed, Sergeant, that women fall at your feet."

"True, but mostly because they trip over in front of me on purpose hoping to gain sympathy and a husband. There is no way I will ever marry again."

"You may well change your mind if you meet the right lady." I take a half full bottle of Clump's best whisky out from his drawer. "This has your name on it, Sergeant."

He takes it from me and reads the short note tied around the neck: 'Get sloshed. Get yourself a nice woman. Cheer yourself up'.

I realise Head needs a bit more socialising. "Why don't you come to the theatre tonight with me and Betty, Sergeant?"

"I'd just be in the way."

"Nonsense. Betty would love for you to come along."

"Very well, sir. I will."

"Good. Meet us outside the Starlight Theatre at seven-thirty."

"How much will it cost?"

"We shall get you in for free. Anyway, we'll achieve nothing more here today so let us go home."

We leave the Yard and go our separate ways and shortly I am back home.

I find Betty sat in the parlour knitting. I hide the Champagne behind my back.

"You're home early, Detective Inspector. How lovely. Shall we get back to it or do you want tea and something to eat first?"

"A ham and pickle sandwich with a cuppa would be nice my little firefly."

"And then we must open our presents. Are you hiding something behind your back, Detective Inspector?"

I produce the presents from the Clumps.

"How lovely," smiles Betty. "Theatre tickets as well. What's on?"

"I don't know. Sergeant Head will be joining us. I hope that's alright with you?"

"Of course, it is." She gives me a peck on the cheek, takes charge of the presents and sets them down on the sideboard.

I follow her into the kitchen and sit down. Betty puts the kettle on and makes me a huge crusty bread sandwich and a smaller one for herself. While we munch away I tell her all about the latest flying suicide.

"It's all very strange, Detective Inspector," says she. "Fancy thinking you can fly."

"Believing is a word that transcends thinking. They didn't think they could fly, they actually believed it."

"Um…" ums Betty. "And that belief led to their deaths."

"It seems so," sighs I, dropping the subject. "Today is a special day, my love. Let us forget about my work and just indulge in each other."

After a couple of hours of testing how much more our mattress can take before the springs give out, we get scrubbed up and don our best outfits. Betty looks radiant in a bright yellow crinoline dress with matching bonnet and a blue woollen shawl over her shoulders. I put on my black suit, white cravat and black top hat. We are ready to go. It is four-thirty, plenty of time for a leisurely meal and then on to the theatre. On the way out I pick up my silver topped cane and we set off to catch the tram at the end of the road. The tram drops us off right outside the Ocean of Fish Restaurant, Betty's favourite place to eat. We both order fish, chips and smashed up peas with a bottle of French Chardonnay.

The food is delicious, the service exemplary and the charges acceptable.

By seven-fifteen we are outside the theatre where Head is already waiting for us. There are long queues waiting to buy tickets but as we already have ours we go to the front and I show them to the doorman. He knows me and barely glances at them before allowing all three of us in.

"I thought you only had two tickets, sir?" queries Head.

I hold them up for him to peruse. I had cut one in half and fanned the two halves out behind the uncut ticket so that it appeared I had three tickets.

"Sneaky," grins Head.

"Typical," chides Betty.

"Magical," laughs I. And a magic act just happens to be the main event on tonight's show.

We settle down in our numbered seats near the front and hope that no one challenges Head and accuses him of being in the wrong seat. Seats bought on the day are very much sit where you can, providing you're in the correct area that you payed for. However, if someone has prepaid tickets for Head's seat, then in theory Head will have to move to accommodate the challenger.

As the gas lights are dimmed, announcing that the curtains are about to go up, Head receives just such a challenge from a well-dressed short man wearing a monocle.

"Excuse me, my friend," says he, flashing his ticket "I believe you are sat in my seat."

As there doesn't appear to be a vacant seat anywhere near us we are in a quandary. I flash my warrant card. "My apologies, sir," says I, conspiratorially. "We are on surveillance."

He leans closer to peruse my card and whispers, "For what reason, sir?"

"Keep it to yourself, sir. We have reason to believe that there may be a mass murderer in the audience. Our information tells us he will almost certainly be sitting somewhere in this area."

"I see," says he, appearing suitably horrified. "How dangerous is he?"

"Very! He is infamous for stabbing his victims through the back of their seats before vanishing into thin air."

"Do you know what he looks like?"

"I am afraid not. But on further information received we hope to arrest him this very evening."

"Then, sir, I shall leave you to it."

And he does, hurrying away as if his very life depends on it.

"You are a dreadful liar, Detective Inspector," chides Betty.

"Actually, Mrs Potter," says Head. "I'd say the Inspector is a brilliant liar."

The show begins; a troop of girls come out unsuitably dressed and dance for us. They are followed by the compere who tells much better jokes than Head, before announcing the next act, a group of foreign acrobats. After them the compere returns and tells a few more jokes before introducing: 'The incredible, the mesmerising, the fantastically sophisticated. Lock up your daughters because he is so handsome, master of all things magical and hypnotic. Ladies and gentlemen, I give to you... the one and only, Count Hugo Strange.'

To rapturous applause Count Hugo makes a flamboyant entrance into the limelight. He is a tall imposing figure in his white top hat and tails. He sports a ridiculously wide, waxed jet-black moustache and a small waxed goatee beard. Playing to the audience he seems to glide across the stage with his arms raised as if the very angels themselves had released him from his heavenly duties just to entertain us.

The Count's act is truly mesmerising, his magic deceives the eye so well you swear it truly is magic. But it is when he changes from magic to hypnotism I realise the man has extraordinary powers. Several volunteers are coaxed onto the stage and within moments Hugo has them all sleeping soundly while still standing up. They perform the most ridiculous feats to his commands, from believing they are chickens, cows, pigs and all kinds of animals to believing they are nobility, even long dead Kings or Queens. The man seems to have the power to control the volunteers' every thought, every action, and every single sound that comes out of their mouths. The audience are ecstatic, mesmerised and enthralled by it all, they are also in pain through laughing so much. I have never seen Head laugh to the point of choking. Betty is almost drunk with laughter and I must admit Hugo has captivated the entire audience, including myself. I also admit to myself that I may have found the real drug behind the Flying Women suicides.

Count Hugo's act finally ends with all the volunteers sent back to their seats, seemingly none the worse for their experiences. The applause is deafening and repeated over and over as the Count takes umpteen curtain calls before finally disappearing behind a side curtain. The compere returns and announces a thirty-minute interval. The lights go up and the entrance doors are opened allowing those seeking refreshments and the lavatories to rush out along with the clouds of smoke from all those cigars, pipes and cigarettes that had been smoked throughout the performances. Betty and Head need the lavatory and a coffee. I ask them to bring me a coffee back. As soon as they've gone I take myself backstage where I am instantly challenged by a strapping great brute who looks like he's survived a battle with a sledge hammer.

"No audience allowed back here," says he.

I show him my warrant card, "I am Detective Inspector Potter and it is imperative I speak to the Count, immediately."

"You the famous copper they call Jerry Pot?"

"I am."

"Alright, as it's you." He points, "Down that corridor, second door on your left."

I thank him, follow his directions and rap hard on the door.

"Come," says a commanding voice.

On entering I find the Count removing makeup from his face while sat in front of a large wall mirror, he is also assessing me and I sense he is reading my mind. He turns around on his seat to fix me with incredibly dark, penetrating sparkling eyes.

"You, sir, are not the usual autograph hunter. I would guess you are an official of some sort."

His English is excellent with only a hint of an accent.

I introduce myself, congratulate him on his brilliant performance and then get straight to the point. "What do you know about the unusually high amounts of odd suicides that have occurred in and around London over the past three weeks?"

"Only what I read in the paper last night in my hotel room. Now, Inspector, you have come here because you have realised that such a man as myself has the power to control people to the extent that should I wish to, I could make them do anything that I wanted them to do. Well you are correct in your assumptions. But you are questioning the wrong man. You see I only arrived in England yesterday morning. Tonight, was my first appearance here at the Starlight and even I, brilliant though I am, cannot hypnotise people from hundreds of miles away."

"Ah…" says I, utterly deflated.

"Ah indeed. I suggest Inspector that you find out who else has my abilities. I suggest you visit not only theatres but funfairs, clubs and societies, especially those so-called Gentlemen's Clubs that cater for the more perverse. Be warned that there are a lot of charlatans out there who couldn't hypnotise so much as goldfish."

We talk further for ten minutes or more before I thank him for his time and ask him for his autograph for Betty. He is happy to oblige and writes a small piece to Betty in my note book and then autographs below it. I head back to my seat, of course I will check out the Count's story but after years of detective work I know when someone is telling me the truth. However, the Count assured me that I am on the right track. Out there somewhere there is a hypnotist with the power to control minds to such an extent that they can even persuade them to kill themselves.

"Where have you been?" demands Betty as I retake my seat. "Your coffee is getting cold, Detective Inspector."

I take it from her, "I shall tell you later."

The second half of the show entertains but cannot live up to the first part and we are content to go home once we've done the God Save the Queen bit.

Once outside we move away from the crowd scrambling for cabs and I tell Head and Betty what I found out. Head is overawed by the revelation, while Betty is overjoyed with the Count's autograph.

An urchin appears, "You've stepped in a puddle, mister," says he. "I'll clean ya shoes for a penny."

On gazing down, I see my shoes reflecting the street lights via something wet. The urchin bobs down and wipes away at my shoes with a dirty rag.

"All done, mister," grins he, standing up and holding out his hand.

I place a penny into it, he grins and is on the point of hopping for it when Head suddenly gives him a ringer.

"What's that for?" complains he, rubbing at his left lug.

"That's for pissing on the Inspector's shoes."

"Get stuffed, Copper," spits the brat before disappearing into the crowd.

Betty thinks it is funny and even Head has a grin on his face. I too, have to smile as I take Betty's arm, glad that Head has at last cheered up. We say goodnight to the Sergeant and head off home our separate ways having agreed to rest up on Sunday and continue our quest to unearth whoever is behind the suicides first thing Monday morning.

Come Monday morning we find that there were three more suicides investigated by other detectives and plods from the day before. One of which was Shirley from Tannery Street. I call a meeting and take charge as Clump is away. I instruct all those present to seek out anyone who may have the ability to hypnotise people before dispersing them to; 'Get to it'.

The drug theory is totally out the window when Dr Shelley reports to me that he couldn't find a trace of drugs or even alcohol in Gloria's blood, stomach or guts.

Head and I head down to Tannery Street.

We find Chloe in a state of terror. She has gone even further this time by chaining herself to the bed by both ankles while leaving enough chain length so she can still do her job.

Ned Bucket is also there, he is genuinely upset at losing Shirley because she was, 'One of me best earners'. He is however quite pleased that his bondage idea has been reaping in extra rewards. I note that there is also an extensive array of alcoholic beverages stacked on the chest of drawers.

Having read the report on Shirley's death I find myself asking Chloe and Baldy the same questions they'd been asked the day before, in the hope that they may have remembered something new.

"I remembered something else last night when I had a Tom giving me one," says Chloe. "I often come up with stuff when I'm bein' shagged cause I get so bored an' it stops me from droppin' off. As Glo' weren't around that posh bloke took Shirl' out in his carriage on Saturday night instead."

"According to the report I read this morning you told the Detective all about that yesterday."

"I did, but I forgot to tell him where the toff took Shirl' that night."

"Where was she taken?"

"Battersea Funfair. An' she had her future read by a weird bloke wearing a funny hat."

My brain begins to work overtime, "How would you like to earn a couple of pounds, Chloe?"

She gives me a suspicious look, "Doin' what? I don't do anything with animals."

"You won't have to. I need you to accompany me and my Sergeant to the fair tonight."

"Really? You're goin' to take me to the fair and pay me for it? What's the catch?"

"If we are successful, the man behind the suicides will be the catch."

"How long will you need her?" butts in Baldy. "Every hour she's out will cost me money."

"As long as it takes."

"Then she ain't goin' unless you pay me a fiver as well."

Head gives me a knowing look that tells me to leave it to him. "That sounds fair to me, Mr Bucket. What say you, sir?"

I nod.

"In advance," demands Baldy.

"I shall bring you the money tonight when we pick up Chloe, Mr Bucket," says I. "Say about six."

He glares into my eyes, "Very well then. But she don't leave here until I've got the money in me hand."

"I need a pee, Ned," cries Chloe.

"Alright, alright. Keep ya drawers on."

"I ain't got any on anyway,"

We leave Baldy undoing Chloe's chain and head back to the Yard. Once there I fill Head in on my plan to expose our villain, that's if the man with the funny hat really is our villain.

"We could be on a wild duck chase, sir."

"Or we could just be on the right nest. So, Sergeant, are you game?"

He grins, "I am, sir. Especially about putting that bloody pimp in his place."

Satisfied that we have covered everything we can for now we leave the Yard and Head back to mine for something to eat, stopping on the way to borrow a couple of outfits from a theatrical friend of mine. By just after five we are dressed as ordinary slum folk complete with floppy hats, jumpers with holes, patched trousers, scruffy jackets and well-worn boots. Both of us carry our usual weapons concealed beneath our clothes.

We find Chloe excited and ready to go when we call for her. She is dressed in a white dress with blue flowers upon it, around her shoulders is Gloria's fake boa. Her bonnet is pale blue and she is carrying a small straw bag. She looks very pretty and I have a pang of sorrow that the poor girl has such a rotten life. But that is how it is in these times.

Baldy puts a hand around her throat, "You do any tricks out there you make sure you bring the money back to me or you'll be bleedin' for it."

The thug seems oblivious to Head and I believe he has temporarily forgotten who we are, we are about to remind him.

It is one hell of a feat to clap Baldy's wrists in chains, he puts up one devil of a fight, but a knee in the roundies by Head finally subdues him enough to be able to chain him to the bed as well. I slip the keys into my pocket. As we make our way downstairs and out into the street Baldy's ear shattering curses can still be easily heard if not so easily deciphered. Head links arms with Chloe and I must admit they look rather suited. Battersea Funfair, here we come.

We finally arrive at the fair at seven o'clock. It is still light and won't be dark for another hour or so, but several of the rides are already lit up. The carousels, helter-skelter and side shows, such as the ghost shows, the strongman and the bearded lady have queues of men, women and children all eager to pay a penny or two to be entertained. Barrel organs and wandering musicians fill the air with sound, the atmosphere is one of excitement and laughter. There are also a lot of urchins about.

Chloe is having the time of her life and we allow her to enjoy a few rides before we get down to the more serious business of why we are here. However, Head and I can't resist having a go at the shooting galleries, the darts and ring the bell. Head wins Chloe a rose designed brooch and pins it onto her dress close to her heart, she places a hand over his and their eyes meet. Either they're acting their parts extremely well or they are becoming genuinely lovey-dovey. It is time to get on with it.

The richly decorated tent of 'The Great Marco' finally materialises before us. According to his billboard: 'The Great Marco knows all, sees all and can tell you your future and fortune for just crossing his palm with silver'. Head and Chloe go around to the side of the tent and I step in through the open flap. Before me, sat on a brightly coloured elaborately decorated throne several feet to the rear of the tent, sits a dark-skinned man who stares at me through black, unblinking eyes. He wears a blue coloured turban with matching robe, both of which are decorated with silver crescent moons and stars. Around his neck hangs a heavy gold chain with a pentagram, his wrists are laden with gold bangles and chains. He sits in front of a round black enamelled table that reflects the flickering lights from tall candles placed all around the tent. On the table stands the inevitable crystal ball. The entire effect is unnerving but still it draws you in. Marco gestures for me to sit opposite him, there are three gold painted chairs to choose from, I take the one in the middle.

"The Great Marco knows all," he begins holding out his hand. "Cross my palm with silver and Marco will change your life for ever."

Close up, I can tell that Marco's colour comes from a bottle and not from some far eastern, exotic, mysterious place. He is as English as I am, but that doesn't detract from his mesmerising stare or his aura of mystique. I place a silver sixpence in the palm of his hand, he closes his hand and opens it again, the sixpence has vanished.

"The Great Marco needs only to know your name and what you do for a living."

"My name is Gerald Palmer and I am a groundsman for a gentleman near Hyde Park."

"And you always wear gloves when working, do you not?"

There are no callouses on my hands, that much anyone can see. "How do you know such things?" says I, feigning amazement.

"The Great Marco knows all. I sense you have recently lost someone dear to you?"

I drop my gaze and rub at my eyes which begin to water immediately because of the salt I rubbed into them. "My darling wife succumbed to the fever."

His penetrating stare has changed to a mocking sneer and I fear I have underestimated the man and he is about to unmask me.

Marco sits back as a lazy smile crosses his mouth, "Why are you really here, Mr Palmer, or whatever your real name is?"

I sit back and meet his eyes, "Surely the Great Marco knows exactly why I am here?"

"Perhaps he does, perhaps he doesn't."

"Perhaps pigs will fly if they grow wings."

"There are pigs, and there are pigs. How high up the pig scale are you, Mr Palmer?"

"Quite high." I have no choice but to come clean and I tell him that I am a Detective Inspector investigating the recent suicides.

"All you had to do was ask," says he with a frown. "I will be happy to assist you in any way I can. In fact, Inspector, I am flattered that you suspect I may have such hypnotic powers as to be able to control minds and send people to their deaths."

"Think nothing of it," smiles I.

I question Marco for several minutes, he is forthcoming and eager to help and offer advice. However, he tells me that my time is up unless I wish to cross his palm with more silver.

Deflated beyond belief I exit the tent and walk away over towards the beer tents. Head and Chloe follow at a discreet distance and we do not come together until we are safely inside one of the tents. Two pints later and having told them all, despite the fact they heard nearly everything, we decide to give it an hour or so before Head and Chloe give it a try.

Darkness falls and the fairground lights add a new dimension to the sights all around us. We have snacked on roast beef sandwiches, sugary rock and candy sticks all washed down with beer and whisky. Chloe is quite drunk by now and she and Head are all over each other to the point that I fear they may just disappear behind the next tent and shag each other rotten. I also fear our mission will go down in history as one of Detective Inspector Potter's biggest balls ups since he began his career as a plod, by arresting a society beauty for soliciting when she was merely taking a stroll outside her Mayfair home to get a breath of air. But then she was unaccompanied and I *had* been trained to believe all unaccompanied women must be prostitutes.

We walk back to Marco's tent where there is now a small queue of people; three prostitutes who are obviously well drunk as they giggle, swear and fool around, plus a young couple who are embracing each other while frantically slobbering away as if they are trying to gobble each other up.

Head and Chloe join the queue while I sneak around the back. Despite the noise of the fairground and the antics of the prostitutes I can still vaguely hear what is going on inside the tent.

A few minutes later I am desperate for a pee and step a few feet away from the tent and undo my fly buttons. I am unseen providing no one ventures around the back of the tent. Unseen by anyone, except for the urchin who jumps up out of nowhere.

"A mere penny will make sure I don't tell anyone how big your dodger isn't," grins he.

I give him a squirt in the face and he runs off wailing. Is nothing sacred?

Back close to the tent I hear that whoever was in the tent is leaving, apparently overawed with what Marco has told them. The trio of prostitutes go in, still giggling and swearing.

The Great Marco plays to his audience and quickly has them drawn into his aura. He asks for his silver but receives an offer of sexual favours in return but only after he has told their fortunes in case he's 'Some bleedin' ol' cheat just out to con us'.

Everything changes dramatically the moment Marco orders all three women to look deep into his eyes. They giggle and make disparaging comments about Marco's mystic abilities before they suddenly fall into a deadly silence. I strain my ears as Marco has lowered his voice to a velvet tone that is hauntingly rhythmic and deeply disturbing. I catch barely half he is saying but it is enough to know that he has them completely under his spell and at his mercy.

At last he claps his hands and the women return to their giggling and swearing.

"What a load of ol' crap," sneers one. "Nothin' bleedin' 'appened."

"You won't be getting your 'and up my skirts," laughs another.

"Nah," says the third one. "Just a bleedin' ol' trickster. Come on girls lets go."

"That's it, ladies," coos Marco. "Fly, fly away."

I go to the front of the tent just as the three women emerge and stroll off arm in arm still laughing and swearing about 'The Great Marco'.

I tell the slobbering couple to clear off. Head, Chloe and I enter the tent.

Marco has pulled off his turban to reveal a white line where the dye ends, the white line is heavily spotted. Syphilis! He gazes up at us as he raises a glass of drink to his mouth and takes a long swallow.

"Brandy," smiles he. "Good for the heart. I wondered how long it would be before you returned, Inspector. I suppose you will be arresting me. Just for your interest I knew you were outside the tent listening in, as I knew that you wouldn't give up until you had proved to at least yourself that I am the one responsible for sending all those filthy whores, along with their equally filthy pimps to their deaths."

"Why did you do it?" asks Chloe, who has instantly sobered up. "You don't know us. You don't know how 'ard it is. You think I want to be a tart? You think I want to have my body pawed over like some piece of meat?"

"Of course, you do. Isn't it easier to lay on your back than go out and do honest work."

"Work! What bloody work? It's whore or starve."

"Enough," snaps I. "Mr Marco, or whatever your name is, I am arresting you for inviting women to fly out of windows and men to jump in front of trains and horses."

"Don't you mean enticing?" asks Marco.

"Probably," admits I. "Do you have anything to say before we drag you off to the nick?"

"Yes, actually I do. If you think you will be hanging me you will be sorely disappointed."

"And why's that?" demands Head.

"Wait and see." With that he stands up, downs the remainder of his brandy and fixes his turban back on. "I am ready to go, Inspector."

Head goes to cuff Marco, but then puts his cuffs back into his pocket.

Chloe unexpectedly goes to spit in his face only to back away.

I am now beginning to realise exactly what I am dealing with and if it hadn't had been for Count Hugo's hypnotising me on

Saturday night at the theatre to protect me from anyone else doing the same, I too would be under Marco's spell.

As if we are simply out for an amiable stroll we make towards the exit, but just then Marco raises his arms to the starlit sky and cries out in a voice that echoes around the entire place, "Armageddon!" All hell then breaks loose!

Rides start to speed up, barrel organs play dementedly fast, darts are sent flying out in all directions, sticks of rock are pelted at anyone and everyone. The entire fairground has become bewitched, the screaming voices of hundreds of people stun the senses. Hats, bonnets, bags and all sorts fly everywhere as terror struck, people cling desperately to anything that may stop them from being hurled from their ride to serious injury or death. Behind it all are the fairground workers, their eyes vacant, all have been hypnotised, they are not in their right frames of mind. I spy the three prostitutes standing up at the top of the helter-skelter, they are about to jump. There is nothing else for it, drawing my revolver I point it at Marco and shoot him straight between the eyes and he collapses instantly to the ground. Levers are pulled by confused and traumatised assistants to slow down rides. People burst into tears, faint away or collapse in delirium onto the ground. I see the three prostitutes hanging their heads over the helter-skelter and vomiting, several urchins run forward carrying buckets in which to catch the vomit just in case it contains something worth having, like a half-digested sausage. I watch in amazement as two intrepid urchins drag off a wooden statue of a ten-foot-high Red Indian Chief. While others are scooping up armfuls of sticks of rock, coconuts, bottles of booze and anything they can get hold of. One has grabbed hold of a whole leg of ham and is eating as fast as he can at the topside end, while another interloper chomps away at the hock end. Several others run off with dozens of goldfish bowls, carelessly spilling out water and fish, the fish are soon scooped back up and dropped into other bowls before flipping out again. One female brat comes flying by holding on to several bonnets rammed onto her head and a ball of shawls tucked under her other spindly arm. The strongman has been stripped of his leopard skin leaving him naked and confused as some wealthy looking little old dear faints away at the sight of his muscly member. Even his balls and bar weight have been ferreted away along with the biscuit tin of takings. A hand cart comes by with a comatose prostitute in it, her hanging out arms flapping wildly about, the urchin shoving it can't control it and it tips to one side, the woman falls out and is abandoned when the urchin spies a more lucrative prize; the little old lady is quickly bundled onto the cart and wheeled away as fast as the urchin can go. It is utter chaos and can't go on. Raising my revolver, I fire two shots up into the air in an attempt to restore calm, only to receive a coconut to the back of my head, another to my forehead and a large stick of rock across my nose.

At last several plods flood onto the scene, Head and Chloe return to the real world and the crowds start pulling themselves together. Miraculously the urchins have nearly all escaped with their booty and only a few have been caught, and they tended to be the ones who were under three, had wooden legs or were carrying so much booty they couldn't outrun the plods. The plods take charge and quickly restore order by ushering everyone out and closing the fair for the night. The Great Marco is sent off to the morgue on the back of a donkey as nothing else is available. An hour later we are free to go and are soon on a tram heading towards Tannery Street.

Once we get off the tram we have a fifteen-minute walk to Chloe's place. Head has a quiet word with me as Chloe walks ahead of us. He has asked Chloe to move in with him as his maid of all works. "Nothing funny, sir. I just want to give the poor girl the opportunity to get out of whoring and make a fresh start before she ends up old before her time and riddled with disease."

"It is a noble gesture, Sergeant, but I fear you are deluding yourself."

"How so, sir?" retorts he.

"You will not be able to keep your hands off each other, Sergeant. The pair of you need to realise that you have become infatuated with each other very quickly and you would not be able to live together in any other capacity except as lovers. Which is nice, but you must agree to certain rules before you go too far and regret it later."

"I am not following you, sir. Surely if we truly fancy each other, then what is the problem?"

I have a mountain of respect for Head. I also regard him as a true friend, but, I cannot stand by and watch him stampede into a relationship that might have serious consequences, not only for him but also for Chloe. "Shag in haste, repent at your leisure," says I, raising my eyebrows to add dramatic effect. "The first thing you must do is to have Chloe examined to make sure she is free of sexually caught diseases. If, hopefully, she is clear, you then set down some ground rules. Chloe needs to know exactly where she stands, as do you. Do not under any circumstances make the girl idle promises you may not be able to keep. Promise her nothing at the beginning and accept only the same from her. That way you may have a chance to build foundations that will last."

It is easy to see by the look in Head's eyes that what I have just said to him has deflated him. With a touch of anger in his tone, he says, "You don't like her do you, sir? Is it because of what she is?"

I shake my head, "That girl has led a truly rotten life, Sergeant, and deserves the chance of happiness. However, for that happiness to have any hope of lasting it will need to be structured and seriously thought out or she will fall back into her old life. I know how she is feeling right now; she will do anything you ask just to get away from Bucket, and that is not a good basis to start a serious relationship. But, if all you both want is to enjoy what you can while you can, like I say, get her checked out first, and then the both of you can go at it like rabbits and just live for the moment, while making sure she doesn't get pregnant. In short do not confuse lust with love."

"I just want to come home to someone, like you come home to Mrs Potter. I am fed up with washing my own clothes, sir."

I place a reassuring arm around his shoulder, "This is what I am trying to get over to you, Richard. The both of you have decided to live together for very different reasons, and love does not come into that reasoning. You may shag each other stupid, but once the honeymoon is over it all falls apart unless you truly care for each other."

"But, how do we know how much we truly care for each other unless we give it a try?"

"By taking things more slowly. You need to court each other and get to know each other. Spend time together doing all those little things, like going for a walk in the park. By being apart from each other for days at a time so you may reflect on how you really feel for each other. In short, you need to be a normal courting couple instead of two desperate people trying to snatch at a moment's happiness that will inevitably turn to sorrow. Get to know each other's likes, dislikes, habits and aspirations before you get into bed together."

"The thing is, Gerald, I can do anything I want because I can. Chloe doesn't have that luxury. She will still have to survive by whatever means are necessary. Do you know she is only seventeen and has known nothing but whoring since she was just twelve years old?"

"I do not live on the moon, Richard. Of course, I know what girls like Chloe must do to survive and I do not judge them for it, nor can I be soft on them. If I myself am to survive in my capacity as a crime fighter, I have to appear to be a cold-hearted shit bag who couldn't give a rat's knacker about anything except locking away scum or hanging them from the nearest tree."

"You really are a big softy on the quiet though, aren't you Gerald," smiles Head.

"It's sir to you, Sergeant," remonstrates I. "And don't you forget it."

"Will our relationship work? What I really mean is, Chloe has been with a lot of men. Let me put it another way. When you wed Mrs Potter she was a virgin."

"No, actually she wasn't. Do not look so surprised, Sergeant. And do not ever repeat what I am about to tell you."

He crosses his heart, "I swear."

"I trust you implicitly, Sergeant. Betty's first love was a Michael O'Reilly,"

"What! Mick 'The Mauler' O'Reilly?"

"The one and only. Mick and I grew up together in the East End and became best friends from an early age. Betty also grew up with us but was viewed by me and Mick as just another stupid girl who kept hanging around. However, by the time they were in their teenage years Mick and Betty had become lovers. Everyone expected they would marry, they even set a date, but then Mick got his first taste of prison. While he was away, romance blossomed between Betty and me. You see, Richard, Mick and Betty did not love each other in the true sense of the word, they cared for each other but it wasn't love, and once Mick came out of prison he too had changed his mind about getting married"

"Did Mick stove your head in because you'd pinched his girl?"

"No, in fact he was relieved to be released from his promise. We never fell out because of what happened and I have never held it against Betty that she wasn't a virgin when we married. But then she had only the one previous lover, Chloe has had hundreds, which is something else you will have to deal with in your own way."

"That went through my mind. How will I deal with it?"

"If you truly love her, you will deal with it. Now, let us drop the subject for now. I shall formulate a plan that is best suited to you both, but for now, let us pick up Chloe's possessions and then she can come and stay with me and Betty for a while until we sort everything out."

We catch up with Chloe, she and Head hold hands and we walk on. Presently we pass a pawnbroker's that is still open even though it is now gone ten o'clock. Standing outside is a wooden statue that looks suspiciously like the one from the fairground. There is a plaque hung around its neck. I read it out loud: 'This is an exact model of the famous Red Indian Chief known as Geronimo, who was killed at the Battle of Big Little Horn by Colonel Custard. £1.10 shillings ono'.

"I think they've got their history a bit wrong, sir," says Head.

"But at least their spelling is good," grins I.

"Shall we go in and arrest them for selling stolen goods, sir?"

I shake my head, "I have had enough for one night, Sergeant. Let's just get home, Betty will be worrying herself sick by now."

Turning into Tannery Street we find it eerily quiet, a quiet that is accentuated by having so few gaslights that most of the street is in darkness. We are barely twenty feet from Chloe's place when out of the doorway leaps Baldy Bucket, shotgun in hand and pointing it right at us.

"No one takes the piss out of Ned Bucket," snarls he.

How he managed to unchain himself I have no idea, but he didn't do it before wetting himself I reason, judging by the big wet patch around his crotch.

"Chloe," he snarls some more. "Move away from them bastards or you'll get a gut full as well."

"I would think carefully before you do something that will lead you to the hangman's noose," says I.

"The bleedin' hangman can go an' hang," he snarls even more while waving the shotgun all over the place.

"We are dead, sir" says Head. "There's no way out of this one."

Our ears are suddenly assaulted by the unmistakable cracking of hooves on cobble stones coming up behind us, I spin my head around to see half a ton or more of snorting demented stallion charging straight at us.

"Against the wall!" shouts I.

Head slams Chloe against the wall and shields her with his own body while I press myself as hard back against the bricks as I can. "Bucket! Get out of its way, you prat!"

Only Baldy Bucket doesn't move. Instead, he drops the shotgun, sticks his arm straight out, holds up the palm of his hand and shouts, "Stop! I command you..."

His command is interrupted by the horse ploughing right over him and continuing its flight regardless.

Chloe screams loud enough to wake the dead. Head says the f-word several times, while for once I am stunned into momentary silence, but quickly recover to take charge of the situation.

Windows above us are open and a few nosey noses poke out and take a quick gander before disappearing back in and slamming their windows shut, but at least no one dumped their potty contents over us.

"Look at that hoof mark on his chest," says Head as we go over and peruse the body. "It looks like it's been printed on."

"Marvellous," says I. "Anyway, at least he didn't suffer."

"Pity," sulks Chloe. "I would've liked him to have suffered for all he's done to me."

"Never mind, my love," sooths Head putting his arm around her. "You are free of him at last."

I go through Bucket's pockets and find a few wet pounds which I give to Chloe. I can't be bothered to deal with Bucket's body right now and decide to leave him where he is, body snatchers will cart him off and sell him to 'medical science' long before dawn has broken. Besides which I am in dire need of a cup of Betty's lovely cocoa, my bed and Betty's warm cherries massaging my face. We go up to Chloe's room and help her pack what few things she has. Within minutes we are ready to leave, Chloe says a last goodbye and I believe the girl has finished with the place forever.

Head leaves us at the end of Tannery Street and I take Chloe back to mine where we find Betty still waiting up. She takes Chloe in without a murmur of complaint and heats milk up for cocoas all round.

After cocoa Betty shows Chloe to her room and settles her in. I can hear Chloe sobbing and Betty soothing her and know that I did the right thing by bringing the girl here, even though I know tonight's face massage is probably off the menu.

Tuesday morning, Head and I are back at the Yard. We receive applause and commendations from all and sundry for putting an end to The Great Marco's murderous reign, there are still a lot of unanswered questions, but we'll find those answers in due course. Doctor Shelley comes to visit us in our office in the early afternoon to inform us that Marco was riddled with syphilis, as I had suspected. Between us we conclude that Marco had been motivated by revenge for catching the disease from his apparently frequently accepting sexual favours from prostitutes in place of silver to tell them their fortunes. Case concluded. Clump fails to materialise and telephones to inform the Yard that he's having such a wonderful time up in Scotland salmon fishing, he has decided to stay on for a few more days.

At last Head and I settle down to go through the backlog of outstanding work that has piled up on our desk over the past few days.

"Um…," ums Head as he reads a report on two new murders that were committed over the weekend. "You best see this, sir." He hands me the report.

I read it out loud, 'Two people murdered, one on Saturday night in the Starlight Theatre and one on Sunday night in the Music hall. Both victims were stabbed in the back through their seats. Here is a profile of the suspected killer. He is well dressed, quite short, very polite and sports a monocle'.

"We could do with a holiday, sir," groans he.

"Or better still, Sergeant, let us assign this one to anyone other than ourselves."

"Agreed," says he. "Time for a pint, sir?"

"It is indeed, Sergeant."

On the way out, we sneakily drop the report regarding the Theatre murders onto the desk of a pair of Detectives we don't like and run off to the Dirty Duck Inn, which is another, *very* different story.

The Gut

Head and I are in the briefing room, just us and C. I. Clump. It is a bleak room, grey painted walls, a couple of high barred windows letting in weak fanned light, a few chairs and a desk.

We are sat looking across the desk to a blackboard screwed up on the wall, on which are pinned half a dozen silhouettes of heads, above half a dozen sketched pictures of eyes and eye-brows.

Clump is clumping up and down in deep thought while continually scratching with his left hand at the recently grown, full set of fuzzy grey hair around his chops, while his other hand's playing a frantic game of pocket billiards. Head and I follow his every movement while pondering over the reason we are here. Whatever it is, it must be serious.

At last Clump comes to a halt, parks his bum on the desk and gazes studiously at us, "Whatever is said in this room *lads*, whatever is said," he repeats with a knowing wink that tells me Head and I are about to get shafted. "Must be kept between us three, and only us three, plus of course the Police

Commissioner, therefore making four. Lives depend on it, men could get killed, good men, police men, Scotland Yard men." He smiles at us just like a mad man about to attack us with an axe. "Now *lads*. Here it is. The Commissioner has been up my arse big time over the past few weeks. And I mean big time. So far up I've struggled to breathe."

Head and I shoot each other looks of questioning astonishment that Clump quickly picks up on, "When I say up my arse, I am speaking metaphorically. What I really mean he has been on my back big time. Now! Do you recognise any of these faces on the blackboard?" he points.

We shake our heads, "Um…" ums I. "They are merely profiles, sir. Haven't you anything more defined that actually shows their faces?"

He shakes his head, "No, I am afraid not. These are the profiles of the Phantom Gang."

"The Phantom Gang?" we echo back.

"Have either of you heard of them?"

We nod in unison and suddenly I don't like where this is going, one little bit.

"Good. So, you are aware of what's been a foot regarding this gang of murdering scum bags, who are so brazen they not only have the nerve to commit their hideous crimes out of their patch, they have the nerve to commit them right across London and out into the countryside. Not only that, they go for the most lucrative of targets, including: A Member of Parliament, the aristocracy, umpteen, well-healed, wealthy citizens, landowners and God knows, even a Bishop had his ring taken advantage of! Not only did they help themselves to the Bishop's ring, they took his bloody finger with it!"

We gasp in horror.

"Yes *lads*. When the poor old Bishop couldn't get his ring off quick enough they chopped his finger off, just like that!" he makes a chopping action in the air with his right hand, but at least it stops his game of pocket billiards which was becoming very disconcerting. "They chopped it off, whipped off the ring and then calmly handed him back his severed finger. Any questions thus far?"

"Is that where the famous Bishop's Finger beer gets its name?" asks Head.

"I doubt it," growls Clump, fixing Head with a demolishing glare. "This gang is utterly ruthless, and so far, has committed acts of murder, extortion, blackmail, torture. rape, buggery and all manner of thuggery. You name it and they've done it. And they have gotten away with it all. We are nowhere nearer catching them now than we were a year ago when they first reared their ugly heads. In truth, we are clueless. All we know is that they hide out in the notorious Gut, where they can move around with absolute impunity. And do you know why?"

"Because no one knows who they are?" asks Head.

Clump shakes his head, "Everyone knows everyone in the Gut, Sergeant. It's how they stay alive. You should know that, shouldn't you?"

"I do, sir. But if their faces are always black like in those pictures how would anyone know who they were?"

Clump's face, what little is visible through his fuzzy beard, goes red in frustration, "Are you being unedifying?" he demands.

"Um...I don't know what you mean, sir," puzzles Head.

"Are you taking the piss?" I put in.

"Exactly!" roars Clump. "This is no piss taking matter, Sergeant. Lives are at stake and if you do not get your wooden brain into gear it could be your life at stake. Do you understand me?"

"Yes, sir," he replies, but I know he hasn't clicked as to what's coming up, but I have.

Clump continues in a more amiable tone, similar to a mesmerising cat just before it pounces on the cornered mouse, "The thing is *lads*, as you may know, D. I. Spencer and D. S. Brown have been leading the investigation into the gang since day one but have failed to come up with anything that may lead to us capturing the gang, except for these profiles, or silhouettes as they are better known. Let me explain how they got them. The Bishop who lost his finger, without revealing who he is because he wishes not to be exposed to public ridicule, is very short-sighted, or is that long-sighted? Whatever. When he was robbed, in his Palace, one dark night, having been dragged naked from his bed with a carrot up his bottom, the gang, who normally wear woolly hats and scarfs around their faces…"

Head cuts in by raising his hand.

"What is it?" demands Clump.

"Why do they put woolly hats around their faces, sir?"

Clump stares at Head, he is so dumbfounded by the Sergeant's ignorant question he is lost for words, but I can see where Head is coming from; the crafty devil is playing the fool in the vain hope Clump will tell him to clear off and replace him with someone else for the nightmare we are being groomed for.

Having regained his composure, Clump continues, "The gang had not bothered disguising themselves that evening, because they obviously knew that the Bishop's eyesight is so bad he would never be able to give a clear description of his assailants. But, what they didn't know was that the Bishop can clearly define shapes and profiles like a master painter, and was able to draw these brilliant silhouettes himself, some from a side profile and others front profiles. The eye descriptions come from all those victims who looked into the thug's eyes. Several of who agreed with each other, although there were a few disagreements among others."

"May I ask," I cut in, "how many agreed with each other compared to those who disagreed?"

"About half, roughly."

"In other words; the eye descriptions cannot be relied upon?" sighs I.

"But," he smiles," they all agreed that one of the gang only has one eye and that another is cross eyed."

I am getting tired of this and cut to the chase. "So where do we come in all this, sir?"

"Ah…I was coming to that, Inspector. Now," he points a waving finger at us and springs away from the desk. "You two are two of the Yard's finest detectives. You are legends, heroes and unconquerable warriors who are looked up to by every man jack in the force, while the criminal fraternity live in terror of you both. Once we have set you lose on them they know you'll pursue them like a pair of bloodhounds sniffing at a bitch's fanny and won't give up until you've seen the buggers in prison or swinging from a rope. And that is why the Commissioner has demanded I take Spencer and Brown off the case and hand it over to you two. Yes, *lads* you capture the Phantom Gang and it is promotion for you both. How does Detective Chief Inspector Potter and Detective Inspector Head sound? So, what say you *lads*, are you up for it?"

Head changes his tune, he dreams of being a D. I. "I'm in, sir," he cries.

"Good man," beams Clump. "And you, Inspector? What say you?"

"I'd say we're so well known around the area we'd have our throats cut the second we step within fifty feet of the Gut, and that is the very reason we weren't given the assignment in the first place. Is it not, sir?"

"True…" he drawls.

"The other thing is, no one will talk to us or any other policeman because they are all terrified of the gang, while adhering to honour amongst thieves plus seeing the gang as Robin Hoods. I know the gang have handed out loads of money and incentives to ensure that it's in everyone's interest to keep the gang's secrets. That gang has got everyone licking their bottoms. They don't even encroach on anyone's scams or criminal activities in any way shape or form by carrying out their evil crimes well away from the Gut."

"You are as well informed and up to date as ever, Inspector," beams Clump like a jovial fisherman slowly reeling in the catch of the day so it doesn't drop off the hook. "Precisely why the Commissioner insists you take over and lead the investigation. So, what say you, Inspector. Are you in?"

"Is it an order or a request?"

"A request. The mission will be dangerous in the extreme and we have no right to order you."

"So, if I refuse, sir? That is, it? End of?"

"Not exactly," he grins reeling me in a lot faster. "There's the small matter of you and your Sergeant excepting, shall we say, gratuities from certain quarters in which to line your own pockets. In short, Inspector, if you do not take the case, you will find your arse up in court so fast you won't have time to fart or go home and give that lovely wife of yours a quick comforting poke, before you're dragged off to spend the next few years gazing through iron bars! I ask again, what say you, Inspector?"

"I am in, sir," I sigh. "But you realise it could see us dead."

"Not if you slip into the Gut in disguises so clever you'll not only blend in with the rest of the stinking-raggedy-flea-bitten-illiterate-diseased-pox-ridden-scum, even your own mother wouldn't recognise you."

"She wouldn't anyway," I put in caustically. "She dumped me in the poor house once she had given birth."

"Did she really?" muses Head. "Well, I never knew that."

"Never mind all that," cuts in Clump. "Let's get down to it." Sliding behind the desk he sits down and opens a drawer. "Bring your chairs up closer, *lads*, let's have a toast to your future success."

We pull up our chairs as a bottle of scotch and three glasses are banged theatrically onto the table. Clump fills them up to the brim, "To the destruction of the Phantom Gang," he toasts.

"To destruction!" we cry, raising our glasses.

The scotch he usually serves us would burn the hairs of a chimp's chin but this one goes down smoother than silk. We are then presented with cigars, even though we don't smoke. Shortly, Head and I are half cut and coughing away as clouds of grey smoke fill the room.

"To promotion," toasts Clump.

"Promotion!" we cry.

"May I give a toast?" I ask.

"Of course," he grins topping up our glasses.

"To our suicide," I toast.

"But with honour, glory and promotion," adds Clump.

"Plus, a bigger pension," cries Head.

"That's the spirit me lad," laughs Clump.

We drain our glasses dry and clink them together.

"Right lads," sighs Clump. "Unfortunately, I have to bring these jollities to a halt. The Commissioner will be here in a moment and he will want to give you his blessings."

Just as that moment the door opens and in comes Commissioner Jenkins himself. He is a short, thin, waxed moustachioed, Savile-row suited and silk top-hatted man, known to be more slippery and poisonous than a bowl of Thames-caught jellied eels. He is carrying a couple of carpet bags which he dumps close to our feet. "Gentlemen," he smiles. "I take it you have agreed to take over the case?"

We are already up to attention, "With gusto," I lie.

"To the death!" roars Head.

"Good men," he says shaking our hands enthusiastically. "Now, I cannot stay long, lots to do and no time. I just want to commend you both for your selfless bravery, your commitment to the force, your detective brilliance and, as of now, your unblemished records. Other than that, you'll find in those bags, one each, suitable attire for your mission, guidance notes with help and advice, dossiers on the case thus far by Detectives Spencer and Brown, plus copies of the criminals' profiles and the pictures, etc., etc. If you require anything else do not hesitate to ask your Chief. Well done men, good luck and God speed."

"Thank you, sir," we say in unison and receive another greasy hand shake.

"Good lads," bellows Clump jovially. "Pick up your bags and off you go. Take the remainder of the day off to acquaint yourself with all you've been given, and get to it tomorrow, first thing."

Back in my office I clear my desk and we empty the carpet bags onto it. The clothes and boots we have been given are ragged, dirty and very smelly.

"Cor, the bum on these trousers don't half whiff," moans Head as he lifts them up to his nose.

"Look inside them," suggests I.

Head does just that only to recoil in disgust, "They're full of skid marks," he protests. "What dirty bastard wore these I wonder?"

I enlighten him, "The same dirty bastard who shat himself when he was hung in them."

Head drops the trousers like they're hot pants, "I am not wearing them, sir. It's disgusting expecting me to wear a dead man's shitty trousers."

"Do not fear, Sergeant, we shall not be wearing any of these items from the bags, and I shall tell you why. I recognise some of these filthy rags. For instance," I hold up an expensively tailored black suit that has seen much better days. "The more charitable of the upper classes patronise the poor by handing down items of clothing they no longer require. The poor will then wear those clothes until they have rotted away from their odious bodies, or they die in them, whichever is the sooner. Because they have worn them for so long, everyone knows what particular garment belongs to which particular person. For instance, this particular suit, has been seen on one Reginald 'the Slasher' Kerridge for the past two years or more. Kerridge was recently dispatched to hell via the rope and was hung in this very suit and not in prison garb, as was his last request along with a steak and kidney pie and a bucket of ale. I know that's what he wore because I was there."

"Didn't we arrest him a few months back?" puts in Head.

"Indeed, we did, Sergeant. We arrested him for the ripper style copy-cat murder of a prostitute he blamed for giving him diarrhoea."

"Don't you mean gonorrhoea?"

"That as well. Anyway, Sergeant, if I can recognise these clothes and footwear after only seeing them a few times how many others will recognise them? And how long before you and I are left in some alleyway minus our testicles should we wear any of this stuff? No, leave it to me, Sergeant, and I shall obtain more suitable wear."

After studying the evidence gained thus far by Spencer and Brown, Head and I learn a lot about the gang's peculiarities and the way they operate. We study the silhouettes and the eye pictures and begin to realise just what a hopeless task we have been given. It is going to be like looking for a mouse dropping in a coal yard. At last we call it a day and head home with Head agreeing to call for me about eight the next morning.

Betty is there to greet me the second I enter the house still carrying the bags of clothing, we trail off into the kitchen.

"You're home early, Detective Inspector," says she, giving me a kiss on the lips. "Is anything wrong, Detective Inspector?"

"A lot," I sigh. "Put the kettle on my little fire-fly, I need a coffee, then I shall tell you all."

"You smell of bonfires and whisky, Detective Inspector. Have you been smoking?" she slaps a hand over her nose, "And what is that horrible smell? It smells like shit, rotten rags and acute body odour."

"Exactly," I groan. Dumping the bags outside the back door, I take the dossiers from inside my coat pocket and place them on the kitchen table. "Have a gander through this lot," says I.

While she's doing that I take the carpet bags out back and drop them into the 'fire bin', pour some paraffin on and set it alight. Within a minute they smoke like damp seaweed and smell even worse.

"Oi!" yells a rough voice over my neighbour's side of the wooden fence. "Put that stink out or I'll come an' put you out!"

I know that voice! "Mauler, is that you?"

A pair of busted knuckle, gorilla hands slap onto the fence followed by a face that looks like it's been hit by a tram.

"Well, bugger me granny, as I live an' breathe, Jerry Pot! What the 'ell is you doin' 'ere?"

"I live here. More to the point, what are you doing here? I thought you were in Pentonville?"

"Just got out," he beams, displaying a gapped row of chipped, broken teeth. "Got a year off for bad behaviour. Course if I'd a been a 'good' boy I might 'ave got two off. But as the Warden said: 'O' Reilly, me ol' son, you've been pretty good for you, and we're going to let you out early,'" he grins. "They got rid of me before I could finish demolishing the place"

"Fair dos, Mick, I always thought it was a bit harsh you getting six years, just for beating up six plods."

"Yeah, it was. One year for each of the buggers. But they did jump me down that dark alleyway, Jerry, just as I was trying to find me dick so's I could piss. Jesus Mother of Mary, it comes to something when a man can't 'ave a piss an' a fart in peace."

"Anyway, what are you doing in my recently widowed, little old lady's garden?"

"I've been workin'. Landscaping's my new business. Determined to go straight, so I am. No more clink for yours truly me ol' mucker."

Stepping up to the fence I stand on an upturned pot and scan over next door's garden. Martha, my neighbour, has been looking for a good gardener for ages now she can't do much herself. Mick is anything but a good gardener; Martha's prize roses have been chopped down to two-inch-high stumps, her beloved delphiniums have been pulled out of the ground and dumped at the top of the garden amongst a shed-high pile, of other slaughtered flora. Her apple, pear and plum trees have been felled and then chopped into fire-sized logs. It is carnage! Even worse, her favourite gnome's head has disappeared from its neck and looks like it went through the next door's fence, judging by the shape of the hole.

I hardly dare ask, "What happened to Martha's gnome?"

"I caught it with me axe," says he, grimacing guiltily.

"It appears you caught everything else with the same axe."

"I did," he grins. "Didn't take long. The ol' girl said: 'Michael, don't be afraid to prune them roses right down. Pull up any weeds, and if there's anything would do for a bit of fire-wood I'd appreciate it. I'll go off and have a dump, then I'll put the kettle on. Back in a tick'."

"How long ago was that?"

"'Bout an hour."

"I'll come around." I go down our path beside the house, outside and around down my neighbour's path and let myself in the gate.

Mick, all six-feet-four of him is waiting for me, "I've just spied the ol' girl through them French doors. Looks like she's dropped off on the floor."

With Mick following, I go into Martha's back room through the French doors to find her laid out on her back clutching at her heart, stone dead. "The shock must have killed her," says I.

"What shock?" asks he.

"The shock of seeing the beloved garden she and her husband took sixty years to cultivate reduced to bonfire material in less than an hour."

"Oh," he sighs. "Don't think I'm cut out for this landscaping, after all."

"Which brings me to ask you, my old childhood friend. How do you fancy working for Scotland Yard for a while?"

"Now that *would* be a bloody first, be Jesus. Tell ol' Michael a bit more."

"It will be dangerous. Suicidal in fact. The pay is crap, but there might be gratuities to boost your pay."

"Will I get to smash heads and kick balls without getting arrested?"

"You would indeed."

"Would it be legal?"

"It would when you work for us."

He spits into his hands and rubs them together. "Fuck it! I'm in be Jesus."

"Fabulous," smiles I. "Be here tomorrow for eight-thirty."

"What, here in this garden?"

"No, next door at my house."

He gives me a friendly jab in my shoulder, probably causing extensive bruising, before picking up his axe and heading towards the exit. "Thankfully the ol' girl payed me in advance," he throws back at me. "Sees ya tomorrow me ol' Jerry Pot."

The following morning, I sit yawning up at the kitchen table while Betty fries me some bacon and egg. Last night after dinner I went and got the doctor and the local plod in to sort Martha out. Then I went to see a theatrical friend of mine to borrow some 'gear' from him, and then I came back home and burnt the midnight oil while working out a plan of action for today's mission.

"You should have told Clump you wouldn't do it," Betty says for the umpteenth time as she bangs my plate of food down on the table. "Let the hairy old bastard do his own dirty work, Detective Inspector."

"If I had done that you wouldn't be calling me Detective Inspector any more you'd be calling me prisoner 25566, or similar."

"Well I'm not happy about it; what if you get killed? What would I do then Detective Inspector?"

Luckily the door knocker sounds and Betty goes and lets Head in.

"Morning, sir," says he.

"Morning, Sergeant. Take a seat. Do you want anything to eat or drink?"

"Just a tea please."

Betty makes him a cuppa and then takes herself upstairs to keep out of the way for a while.

"Michael O'Reilly is going to join us," I tell him, matter-of-factly.

His face turns white, "That madman! Are you mad, sir?"

"Probably. But then we would have to be mad to venture into the Gut without a dozen armed plods with us, Mick's the nearest equivalent"

"I've written up my will," says Head, soberly. "Left everything to my sister."

"Good. Let us pray she doesn't inherit too soon." I am about to say more when there is a banging on the door so loud it sounded like a bomb went off. "That'll be Mick," I ponder and go and answer it. Mick is standing there with the biggest grin on his face, he's also carrying a carpet bag that looks stuffed with stuff.

"Mornin' Jerry," he beams, pushing past me and tramping off into the kitchen. "Bloody shit! Dick me ol' mate. 'Ow the 'ell is ya?" he roars on seeing Head.

"A bit sick," comes the sickly return.

"It's fear, Dick 'ol son. I always get it every time I spy one of me ex-wives comin' up the road."

"Take a seat Mick," I offer. "Tea or coffee?"

"Nar, thanks," he returns and sitting down he takes a bottle of whisky from his bag, uncorks it and takes a long swallow, corks it and puts it back in his bag. "Hair of the dog," he winks. "How's the ol' girl next door, Jerry?"

"Still dead, I am afraid. Anyway, gentlemen, let's get down to business."

Over the next hour I instruct them on what we are about and how we will go about it. Mick is disappointed that the initial plan of action is to spy and see what we can unearth about the Phantom Gang. His plan of action would be to go in and terrorise anyone he comes up against and make them talk, go after the gang and then kill the lot of them. It might work but would be far too messy. At least now I am confident that Mick has no hidden agenda, I show him the silhouettes and the eye pictures.

"Well bugger me ol' gran," he laughs. "I know who these are. This one wiv no ear is Charly 'The Chopper' Granger. I know it's 'im because I was the one who bit off his ear, so I was. Now he's a real, bad bastard, big like me but ugly wiv it. This one wiv the broken conk is Walter 'The Flasher' Cutler."

"Does he flash his privates?" buts in Head.

"Nar. He got 'is name for flashing knives around. He's a tall, skinny, evil bastard who'll slice your nose off wiv ya finger wiv it, if it's up there at the time. He's also the cross-eyed one, so, you have to watch him, you never know if he's goin' where he's lookin', or lookin' where he's goin'. This one is Stumpy, no one knows 'is real name, but you can't miss 'im, he's only about four-foot-three, and he's the one missing an eye, but has a gold coloured false one in its place."

"Did you have anything to do with his missing eye?" asks Head who seems enraptured by Mick's rendition.

"I did!" he returns gleefully. "Little bastard thought he was goin' ta sink his teeth in me balls and get away wiv it. No chance, got him by the hair and poked the buggers eye out, so I did."

"When was all this?" I venture to add.

"Just before the six coppers' scrap. I was in me bath at the time."

"In your bath!" we cry in unison, but I know Mick, we are about to hear one of his true but heavily embellished stories.

"Yeah. I'd just fought Charly in an arranged fight, ya know with all the toffs there bettin' money. He were a dirty fighter, nearly bit me bloody nipple off so he did, so I bit his ear off and then I got real dirty and pulverised the shit. 'Cause I'd bet on me winnin' an' I won a lot, then went home and climbed into me bath for a soak an' dropped off. Next thing I know, Charly an' his gang come bustin' in an' go for me, with Stumpy stickin' his head under the water an' sinking his teeth in me knackers, so he did, while Charly swings his chopper at me and Flasher stabs at me with a blade but misses and sticks Charly in the arse, cause, Charly falls back an' I stab a finger into Stumpy's eye and out it pops, Stumpy runs off screamin', I manage ta get out the bath and break Flashers nose and force the buggers out me washroom an' lock the door. I hear 'em goin' through the place an' know they're after me 'ard earnt winnings, but me balls are bleedin' awful an' I don't like fightin' in the nuddy. So, they make off wiv me dosh an' I swear I'll get 'em for it, trouble is, the next thing I know I'm in the nick for six years."

"Do you still wish to be a part of this operation?" I ask.

"Put it this way, Jerry, now I know them bastards are somewhere in the Gut, I'd go for 'em on me own if I have to. But if I do it wiv you it'll be legal an' I won't go back to prison. See I hate prison, ya can't get a proper shag in there unless you don't mind where you stick it."

"What about the others in the pictures, Mick, any idea?"

"Yeah, there's Jimmy 'Peg-leg' Smith, Sean O'Malley and 'Fat Sam' Brady. Now, havin' said what I said, do ya want ta change your plan a bit?"

"What do you think, Sergeant?" I ask.

"I think we should give Mick every penny we have and pay him to go and kill the gang like he suggested."

"We are officers of the law, Sergeant. We have sworn to uphold that law and protect the public from the criminal fraternity, even at the risk of our lives. However, that is a bloody good idea of yours, but I am afraid it will not happen. Now, let us prepare ourselves for the Gut."

Taking them into the parlour I show them the disguises I have borrowed from my theatrical friend. Mick refuses to 'dress' up and Head isn't keen to wear a big false shaggy beard, big floppy felt hat and several layers of made dirty and smelly clothes. But, as I have to wear similar, then so shall he. We get ready while Mick pulls out a leather railway navvy's jerkin from his bag and puts it on. It has several pockets inside and out and he begins to fill them up with different items, including; a two-shot derringer, a hammer, flick-knife, knuckle-dusters, short iron bar, a bag of humbugs, cigars and matches and a toilet roll, just in case. Finally, a sawn-off shotgun briefly appears before being put back in the bag, a steel reinforced bowler hat goes onto his head and of course out comes the bottle of whisky which he takes another long swig from, "Arfties," he grins and offers the bottle around. I turn it down but Head takes a good go at it but makes the awful mistake of lifting up his fuzzy beard and sticking the bottle in his mouth.

"You do that out there, Sergeant," I remonstrate through my own beard, "and we shall be exposed immediately."

He mumbles something back, but I can't understand him and tell him to take the beard off.

"This beard doesn't have a hole for the mouth," he complains. "I'll have to keep lifting it up just to breathe, let alone anything else."

"That's cause it's a hairy-chest piece an' not a beard," puts in Mick. "Or it might even be a wig or a hairy mott piece, who knows?"

"What is a mott?" I venture to ask.

"Slang for a woman's bushy bit down below."

"Really," says Head, amazed. "Why I've never heard it called that before."

"Never mind," I snap. "Let's get going."

Along with our false beards, Head and I are also wearing long coats to hide the revolvers under our armpits, and the full-length truncheons strapped to the inside of the coats, and like Mick we have knuckle-dusters and the inevitable flick-knife, Head also carries a pepper-pot and a clean pair of pants, just in case.

Betty runs down stairs crying, to see us off, she is inconsolable at the thought of my being killed. Mick tries to placate her by offering to give her a good shag like he used to before she married me, but even that doesn't work. We head off to the Gut with Mick swinging his bag and whistling as if he's going on a jolly caper, while Head and I miserably concede that this is how murderers must feel on their way to the gallows.

A cesspit is the shortest way to describe the Gut. A more detailed description would be; rows of dilapidated buildings going back centuries and in danger of collapse at any time (which they often do) scores of costermongers selling everything from rat poison to food poisoning in the shape of home cooked foods such as jellied-eels. A jam-packed muddle of society's poorest, dirtiest and most villainous, all crammed into a few acres of filthy streets and overflowing tenements. Dirty dogs fornicate everywhere while urchins and chancers roam the streets looking for any opportunity to make a penny, steal a penny, or beg a penny so they might eat that day. But it doesn't pay to feel sorry for anyone here, because while you feel sorry for one, another will pick your pocket or knock you unconscious and strip you bare. However, there is still a semblance of community here, once your face is known, and provided you follow the rules, you are accepted and everyone looks out for everyone else when they are not fighting or killing each other. But *really* dangerous criminals don't have much to do with anyone except their own kind. They frequent certain bars and certain areas that are the most inaccessible to the outside world, especially the police. Step into these areas at your peril, which is exactly what we are doing. In the daytime, it's not quite so dangerous, but at night it is deadly.

As we walk we attract attention, most of it is directed at Mick, he is well-known and of course hasn't been seen for over five years, women call out to him: 'Oi, Mick, when ya gonna give us money towards the brats you've fathered?' And the hapless urchins are shoved forward to meet their long-lost father. Mick brushes them aside, particularly the ones who don't look old enough or ugly enough to be his. Head and I also attract attention, urchins run up asking if they can have our beards when we shave them off as they can sell them for a few farthings, others demand money or they'll tell everyone we're really coppers in disguise, which sends Head into a panic so he can't stop farting. I assure him that they are just trying to intimidate us, but he isn't convinced. As we near where we can expect to find Charly 'The Chopper' Granger and his gang of cutthroats, Mick suddenly veers off and heads into The Spread Parrot Inn and we follow him in and take stools around a round table. It's too early for drinkers and the place is empty apart from a vagrant who's asleep on a bench, the room reeks of stale air, smoke and cheap beer, it's also dark and dingy. However, a comely wench with enormous barely covered breasts comes bouncing over to us, "What's ya poison?" she demands.

"Three beers," answers Mick. "And tell Tel, Mick O'Reilly wants to see him."

"He's in bed with his tart and he don't like to be disturbed," she comes back with finality.

"You tell him or I will," snarls Mick. "But bring our beers first and be quick about it."

She flounces off and I lean closer to Mick, "Why have we come in here?"

"Tel's an ol' mate, he'll be able to tell us what's what, so we know what's what."

"Can he be trusted?" asks Head.

"No. You can't trust anyone in the Gut, Dicky me ol' mate. Not even your muvver. But Tel owes me and he hates Charly, especially his chopper."

"Why is that?" I venture to ask.

"Charly put it in Tel's head once, years back, and Tel's never got over it."

The wench returns with our beers, "Three-pennies," she demands holding out a grubby hand.

I pay the woman and she suddenly smiles at me, "Anything else, me duck, I like a hairy man."

"Not just now, thanks, I'm on…"

"Medicine for the clap," cuts in Mick.

"I wasn't askin' you," snaps the wench. "I couldn't care less about your clap. It's probably up your arse anyway. I was asking the hairy bloke."

"I'm on it as well," I put in. "The medicine that is."

"What about you then?" she says to Head. "Care to juggle me jugs?"

"Give her a sixpence," demands Mick. "Or we'll never get rid of the cow."

I give her a sixpence which she drops down her cleavage, "I'll go get Tel," she smiles.

"You nearly said on duty just now," accuses Mick. "You'd best be more careful in future and think before you speak or you'll give us away too early."

Just then, a short, pot-bellied man with a long, indented scar on his bald head and wearing a dirty white apron, while carrying a half-eaten family sized jam tart, comes and sits down at our table.

"Mick, me ol' son, how are ya?" he asks, giving Head and I the eye.

"How's it hangin' Tel?" asks Mick as they shake hands.

"Good. Gets bigger every time I look at it."

Mick laughs and then goes serious, "These here are coppers, Tel. I'm workin' for 'em. We're after that bastard, Charly Granger an' his gang, thought we'd come in here an' get what's what."

"You did right, Mick. Charly knows you're out. He said if you dare come into the Gut he'll 'ave your balls on a plate for his tea, while you watch." He points at me and Head. "He also knows about these two."

"How the hell does he know?" asks I.

"Because someone obviously told 'im," puts in Mick. "So, who else knew you was comin', Jerry?"

"The Commissioner and C. I. Clump, and probably D. I. Spencer and D.S. Brown."

"One of them must be a snitch," puts in Head.

"Or more than one," ponders I as all starts to reveal itself. "We know the gang get their information about who to target from someone in the know. No one knows the doings of the upper-classes better than the Commissioner, he moves in their circles and has apparently been spending a lot of money lately."

"Well. Well," grates Mick. "More bent coppers, hey, Jerry me ol' son."

"The bastards!" puts in Head. "I reason we should abort the mission for now, sir, until we find out who's behind the gang."

"We should, because it's obvious we have been set up and sent to our deaths. But why?

Because the gang has gone too far and Jenkins wants out. Once we have been topped, Jenkins will be justified in sending in an army of armed plods to make sure the Phantom Gang never operates on this earth again. The plods will be so fired up over our deaths, even though they don't like us much, but we are still one of them, they will come in here and shoot anything that moves. It will be a blood bath, but rest assured, the gang will be annihilated and Jenkins will escape any form of retribution."

"What about Spencer and Brown?" asks Head. "Why send us in and not them? Why not sacrifice them?"

"Because them buggers 'ave got to be in it as well," puts in Mick. "The shits are lookin' out for each other, to be sure they are."

"And Clump?" queries Head. "Has he betrayed us as well?"

I shake my head in disbelief, "Who knows, Sergeant. What I do know is, no one except for us knows Mick is with us, I did not tell the Chief because he would not have allowed it. I'll bet this Charly Granger won't be expecting to see Mick with us either."

"He will now," says Tel nodding over towards where the vagrant had been asleep but was now gone. "That was one of Charly's spies. He's got 'em all over the place, gives 'em some beer money and they hang around listenin' in an' then reportin' back."

Mick is up on his feet and out the door before you can blink, two minutes later he returns. "Vanished, couldn't catch the bastard," says he, re-taking his seat. "Where can we find Charly, Tel?"

"Charly took over the Old Bull down Bullock Lane some months back. You'll find 'im an' his gang in there every night if they're not out on jobs."

"Well let's hope they're in there tonight," grimaces Mick. "'Cause me and the lads mean to kill the buggers."

"You got a plan?" asks Tel.

"No. Jerry, you got a plan?"

"No, not really."

"I've got one," smiles Head. "It's called the abandon ship plan, every man for himself."

"You are the bravest Police Officer I have ever known except for myself," I tell Head. "And I know you will do your duty this day. As indeed we all shall. So, no more defeatist talk. Onwards and upwards."

"Yeah!" yells Mick. "Let's get on, throats ta cut. Eye balls ta poke out. Brains ta spill and guts ta gut." He gets to his feet raising up his tankard. "A toast, gentlemen," he roars. "To the annihilation of the Phantom Gang."

"To the annihilation of the Phantom gang," Head and I join in.

We sit down again and Mick says to Tel, "You gonna join us, Tel?"

"I'd like to, Mick me ol' mate. But me arteritis is bad, I'd be no good for it."

"Fair dos, Tel. Come on Dick and Jerry, time we got off."

We follow Mick out into a bright sun and head deeper into The Gut, suddenly a woman who's hanging out a pair of bare wallopers from two storeys up shouts out, "Hey! Mick. Fancy a quickie?"

"Molly, me ol' darlin'. I'll be right up," he grins. "Back in a bit lad's just hang around here till I come back."

The second Mick leaves we are accosted by the same urchins who accosted us earlier, "Oi, mister," says the one with the cutthroat razor. "I'll give ya a shave for a penny plus I keeps ya 'air." It is more of a threat then a request.

I mimic the local language, "Clear off or I'll…"

"You'll what?" he snarls waving his razor around.

"Give ya a ringer round ya lugs."

"I'll shout out coppers, if ya do."

"We ain't no coppers," joins in Head.

"No one knows that, mister. Pay up or get screwed up."

I take out a few farthings from my pocket and toss them in the air, better that then being screwed. Within seconds more urchins dive in and there is a frantic fight between them to see who'll get the most money.

We walk on to the cries of the costermongers.

"Fresh pork-pies a penny each. Stale half price. Near rotten, open to offers."

"Nearly fresh fish. Come an' get it."

The fish is covered in flies and I ask, "How much are the flies?"

"They're free," he growls. "Piss off if ya ain't buyin'."

"Women's underwear, knickers and drawers. Woollen an' silk. New an' second 'and."

They all appear to be second hand to me, "Which are used and which are new?" I ask.

We receive a puzzled glare, "Unused ain't stained and don't 'ave holes in 'em."

"Come in them. Dirty books, filthy photos an' exotic postcards from exotic places where no one wears any pants or knickers."

"How much is a filthy photo?" asks Head.

"Depends how filthy it is. Especially if it's a certain kind of filthy photo."

"Like what?"

"These," he holds out a few photos. "Taken in the Kasbah. That's a place in Hamburg."

I look at one of the photos, it shows a hairy man doing something disgusting to a donkey. I quickly hand it back and we walk on but the costermonger comes after us, "You don't know what you're missin', gents. Look at this one."

We look, it is the same donkey, now doing it to the same man, "These are an affront to public decency. You should be locked up for selling these. Do you have any feelings for that poor animal's welfare?"

"I ain't the one rogering it, am I?"

"Just clear off," warns Head and the scumbag goes sulking back to his stall. "Glad I don't have to live here, sir."

"So am I, Sergeant, and I long for the day when slums all around the world will have vanished and be replaced by decent housing, so that no one has to live in squalor ever again."

We move on but come to a halt at the start of a narrow alley, that's called Narrow Alley. It is a dark forbidding place that smells of raw sewage and where sunshine probably never touches the filthy cobbles. Most windows in the four storeys-high dilapidated terraces are closed to keep the putrid air out.

Head reads out a sign screwed to the wall. "'Beware of falling chamber pot contents. I don't think we should venture down there, sir."

"I think you are right," agrees I as I read another sign that says: 'Give way to traffickers'.

Turning around we amble back towards the dirty book seller, "I knew you'd be back," he beams. "How about a copy of the Karma Sutra ta take 'ome to the ol' woman. That'll get her frisky."

"How about a copy of my knuckles on your kisser?" snarls Head.

"Hot chestnuts," comes the call from across the road. "Only tuppence a bag."

"Hot chestnuts, sir," says Head. "They'll be no danger there of picking up a terrible disease. The heat of the coals will kill any germs."

"I agree," says I agreeingly.

We veer over to the nutty man who shakes up his hot tray to roll the chestnuts over, "Bag each, gents?"

We nod in uniformed excitement.

The nutty man begins to shovel the unusually large, half burnt, chestnuts into a paper bag.

"Hold on," frowns Head. "There not chestnuts, they're bloody conkers!"

"Yeah, but they're still a type of chestnut," he counters.

"Technically he is correct," puts in I. "They are in fact horse chestnuts."

"Well I don't want any," sulks Head.

"Why not?" demands the nutty man.

"Because they're bloody conkers and taste horrible."

"Hot bloody conkers," shouts the nutty man. "Good for the gout and bodily functions."

We move away to go and stand beside a horse trough and a water pump. Head splashes water onto his face and to my horror his beard falls off and lands in the trough where an urchin leaps forward and runs off with it.

"Oi! Come back with that," demands I. "Stop thief!" Which instantly starts up a chorus of 'Stop thief' amongst everyone else.

"There's the thieves," shouts the urchin with Head's beard. "Over by the 'orse trough."

"Get 'em," yells the dirty book seller. "They tried to steal my Karma Sutra."

"Get 'em," yells another urchin. "They're bloody coppers in disguise. Look 'is false beard's fell off."

Normally we'd run for it, but a half circle angry mob, waving knives, coshes, walking-sticks, coconuts and cucumbers are closing in on us and there is nothing for it but to pull out our truncheons and revolvers, but the mob doesn't seem the least bit perturbed and edge even closer.

Just then a shotgun goes off and Mick comes to stand between us and the mob.

"These fellas are with Michael O'Reilly," he booms out. "If you want 'em, you'll have ta go through me first."

It does the trick; Mick's reputation is so formidable the mob disperses and goes back grumbling to their stalls and such.

"Can't leave you fellas for a second," grins Mick. "Now, Molly just told me that Charly ain't hidin' out in The Old Bull, he's hidin' out in the Cow and Pat which he owns. She also told me that Charly also owns the Spread Parrot and that Tel now works for Charly."

"So, Tel lied to us?" suggests I.

"Probably did," says Mick. "And he's probably setting us up right now for Charly and his gang to wipe us out the second we show our mugs outside The Old Bull."

"Can you trust this Molly's information?"

"Oh, to be sure. I'm her husband."

"Really?" amazes Head.

"Sure I am. She just doesn't know I got a few more wives as well," he grins, reloading the shotgun and stowing it away in his bag.

Head and I put our weapons away and I realise there is no point in maintaining our feeble disguises and toss my beard away, which is quickly grabbed by a shaven headed, girl urchin, who's either sold her hair or had it shaved off to get rid of fleas and such. "Just what I want," she cries slapping the beard onto her head and skipping happily off.

"Now, I'm thinkin'," says Mick. "We watch and wait until Charly an' his gang go off to set their trap for us, then we'll nip into his place and wait until he comes back, ambush the buggers an' kill 'em."

"That sounds like a plan," says Head.

"If it goes to plan," I doubtfully say. "Anyone sees us watching the place and we are dead."

"Don't worry," says Mick. "I know a place where can watch without bein' seen. Come on let's go."

We follow Mick down the smelly alley and somehow make it out the other side without getting any chamber pots emptied on our heads or getting gassed to death by the high levels of methane gas flouting around, but we all end up with shit on our shoes. Going down Victoria Lane we are accosted by urchins and all manner of ne'er-do-wells but ignoring them we march bravely on despite the stink wafting up from our shoes. Resolved in my own mind that we must do this no matter what, I am also assured that Head is also resolved as he hasn't farted for ages.

At last we come to a halt outside a public bath-house, "Here's the crack," whispers Mick. "We'll go in and bathe until it's time ta go hide in the bogs where we'll be spyin' through a grille in the wall that looks across the street to the Cow and Pat. Do ya understand?"

We both shake our heads.

"Never mind, just follow my lead."

Following Mick, we trail into the bath-house and go up to a tall spotty man behind the counter.

"Good day, gentlemen," he welcomes. "Please read that sign if you can read," and he points to a huge sign on the wall behind him.

It reads: 'The Worshipful Company of Sanitation decree this bath-house to be free of fees for all in the worshipful wish that the odious bodies of the odious people of the Borough should get cleaned and sanitised. Please leave the bath-house tidy'.

"Now do you all want towels, soap and toilet paper?"

We nod and are each handed a grey towel that was probably white once, a small bar of soap and several newspaper squares tied with a piece of string in one corner.

The spotty man stiffens himself up to appear more formal, "No bodily functions to be committed in the bath. No bathing or shaving in the toilet bowls. No stealing of any kind. Keep your possessions as close to you as possible, at all times. Naked bathing is mandatory, no wearing of filthy clothes. Anyone caught committing lewd acts will be arrested and given a good kicking."

"By whom?" I ask.

"By our security warders."

"Understood," says Mick on our behalf.

The spotty man rabbits on, "No fighting or swearing, no blasphemy or ball games. Is that all clear to you?"

"As the Thames," says I.

"Good, enjoy your scrubs, although I must say you don't appear very dirty but you don't half stink. The baths close at six, be sure to have left by then or you'll get locked in until the morning."

We thank him and trail off into the bath area itself. The bathing-pool is a large square of steaming scummy water surrounded by white tiled walkways and walls. There are several cubicles to get changed in and already in the bath are several dirty old men getting scrubbed up. A warder patrols around the bath while swinging a pickaxe handle, while another is sat on a chair in the corner, by one of the two open windows, drinking beer and smoking while a pickaxe handle is laid across his lap.

"I have just thought," says I thoughtfully. "This place closes at six but it won't become dark completely until about eight."

"We'll be staying on," says Mick. "We'll go and hide in the bogs about five-thirty. Until then we'll just wallow in the bath."

We each go into a cubicle and I strip off. I'm not too happy about Head seeing his senior officer in the nude as no doubt he feels the same about me seeing him in the nude, but needs must. I exit the cubicle carrying my bath stuff and neatly folded up clothes, place them on a bench beside Head's clothes and Mick's bag. I gingerly go down the greasy steps and wade into the water intent on sitting down near my comrades.

"It ain't grown much since I last saw it," laughs Mick pointing at my private member.

"How long ago was that?" asks Head in obvious fascination.

"Back when we were kids swimmin' in the Thames," chortles Mick.

"It has grown a great deal since then," I counter angrily. "It has just shrivelled up at present out of shyness. Anyway, you shouldn't be looking."

"Just foolin' around," grins Mick. "Now it might not be so big but I wouldn't want the bugger on the end of me nose for a wart, now would I?"

"Indeed" agrees Head.

"Now," Mick goes on. "I've ordered us some beers, but don't forget if you want a pee go to the bogs or these warders will start a ruckus that we don't need."

"Will do," agrees us as we settle down in the warm water that doesn't smell any worse than cheesy feet.

Three beers in wooden tankards are brought to the poolside edge by the counter assistant and for the first time since we set out on this venture I find myself totally relaxing. The clock on the wall says it is three-thirty, so we have a while to wait.

The time passes slowly, we chat, drink beer and take turns to go off and pee. My skin starts to crinkle up in the soapy water, but at last at five-thirty we get out, dry off, get dressed and slip off to the toilet area. Mick produces a piece of black chalk and writes: 'Out of order' on one of the three white painted peeling toilet doors, underneath that he draws a picture of a man with his trousers down squatting over the pan. I know it's a man because Mick also draws a pair of over large testicles hanging down, he then puts a large cross over the man's buttocks.

"That'll keep 'em out," he grins admiring his work."

"What if the warders come in, Mick?" asks I.

"No problem. I've bought the buggers off, so I have."

We cram into the cubicle, it is only about five-foot-long by two feet, with a stained bowl and a flushing system above that, and above that, fixed into the wall is a foot-square holed grille close to the ceiling that lets air in and the smells out.

"We'll take turns watchin' out," says Mick lighting up a cigar.

I take the first watch and standing precariously on the wooden toilet seat, I put an eye as close as possible to the grille and peer out, "I can see the front of the Cow and Pat quite clearly," says I.

"Good," says Mick.

"Marvellous," says Head. "What else can you see, sir?"

"Just folk going about their business. There's a few rough types seated outside the pub, drinking and smoking. A couple of prostitutes plying their trade. A pair of dirty dogs fornicating..." My rendition is suddenly interrupted by a load bang which makes me jump out of my skin and nearly fall off the toilet seat.

"What the hell was that?" hisses Head.

"Someone just shot one of the dogs," replies I. "The shit-bag!"

"Probably wants it for 'is tea," puts in Mick. "Not bad meat is dog."

"Well I don't fancy it," grimaces Head.

"Me neither," adds I. "My God the man who shot the dog's started skinning it!"

"Told ya," says Mick. "It'll be in the pot in no time. You see if it ain't."

"What happened to the other dog?" asks Head.

"It is sitting with the man who shot its lover. It seems happy enough, its tail is wagging and its tongue is out drooling all over the place."

"Waiting for its share of the dead dog," puts in Mick. "Let me up there a minute, Jerry."

Shuffling around in the confined space we change places and then Mick informs us; "That's Bill 'The Cook' Chapple, skinning that dog, and the other three are his henchmen, they're killers for hire. That bastard Charly must have brought 'em in for back up."

"Why's he called 'The Cook'?" asks Head.

Mick gazes down salubriously at us, "He likes torturing his victims by boiling parts of their bodies in boiling water."

Head looks horrified, "What parts?"

"Any parts. They say he once boiled a copper's balls right off just for the fun of it."

"Take no notice, Sergeant," says I. "Our Irish friend is joking. Are you not, Mick?"

"Course, I am," grins Mick. "Bill used to be a chef and that's obviously why he's known as 'The Cook'."

We suddenly hear the distinct sound of the baths being locked up for the night and can now open the door, leaving Mick on watch, me and Head, step out of the toilet.

An hour later, just as dusk is setting in during Head's watch, he says, "They're all coming out."

"Good," says Mick as he and I go into the other cubicles and peer out through the grilles.

"They're all out all right," growls Mick. "And it looks like they're 'all' going to the Bull armed to the teeth. And why's that bastard Charly got a small bottle of something in each hand?"

I watch as the six gang members and the four further rough necks exchange greetings and shake hands before Charly starts to obviously give them their instructions. "Ten of them altogether," grates I. "We'll never take out ten of them, Mick."

"We'll be dead before we take half of them out," puts in Head.

"Time for plan B," laughs Mick as he comes out of his cubicle and calls us together.

"Now," says Mick, reaching into his bag. "I had been thinkin' of tryin' ta take one of the buggers alive so we could find out where Charly hides his loot. But plan B don't allow for that," he grins as two sticks of dynamite appear in his hand.

"Bloody hell!" exclaims Head. "You've been carrying that around all this time?"

"I have," grins Mick some more. "This is how it goes, and we best be quick while they're still close together. The warders have left a side door unlocked for us, we go out, I light the fuses, we run around front and I toss the dynamite. BANG! It's all over in a flash. But if any of 'em survive and still want to fight, you two will be behind me to finish 'em off."

"But what about if there's any innocent bystanders close by?"

"There's no such thing as innocent in the Gut, Jerry. You should know that. Now, come on, let's get the bastards."

There's no arguing with Mick and we find ourselves charging through the bath-house, out a side door and around to the front with Mick having somehow managing to light the 'far too short' fuses on the dynamite. The second we are exposed to the gang they start to fan out and bring their weapons up, but it is all too late, the sizzling fuses whizz up in the air, mesmerizingly watched by everyone, before arcing over towards the Cow and Pat.

"Down," screams Mick, and Head and I fall face down onto the filthy tarmacadam and cover our heads, just as the explosion from hell goes off, quickly followed by a down pouring of liquorice allsorts of body parts and related parts to those bodies. It takes a full minute or more for the dust to settle before we venture to stand up coughing and spluttering to survey the carnage. A ball of black smoke hangs over a scene of absolute devastation. There's a foot deep, smoking crater, with a circumference of twenty feet or so. The Cow and Pat, all windows blown in, could be renamed The Cow and Splattered, it's walls are pebble dashed with grizzly bits of the gang, bits of metal, wood and clothes. Jimmy Smith's peg-leg is imbedded a foot up in the wall, a half of the half-skinned dog hangs from what's left of the inn's sign, while Fat Sam's, fat head, with a still smoking cigar in its mouth, peers eerily out at us from an upstairs window sill. For ourselves, our heads and backs are covered in all sorts of crap, but we are miraculously unscathed, and it appears that the only one to have survived from the gang is Stumpy, who, wobbling crazily, manages to get to his feet and begins to go around in circles with his arms held out in front of him. His face is soot-black, the clothes on his back have been practically shredded, one shoe is missing and his hair is smoking, other than that, he doesn't look too bad, all things considered.

"Holy Mother of Mary," grins Mick. "I've always wanted ta blow something up."

"Something!" gasps I. "Everything in sight would be a more accurate description."

"One hell of an explosion," adds Head.

"Made worse by those jars of liquid," puts in Mick. "I'm now of the opinion they might 'ave 'ad a bit of nitro-glycerine in 'em. That bein' so, it's obvious ol' Charly meant to blow us to kingdom come, but we got in first. I'd call that a result."

Truth to say, I believe Mick is right and he has in fact saved all our lives, otherwise we could have ended up splattered all over The

Old Bull and my poor Betty would never have known what exactly happened to me or where parts of me ended up.

"All we need now is ta find Charly's stash. Come on fellas."

"What about Stumpy?" asks I.

Mick gives him the once over, "No good talkin' ta him, he's lost the plot. I'll leave his fate to you, Jerry."

"We'll take him back with us when we go," says I.

Mick strolls over to the inn and we step inside to find dust still whirling around, the pair of prostitutes cowering against the wall beneath a shattered window, while a whimpering sound comes from behind the bar. We go over and peer around the bar to find a bar wench and barman locked in an embrace while shaking like jellies. Mick quickly takes advantage of their terrified states and hauling the barman to his feet, drags him out from behind the bar "Where does Charly hide his stash?" he demands.

"In his safe, upstairs," comes the croaked reply just before the man faints away.

Up the stairs we trot, stepping over the odd bit of body that's found its way in through the windows and begin to go through the half-dozen bedrooms.

"In here, sir," calls out Head.

We go into the back bedroom, it is huge and richly furnished and is more akin to the affluent areas of London than the cesspit of the gut, it even has a five-foot-high safe in one corner plus a four-poster bed, and in the bed, someone is hiding beneath a luxurious quilt. Mick pulls it off to reveal a dark haired, fully dressed, very pretty but terrified young woman. "Do you know the combination of that safe?" demands Mick.

She nods.

"What is it?"

"Charly w... w..." she tries to answer only Mick's aggressive manner is obviously scaring her even more, so I take over.

"We are policemen, madam, no harm will come to you providing you cooperate with us. Is that clear?"

She nods, "But Charly will k... kill me when he finds out."

"Charly's been blown ta bits," grins Mick. "The only thing he's likely ta be killin' is the seagulls who'll gorge on his poisonous flesh."

"Really?" she smiles, which lightens up her face and makes her appear even more attractive. "2471."

Head enters the code and the door is opened to reveal a good pile of bank notes, investment bonds, jewellery and other precious items. We stare open mouthed at the hoard; there's enough stuff for all of us to retire in luxury to the seaside for ever and a day.

Mick rubs his hands together, "By the blessed saints, half the bloody wealth of Mayfair must be in there. Jesus, I'll never 'ave ta work again."

"None of us will," beams Head.

"We would also be on the run forever if we help ourselves to that lot," says I. "Even if we go abroad they'll catch up with us eventually. But, if we're clever we can all do well out of this and no one would be the wiser." I watch their faces. Head knows I am right, but Mick's eyeballs are practically revolving in their sockets like a one-armed bandit, will they stop on diamonds or garnets?

"You're right, Jerry me ol' mate. A good cut will do me. I may be a crazy bastard but I ain't a stupid or greedy one."

"Nor me," puts in Head.

"Then let's get to it," says I.

We find a couple of sacks from the downstairs kitchen and fill them up. How much the jewels, bonds and various treasures are worth we have little idea, but in cash we reason there's probably three thousand pounds worth, maybe more. Mick puts three wads of notes into his bag, one each for the three of us, he also takes a diamond necklace and a highly decorated little china egg for himself. Mick will drop our money off at mine and then he'll disappear for a while. Then I find a small black book, a quick scan inside it reveals detailed descriptions of the gang's crimes, along with other details. I shove into my coat pocket. The woman's name is Rosy, we give her a wad and tell her to disappear from the Gut and keep her mouth shut or else. She is ecstatic and gives all three of us a big kiss and asks to walk out with us, we agree, otherwise she wouldn't get further than the end of the street before she's mugged and robbed of everything, including her clothes. It's time to leave and we go back out to be confronted by a maniacal scene of umpteen urchins and chancers frantically searching the area for whatever they can find, but of Stumpy, there's no sign. We are quickly accosted by an urchin who offers us a nice ring for a quid. I look at it, it appears ancient and undamaged, rich solid gold with a large purple stone in the shape of a cross. It must be the Bishop's ring, Charly must have been wearing it when he got blown to smithereens. "I'll have it," says I.

"Do ya want the finger that come wiv it?" asks the urchin producing the bloody object.

"No thank you," returns I.

"Give us ya money first," demands the urchin. "Or I'll swallow it."

I fish out a couple of ten-shilling notes and we do a swap, he runs off blissfully happy but is mugged before he's gone ten feet by a bigger urchin, who is then tripped up by a vagrant, who in turn is then hit on the head by Walter's wooden leg being swung by a prostitute dressed as a nun. The first urchin then manages to grab back hold of the notes from the bigger urchin and makes a break for it again, before being rugby tackled by a crippled beggar in a wheel chair, who flies out of his chair faster than a cat with its tail on fire. It is mayhem.

Then suddenly we hear the unmistakable sound of several marching, hobnailed boots on tarmacadam, echoing from not so far away.

"Plods!" cries Mick. "Scarper."

"You go. Go!" orders I.

Mick and Rosy flee in the opposite direction from where the approaching plods sound like they're coming from, but Head and I, with the sacks of treasure by our feet, stand and wait. Luckily, Mick and Rosy have melted away amongst the ramshackle buildings by the time twenty or so plods, armed with rifles, appear before us where they form a half circle while aiming their weapons towards us and the crowd. A Sergeant fires off a shot in the air and everyone instantly stops what they're doing and stands to attention.

"Anyone who moves will be shot!" yells the Sergeant. "And I mean anyone!"

Through a gap in the plods' formation appears no other than Commissioner Jenkins accompanied by C. I. Clump. Spotting Head and I, they come right up to us.

"Good evening, gentlemen." greets our illustrious slippery Commissioner. "We heard an explosion all the way back to Fish Bone Alley."

"I was wondering how you all got here so quickly, sir," says I, peering into his slippery eyes. "May I ask why you and the Chief were at Fish Bone Alley, sir, along with all these uniformed officers?"

"You may," smiles Jenkins. "We had a tip off as to where exactly we could find The Phantom Gang, and so, Chief Inspector Clump and I decided to act on that information immediately. Only it looks like we need not have bothered."

I give Clump a quick once over, he doesn't appear so happy, and I just know that despite everything he isn't bent enough to be in partnership with Slippery Jenkins' murderous antics.

"The gang's all gone," smiles I.

"Gone where?" asks Clump.

"They sort of split up," says I. "Parts of them went south, others north, and the remaining parts went east to west."

"Meaning what, exactly?" demands Slippery rudely.

"Meaning the nitro-glycerine, they had on them went off and blew them to smithereens."

"Why were they carrying nitro-glycerine?" asks Clump.

"We don't really know, sir. Perhaps they intended to use it on their next job. All Sergeant Head and I know is that we were observing the gang from a safe place while they were having a meeting outside the inn. We noticed they had two small bottles containing a liquid which we reasoned was probably explosive liquid, judging by the careful way they were handling it. We further noticed their leader…"

"How do you know he was their leader?" demands Slippery.

"Our earlier investigations, sir, had not only revealed to us who was leading the gang, it also revealed all their names."

"Well done Officers," beams Clump. "Promotion is on the cards for you both, as promised." He gazes defiantly into Slippery's eyes, "Isn't that correct, sir?"

Slippery appears less than happy, but he is cornered, "Most definitely, Chief Inspector. So, gentlemen, what is in those sacks?"

"A fortune, sir," smiles I. "The ill-gotten gains from the gang's criminal activities."

"Well done, men," beams Clump even more beamingly than before. "You shall receive a reward from police funds for this. Isn't that correct, sir?"

"Yes. Yes, of course," comes the impatient reply. "Well Inspector Potter, did anything else materialise as you bagged up this fortune of stolen goods?" he asks cagily.

"Not really, sir," I reply, rummaging around in my pocket. "But this was found by an urchin outside the inn." I produce the ring and hand it to Slippery. "I will need to make a claim in my expenses, sir, as I had to pay the little villain a pound for it or he threatened to swallow it."

"Of course, Inspector. Of course," smiles he miserably. "Nothing else?"

"If there was, sir, I suspect it's in a thousand pieces and spread all over the Gut by now."

"Good. Good. Well, Chief Inspector, I suggest we search the inn, just in case something else does turn up. Your two fine officers should get themselves home and be back in the Yard first thing tomorrow to make out their reports. Take the sacks of treasure, Inspector and half of the uniformed officers for protection. And we shall all meet up tomorrow."

"Thank you, sir," says I.

Head and I head off with the plods following behind carrying the sacks of treasure, we keep far enough ahead to ensure none of the plods can hear us.

"What now, sir?" asks Head.

"Well, Sergeant, what indeed? We have our 'reward' to look forward to, which we must keep quiet about. We also have Charly's diary, come accounts book."

"We do?" amazes Head. "Since when?"

"Since I took it out of Charly's safe and slipped it in my pocket. I believe, Sergeant, that once I have had time to study it we will have enough evidence to hang the commissioner along with any other bent officers who have been involved."

"Does that mean us as well? We're bent coppers."

"There's bent and bent, Sergeant. We are far less bent than some, but more bent than others."

"How bent are we on a scale of one to ten?"

"About eight."

"That means we're near the top for the bentest of bents. Bloody hell, sir, I reckon we'll be swinging if we get caught."

"Have no fear, Sergeant. We haven't been bent enough to warrant doing a stretch on the rope, but at least ten years in the clink is a distinct possibility."

"That's a relief, sir," smiles Head. "After seeing a few hangings over the years, I must admit I don't fancy it much. I'd much rather go the way Charly and his gang went. Bang. Gone."

"Agreed," says I. "Talking of Charly and his gang, I wonder what happened to Stumpy?"

"Perhaps he recovered and ran off," shrugs Head.

"Then he could be a problem, Sergeant. If he knows who the bent coppers are who were involved with Charly he's going to tell them that Mick was involved, and that we hurled dynamite at the gang and blew them to pieces."

"Leaving us in deep shit, sir."

"Exactly. We must track Stumpy down and get rid of him before he talks."

We arrive at Narrow Lane and I hold my hand up to halt the plods. Their Sergeant comes up.

"What's up, Inspector?" asks he.

I point up to the windows that are open in the houses, which is most of them, "If we go down this alley, Sergeant, I fear we shall be showered in shit from chamber pots and all sorts. The residents, I further fear, are waiting for us," I point some more. "Can you see there are a few bare backsides sticking out of a few windows, ready to deliver their foul insides down on our heads?"

"No problem, sir," grins he and promptly raises his rifle and takes aim at a particularly fat arse that is hanging right out over the window sill three storeys up.

"That's not the way, Sergeant," says I. "We may start a situation that quickly gets out of control and find ourselves murdered instead of just covered in crap. We need another way out."

"As you wish," sighs he, lowering his rifle. "But there isn't a way out of the Gut other than similar lanes like this. And may I remind you, sir, it will be totally dark within the hour and you don't want to be still in the Gut once it's dark if you can help it."

"Let us try anyway," orders I.

We follow the Sergeant and a few minutes later we come to a stop at Even Narrower Narrow Lane, where suddenly all the windows in the buildings slam open and several bare bums appear.

"Let us try further along," sighs I.

Ten minutes later we come to a stop at Tapered Lane. It is so narrow it is near pitch dark and we would have to go down it in single file. At the other end, it appears to taper to a just squeeze through arch. But at least there are no windows that I can see on the walls lining both sides of the lane. "Follow me," orders I. And down I go, the floor is damp and slippery, rats run around my feet and the air is stale and acrid like the trough in a toilet that has accumulated years of dry crusty urine.

"It stinks of piss!" gasps Head, who is directly behind me. "Try putting a hanky over your mouth, sir, or you might get gassed by the fumes."

Glancing behind me I notice that none of the plods have followed us in. "Where are the plods, Sergeant?"

He stops to look behind him, and mumbles something incoherent.

"What was that, Sergeant? Take the handkerchief away from your face."

"The buggers have hopped it with the sacks of loot, I reckon. Bastards!"

"Not only that," worries I. "We are now on our own, Sergeant, and once we show our faces out the other end and the locals see we're on our own we shall be turned into mincemeat."

"Perhaps they won't recognise us, sir. Perhaps we can just merge into the crowd."

"Perhaps the Queen will take up holy orders and the Pope will become an atheist! No, Sergeant, we'll need to come up with something special to get us out of this."

"How about this?" he says handing me something over my shoulder.

"Dynamite! What on earth are you doing with dynamite, Sergeant?"

"Mick give it me."

"No, he didn't, he 'gave' it to you."

"That's what I said."

"No, you said, He 'give' it you."

"No, I didn't. I said; Mick give it me."

"You cannot say; 'Mick give it me'. You should have said; 'Mick gave it to me'."

"All right! Mick gave it to me."

"Good, let us proceed." We walk on, I have one hand holding a handkerchief over my nose while the other hand holds the dynamite which is feeling rather sticky. My eyes are watering through the ammonia fumes and my head is aching. Other than that, I feel all right.

At last we reach the end, where I peep out the arch and comb the area. The gas lights have been lit, those that work. They cast eerie shadows around the place where costermongers are still selling their wares, prostitutes are selling their bits and the usual urchins and chancers are begging, stealing and accosting people. The place is packed with all sorts of dubious dubiousness. But there is nothing else for it except to go for it. "Are you ready, Sergeant?"

"For what, sir?"

"Whatever happens the second we poke our noses out onto the street."

"I'm ready as ever I will be, sir. Should we need it, have you matches to light the dynamite with?"

"No, have you?"

"No. But we could always throw it onto a chestnut seller's hot coals."

"Or throw it up in the air and shoot it with our revolvers."

"I like my idea best, sir," says he smugly.

"But it is flawed, Sergeant," returns I. "What if there are no chestnut sellers out there?"

"What if we shoot at the dynamite like you suggest and we don't hit it?"

"Good point. I know what we'll do, we'll just toss it in the air, scream out: 'DYNAMITE!' and while everyone dives for cover we'll make our escape."

"I think that's a cracking idea, sir. Let's just hope it works or we're dead."

"Right, Sergeant, are you ready?"

"Just one thing, sir. I'd just like to say it's been a pleasure working with you over the years. And I consider you to be a friend as well as my superior."

"Thank you, Sergeant Head. I also consider you to be my friend as well as my inferior."

Suddenly a face appears before me and I jump out of my skin.

"That you, Inspector?" asks the face.

"Sergeant?" gasps I.

"Watt, sir."

"Is that you? I can't see you very clearly."

"It's me all right. Are you coming out or what?"

We step out to see all the plods are there, plus the sacks of loot, even if they do appear to be somewhat smaller. "Are we relieved to see you, Sergeant…um…?"

"Watt, sir. Sergeant Robert Watt."

"How come you got here before us, Sergeant Watt?"

"We went straight through the houses without being challenged. There wasn't anyone about because they were all upstairs waiting to dump on us."

"Right. Well done." Head and I head out of the lane into the street, with ten armed plods by our side no one would be suicidal enough to attack us, but that doesn't deter the urchins.

"Oi, copper," shouts one. "Giv' ya a bag of marbles for that dynamite."

"No thanks," says I.

He holds out his hand and what do I see nestling between two blue-green marbles? A gold coloured false eye. "But I shall give you a shiny sixpence piece if you give me that gold marble and tell me where you found it?"

"Shilling, or I'll swallow it."

"Haven't we met before?" I frown.

"Yeah," he beams. "You was the one bought that ring off me. And you an' your..."

"A shilling it is," I cut in before he says something I might regret.

We do our swap and he says, "Saw this short arse goin' along the street, funny bloke, walked like this he did," and mimicking a zombie proceeds to go around in circles. "But then he'd walk off like normal. Then he comes to the Spread Parrot and starts goin' 'round in circles again, but bumps into a wall an' falls over. Then up he gets and just goes into the inn like, how's ya granny off for spots, leavin' this marble behind which must 'ave fell out of 'is pocket."

"Marvellous," smiles I. "Thank you. Now clear off before you get mugged." He runs off and I say to Sergeant Watt, "We need to make a detour to the Spread Parrot, I have information that the last of the Phantom gang could be hiding out there."

"Very well, sir," agrees he.

Within ten minutes we are at the inn and we go straight in. The barmaid with the jugs stares at us in horror, "What the bloody 'ell do you lot want? I don't do groups above four at a time."

"We are not here for you, we're looking for Tel and a small man called Stumpy. Where are they?"

"Dead," smiles she.

"Dead?" smiles I not. "How?"

"That big ugly bugger of an Irish man you was in here wiv earlier came in an' shot 'em both."

"What, dead?" gasps Watt.

"Yeah. Dead as ducks they were. Then he just buggered off. Had a real pretty little thing with him called Rosy. Seen her before I have. She used to belong to old Charly Granger..."

"Yes, thank you madam," I yawn. Give them an inch and they'll ramble on for ever. "Where might I find Tel and Stumpy's bodies?"

"God knows," she grates. "They was shot an' then sold to body snatchers before they'd even finished bleedin'."

"And are you sure they were dead?"

"Yep. Deader than dead, that's for sure."

Another problem dealt with thanks to Mick I ponder as we continue our journey.

At last we are out of the Gut where we split up with the plods. I thank them for their help and quietly inform Sergeant Watt that I know he and his men have lightened the load on the sacks of loot. I promise not to mention it if he promises not to mention anything about dynamite, the Spread Parrot, Mick, Tel and Stumpy. We shake hands and take our leave. I part from Head once we are out of Fish Bone Alley and twenty minutes later I see the welcoming sight of oil lit lamps flickering out through the windows of my home. Betty must have been keeping a look out for me because she's out and in my arms before I can get the key in the door.

"Detective Inspector," she cries. "I thought you were dead!"

"I often thought I might be. Still, I am home safe and sound, my little rosebud."

She breaks away from me, "You don't half smell, Detective Inspector. Have you been down the sewers or something?"

"As good as," laughs I. I take off my filthy shoes and leave them on the step before we trail off into the house and close the door behind us.

Betty puts the kettle on the stove, but I am in dire need of something much stronger and head for the parlour.

"An urchin delivered a message for you, Detective Inspector. It was from Mick," says Betty following me in. "He's going to hide out with someone called Rosy for a few days and will call on you later."

"Good," says I. Taking my revolver out of its holster I set it down on the sideboard, then pour myself a stiff scotch and am about to sit down when Betty stops me.

"Not on my sofa, Detective Inspector. Get those smelly clothes off first. I shall fetch your dressing gown, you can sit around in that while I fill you a bath."

I take off the coat, the trousers and my socks that reek of urine and hand them over to Betty who promptly heads off to the kitchen with them.

Plonking down on the sofa I take a long drink of the scotch and start to relax just as the back-door slams shut. "Fucking hell!" roars I. Throwing the glass of scotch away I tear out the room, through the kitchen and out into the yard where to my terror I see Betty is about to do what I thought she was about to do, "Stop!" yells I. "Do not strike that match Betty or you will blow us to kingdom come."

"Why?" she asks in confusion, her pretty face looking fearful.

"Because in the pocket of that coat there is a stick of dynamite."

"Oh, really, Detective Inspector. Why do you have a stick of dynamite in your pocket?"

"It's a long story," says I, going up to her and taking the matches from her trembling hand. "Now, my love, those clothes belong to a friend of mine and he would not like to see them burnt in our fire bin. So, I am afraid they will have to be washed and then returned."

"But they're all tatty and stinky, Detective Inspector. The best place for them is the bonfire."

"Probably," I sigh. "However, as I have said they have to be returned. So, let's fish them out."

We fish them out and take them into the kitchen where I go through the pockets, inside and out. The diary is there, my truncheon and other bits and pieces but *no* stick of dynamite! That bloody urchin, the crafty little pick-pocket must have nabbed it off me. Heaven only knows what the consequences will be! "I have to go out," I tell Betty. "It is urgent."

"What in your long-johns and shirt, Detective Inspector?"

"No, I shall dress first," I say, going into the parlour I pick up my revolver and holster it, then it's upstairs and dress. A few minutes later I am outside kissing Betty goodbye.

"How long will you be, Detective Inspector?" she asks worriedly.

"Who knows," sighs I and turning away I head off back towards the Gut.

Just as I reach Fish Bone Alley there is a large explosion up ahead of me, I see a bright light fanning across the night sky, a big ball of smoke and hear a chorus of screams. Turning around I head back home.

"That was quick, Detective Inspector," smiles Betty as I step into the hallway. "Good job I have your bath all ready." And she is also ready, wearing a see through white nighty and smelling delightfully of rose water. It is going to be a long night.

As I walk into Scotland Yard the next morning I am met with an aura of doom and sadness. Head heads over to me and heading down a long corridor towards Clump's office he says, "Have you heard, sir, the Commissioner got blown up last night?"

"Is he dead?"

"He is, but luckily no one else got killed. Four plods sustained fairly serious injuries as did several locals. Which was a miracle really."

"What happened?"

"Apparently several urchins were playing bat and ball, but using a stick of dynamite as the ball, one wacked the 'ball' which flew through the air and hit the Commissioner in the kisser just as he was squeezing himself out of that arch we went through."

"So, the urchins had lit the fuse before they battered it at the Commissioner?"

"Um..., not exactly, sir. The commissioner apparently was smoking a big fat cigar when the dynamite hit him."

"Well, at least that saved him from getting strung up, Sergeant."

"Strung up?"

"Indeed, Sergeant. I was up all night in one way or another, but I still found time to go through Charly's diary. There is enough evidence in there to prove beyond a doubt that the Commissioner has won the award for the bentest of bent cops that ever drew breath."

"Well, well," wells Head. "What about Spencer and Brown? Oh, and Clumpy?"

"Spencer and Brown were up to their necks in it, but Clump obviously had nothing to do with any of it. So, Sergeant, let us go and tell the Chief the good news."

Clump is sitting behind his desk as we go into his office. He appears supremely miserable; his hairy beard and moustache have been singed back to a stubble that looks like someone had a go at with a flaming torch and a pair of pliers, his bushy eyebrows look like the floor from a forest fire and his unruly singed hair is oddly standing on its end. With his scorched skin and eyes like saucers surrounded by Saturn rings he really does look an absolute sod!

"Smiling miserably, he says, "Take a seat, gentlemen. Please excuse my sorry state, but it isn't every day one gets blown up."

"Indeed not, sir," says I. "But at least you are still with us, Chief."

"Thank you, Inspector," he sighs as out comes the scotch and three glasses. "Still, we have something to celebrate, but unfortunately we also have something not to celebrate. I take it you have heard that the Commissioner was killed last night?"

"We did, sir," says I. "Please accept our condolences."

He pours the scotch, it is far too early for me, but what the hell.

"To the Commissioner," croaks Clump, raising his glass, "And to the uniformed officers still in hospital."

"God bless them," croaks Head and I as we chuck the burning cheap booze down our necks.

"Ah...," smiles Clump. "Not a bad drop of stuff." He refills the glasses. "To Detective Chief Inspector Gerald Potter and Detective Inspector Dick Head."

"To us!" we roar and chuck down the booze which is starting to taste better, as do all crap alcoholic drinks, the more you have.

"Right, men, let's get down to it. You are both going to receive full recognition for your bravery, your devotion to duty and of course for destroying one of the evillest gangs of cutthroats that ever walked the streets of London. You should be proud of yourselves. Well done indeed," suddenly his smile turns to an accusing glare. Here it comes. "However, there is the slight matter of how you went about your duties," he raises his charred eyebrows. "The Commissioner, God bless his soul, after questioning several locals from the Gut found out that there were three of you, the third one being no other than that notorious criminal, Mick 'Bloody' O'Reilly, and that it was Mick who tossed dynamite at the gang and blew them to pieces. The Commissioner has also questioned whether your actions were carried out, out of a sense of duty or more to cover up your own involvement with the gang. What have you to say to all this?"

"Nothing just yet, sir," replies I. "Anything else?"

"Yes, there is," he growls. "I saw how much loot was in those sacks last night, but when I went to inspect them this morning I found they had shrunk to half their size. Have you any idea were the rest of the loot has gone?"

"I do indeed, sir," says I. "And all shall be revealed. But first, you may want to top up the glasses, sir. You will need to be slightly inebriated to take in what I am about to tell you."

If nothing else, Clump knows me well enough to trust me when I speak to him this way. Even so he fills the glasses while keeping one eye on me as if I might shoot him at any moment.

"Have you nothing to say, Inspector Head?" demands Clump, obviously annoyed at Head's apparent indifference to what's going on.

Head is pissed already, I can see it in his swimming eyes, but then, like me, I am sure he's absolutely knackered. "Yus, Chef," he drawls rocking back and forth in his chair. "I stink…, think. I mean, blink…. Billicks. No, no sings to spray."

"Prat!" snaps the Chief. "He will have to drink a lot more than that if he wants to be a great detective. Do you not agree Detective Chief Inspector Potter?"

My new title rings wonderfully clear in my ears, Betty is going to be so proud. "He is a beer man, sir. But I am sure he will learn. Now in answer to your doubts about us, perhaps I can lay them to rest." From my pocket, I hand over Charly's diary and watch in fascination as Clump opens the pages and scans through the diary. A smile spreads right across his charred cheeks, his blood-shot eyes light up with glee. "Bloody marvellous," he laughs. "I bloody knew that cretinously bent scumbag was as bent as bent could be. Marvellous. Well done again, Chief Inspector. Another toast me thinks and this is to yours truly. I am to be the new Police Commissioner. What do you think of that, Chief Inspector Potter?"

"Bloody marvellous, Commissioner," I laugh as we raise our glasses.

"On a sourer note," he goes on. "There is still the small matter of the missing loot."

"I will have it returned before the day is out, sir. On one condition."

"Which is?" he asks suspiciously.

"That no one is prosecuted for it, because if they are, you will have to lock up half your uniformed offices. And the ensuing scandal will rock the very foundations of the Yard."

"I see," he drawls. "Just make sure that a good portion of the returned loot ends up in the Police Benevolent Fund, we have several poor bastards in hospital who may never pound the streets again and end up in poverty, Chief Inspector. If we don't look after them no one else will."

"Agreed, sir."

Suddenly, Head falls off his chair, farts loudly, struggles to his feet and swaying dizzily attempts a slurred speech, Clump cuts him off.

"Piss off home, Detective Inspector," he growls. "Come back when you've slept it off."

Head salutes, "Yus, sir." He slurs and sways out of the room.

"That will be all for now, Chief Inspector," smiles Clump. "Get your report done, sort out the missing loot and get yourself home as well. You deserve an early day."

"Thank you, sir," I nod, not bothering to tell him it's my day off anyway.

Leaving the new Commissioner to carry on drinking and reading the diary I go and find Sergeant Watt and order him to return the loot he and his men have snaffled. Naturally he is pretty pissed off about it but knows it is for the best if he wants to remain in the force while also avoiding prison. An hour later I put my report in to a snoring Clump's desk before I head off for home. I am barely a hundred yards from the station when an urchin jumps out in front of me.

"Remember me, copper?" smirks he.

He's the same rat who sold me the Bishop's ring, "How can I ever forget?" growls I.

"I want ten-bob off you or I'll be shoppin' ya to your boss," smirks he some more. "I know you and that Paddy stole some loot from old Charly Choppers safe, cause I saw ya, cause I was up there me self, but had ta hide when I 'eard ya comin'," he grins evilly and holds out a grubby bony hand. "Pay up or else."

"How about I just throttle you and dump you in the Thames?" I grin even more evilly.

"What right outside the cop shop? Nar, you're done for copper," he grins so evilly I expect to see little horns shoot out of his head any second. But then I have an idea, "How do you fancy working for me?"

"What as a nark?" he says narrowing his ratty eyes.

"You would be good at it," assures I.

"What's the pay?"

"A retainer of one shilling a week, plus bonuses depending on the information you bring forward."

He scratches at his chin and you can see his devious little mind churning my offer over. His right-hand index finger is suddenly shoved up his nose to be rooted around with enthusiasm, presently it is extracted and he peruses the green gilbert stuck on the nail, he then flicks it off using his thumb and I just hope it hasn't landed on me. He grins, "The bogey went to the right which means I'm in. If it 'ad gone ta the left I'd a been out."

"What if it had stayed stuck to your finger?" ponders I.

"Then I swallow it an' try again," he laughs holding out his hand.

Reluctantly I shake his hand, God knows what diseases I've just picked up, certainly as his hand is retracted I can feel a squishy bogey in my palm.

"When do I start?" he demands.

I pull out a shilling and hand it over to him, "Right now."

He bites the coin before shoving it in his pocket, gazes up at me and suddenly his eyes soften and he appears a lot less rat like, "Me Ma will be chuffed ta know I got a job. But don't worry copper, she won't say nuffin'. I'll be able to buy her some medicine and me sibs some good grub. Thanks copper," and turning away he runs off and I am certain I saw a tear in his eye.

I head off home; suddenly the day seems full of promise, the air feels cleaner and in my new position as a Chief Inspector I am ready, with the help of my new informer, to really start tackling the deprivation, the injustice and the hopelessness that many in the slums accept as their lot because they have no choice. There will always be crime and corruption, from all walks of life, but if I can improve the lives of the slum dwellers, even in a small way, then I must at least try. On top of that I intend to make a packet.

The Neck
Breakers Arms

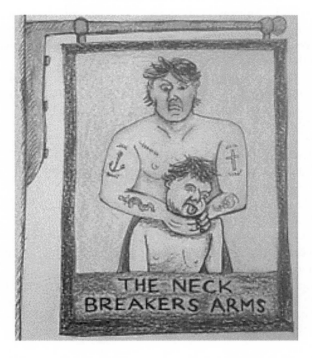

Having been summoned to Clump's office we find the door is shut and Head bobs down to take a nose through the keyhole.

"What can you see?" whispers I. "Is the scotch out?"

"It's out alright and it looks like the good stuff."

"Oh, bollocks," swears I. "I wonder what it's about?"

"Something bad I reason," grates Head standing up. "A mass murderer on the loose who tortures his victims by eating them alive, while having a particular fondness for the taste of Detective Sergeants."

"Or more likely a demonic butcher who's been slaughtering his neighbours and then selling their flesh in his shop. Either way we best go in." says I knocking on the door.

"Come!" shouts Clump.

We go in to find Clump sat behind his desk, he waves a carefree arm around. "Sit down gentlemen," says he. Baggy eyed with his haystack of a beard looking even more wild than normal, he appears depressed and is obviously sloshed despite it only being ten in the morning.

We sit down opposite him and he fills a couple of tumblers up to the brim with scotch and pushes them over to us, spilling a third of the contents in the process.

"What do you know about the French?" says he with indifference.

"They smell of onions and goats," says Head.

"I don't believe they all do, Sergeant. What else?"

"They wear berries on their heads."

"What sort of berries? Blackberries? Strawberries?"

"The Sergeant means berets, sir. A kind of..."

"I know what a bloody beret is Inspector. What else?"

"They also wear stripy jumpers a lot," says Head. "And they invented French letters."

"Really? So, it isn't just the Greeks we have to thank for our literary knowledge?"

Head throws me a confused look.

"The Sergeant means they invented sheaths, sir."

"That as well? So, we owe them for inventing the Harvest festival as well, no doubt?"

I mentally collapse. No wonder he never made 'Detective' Chief Inspector. But then he is pissed and obviously not in his right mind.

"Is something wrong, sir?"

"Hey? Yes, Inspector there is and I don't quite know how to tell you."

"Best just to spit it out, sir," offers Head brazenly.

"That bastard Block, the Chief Constable, has demanded an inquest into the Gut incident. In short, our promotions have been put on hold until a full internal investigation has taken place. I tell you now gentlemen it looks like we may not get our promotion, but worse, we may find ourselves up on criminal charges of fraud, covering up a crime, illegally employing criminals, blowing up criminals without a licence and all manner of shitty things. What do you say to that bastard?"

"It stinks!" snaps Head. "I was looking forward to being a Detective Inspector, sir. Why I've even bought a new suit ready for the celebration afterwards."

"Well it doesn't surprise me, sir," says I glumly. "Block and Commissioner Jenkins were good friends and it could be they were more than friends."

Clump's eyes narrow. "Are you trying to suggest that the Chief Constable may have been involved with Jenkins in shifty operations?"

"I am indeed, sir."

"Marvellous," grins he grinningly and rubs his hands together. "Right," he says leaning across the desk and tapping his nose. "Leave that one to me, lads. For now, keep everything under your hat while keeping your ears and eyes open. Trust no one. And I mean no one. Is that clear?"

"It is," says I.

"Does that mean I'm not to trust you and the Inspector?" puts in Head. "And what about my Chloe?"

"Sometimes, Sergeant," grates Clump. "I really do not know if you are genuine or merely taking the proverbial." He leans back, picks up the bottle of scotch and tops up all three glasses.

"Now, lads, back to the matter in hand." He raises his glass. "Cheers."

"Cheers," cheer Head and I in unison.

Clump bangs his already empty glass down and refills it. "A French cargo ship, called in English the 'Sea Voyager', docked yesterday down by the Victoria and Albert wharf. Aboard that ship there was an extensive array of fine wines and brandies. The ship was due to be unloaded this afternoon and then reloaded with English goods before sailing merrily away back to France, but at present it is impounded. Because it so happens that two of the ship's crew members were found early this morning in a back alley a few hundred yards from the dock having been bludgeoned to death." He slips on his reading glasses and consults his notebook. "I, being the only senior officer in the Yard at six this morning took charge and led the initial investigation. But I must admit I achieved little, other than to confirm that no one knows any bloody thing much at all about what happened to those luckless sailors. Hence, I am giving this to you two. The victims were named as..." he pauses and is obviously struggling with his notes, "A Monsieur Louis Bastard and a Monsieur Henry Ort- something or other."

"May I see, sir?" offers I.

He passes me his note book. It is a sod to read as his hand writing is chaotic.

"I think Louis Bastard is pronounced Loo-ee Basstar and Henry Orteu is pronounced as Onree Ortwar, but I'm not exactly certain as my French is a bit ropey."

"You speak, French, Inspector?"

"Oui. Je peux un peu."

"What does that mean?"

"Yes, I can a little. I think I more or less got that right. But like I say, sir, I am very rusty."

"Perfect," beams Clump raising his glass. "A toast to the Inspector speaking French, even if it is a bit rusty."

"To speaking French," we chorus.

"To the Frogs," cries Head.

"Well men," smiles Clump. "Get yourselves out there and show those Frenchies what brilliant Detectives you are and make the Yard proud. We are the finest Policemen in the world, gentlemen. None equal." He pauses, leans to one side and farts out a real stinker before continuing. "Leave no onion unturned."

"We won't, sir," says I trying not to gag. "Can I have the report on the case thus far?"

Snatching back his notebook he rips out a few pages and hands them to me. "I haven't had time to write my notes out as yet but you should be able to follow on with what's already written down."

I glance through the pages and spot something that causes a slight panic in my long johns.

"The Neck Breakers Arms?"

"The bodies were found just a hundred yards from the place. Apparently, the French men had been in there drinking earlier on that evening. Do you know the place, Inspector?"

"Head and I have had the odd drink in there in the past, haven't we, Sergeant?"

"We have, sir," grimaces Head.

"Bit rough, I found," frowns Clump.

"Just a bit," sighs I.

"Never mind," grins Clump. "They don't come much rougher than you two." He claps his hands together again which is our signal to clear off.

Downing our scotches, we stand up, wish him au revoir, and leave.

"Old Clump's in a state," comments Head as we make our way down to the morgue. "I think he's drinking too much."

"Indeed. He is also pretty pissed off about Block trying to block his promotion."

"And ours as well," grates Head. "I was looking forward to being promoted."

"As was I, Sergeant. Betty will be disappointed too, she was well looking forward to addressing me for ever more as 'Detective Chief Inspector,' and was so excited over the prospect she's already bought a new set of underwear and a bottle of champagne for us to celebrate with. Still, don't lose heart just yet, Sergeant, old Clump won't give up without a fight."

Presently we arrive at the morgue to find Dr Shelley has one of the sailors out on the slab with the other still on a trolley awaiting his turn. Both victims are relatively young, dark haired and clean shaven. I sniff the air but cannot smell any onions.

"Ah, Inspector," says Shelley. "I wondered when you'd be coming to see me."

We exchange the usual pleasantries and the good doctor gives us his report thus far, which is both short and simplistic. Both men were brutally coshed on the back of their heads, the first blow knocked them down and because of the blood on the ground around their heads, Shelley believes they were both coshed several more times while laid prone and then their necks were broken to ensure they were definitely dead.

"A nasty business," sighs Shelley.

"Anything else you can tell us, Doctor?" asks I.

He shakes his head. "As you can see I have yet to open them up, but on initial examination I would say both men are free of diseases and were in good health until someone, or ones, killed them. I will let you know if anything untoward turns up."

We thank him and head back to the office where we holster our revolvers, put on our coats, don our bowlers and head outside to find the sky has thickened up with rolling dark clouds that threaten heavy rain. Once in a hackney I instruct the driver to head towards the docks and I read Clump's notes to the rhythmic clip clopping of the horse's hooves on the tarmacadam road. Clump is of the opinion that this is about crooks falling out over smuggled contraband.

"Any ideas as yet, sir?" asks Head gazing thoughtfully at me.

"Um..." ums I. "We know the Neck Breakers Arms is notorious for receiving smuggled goods. We also know that the place has often been raided but never charged, which leaves me to believe that the landlord has friends in the right places who warn him well in advance of any intended raids. Now, I'm also thinking that our sailors may well have somehow been involved in smuggling and were murdered as a consequence. But it is only a thought, Sergeant. For now, we'll keep an open mind."

"It could be a simple case of robbery, sir."

"Indeed, it could. It's just far too brutal for a robbery. It feels more like someone has sent out a message to warn whoever it concerns not to step out of line. Anyway, we shall see."

I decide to begin our investigations at the Neck Breakers and tell the driver to drop us off a good ten minutes' walk from the place as I feel the need to think a bit more.

Ten minutes later we are on foot and turning into Bent Lane where we find the place is heaving with costermongers, shoppers, prostitutes, urchins and all manner of low life. Further up ahead a costermonger's cry catches our attention.

"Bags for sale or rent. Get your bags here. None finer or cheaper anywhere else in London."

"I could do with a nice bag," says Head.

I shoot him a strange questioning look. "What would you want with a woman's bag, Sergeant?"

He looks horrified. "Not for me, sir! For Chloe. She hasn't got a decent bag."

Obviously affronted by my veiled accusation that he might be into women's things I put him out of his misery. "I was only teasing, Sergeant."

"So was I," he grins.

"Touché," winks I. "Betty could also do with a nice new bag. If they are decent then I shall buy her one. She loves her bags."

"Women do, sir. I'd say bags are so important to the female she almost sees them as some kind of divine gift from the Gods."

"That's very poetic of you, Sergeant. And I agree with you. In fact, I wonder if they worship their bags, and shoes, let's not forget the shoes, more than they do their men sometimes."

Head chuckles. "Chloe moved in with one pair of frayed shoes so I bought her a new pair. She was ecstatic to have a new pair before her old pair had even started letting in water she can't stop going on about it."

"Madness. Women and their shoes. In the old days an ordinary woman would be content to wear a single pair of shoes until they fell to pieces before requesting a new second hand pair. But now, some women believe it should be compulsory to own at least two pairs, plus a couple of bags."

"At this rate, sir, the average woman will own three or more pairs of everything including drawers."

"Probably. In a hundred years, Sergeant, I'll bet you the average ordinary woman will own at least five pairs of shoes, several handbags and dozens of hats."

"Sorry, sir, I can't believe that. It would be ridiculous. Why on earth would anyone want so many shoes, handbags and hats? After all you can only wear one pair of shoes and one hat at the same time, while carrying just one bag."

"Unless you go shopping."

"Ah… But shopping bags are just string or cane and are not considered by the female to be classed in the same league as a handbag or evening bag."

"True," agrees I, agreeingly. "Now the thing is this. What is the point of having too many bags? They'll just spend ages transferring all their junk from one bag to another just to be seen out with a different bag. I mean the junk inside the bag will still be the same, will it not?"

"It certainly would. Just as whatever junk is in one pair of my trousers gets transferred into the next pair I wear."

At last we drop the conversation as we reach the long table where the bags are being sold, only to find there are none left out on display.

A tall shifty hairy faced irk seems to be in charge, so I ask, "Have you run out of bags?"

"Nah. We got a few left."

"Where are they?"

He sweeps a long bony arm behind him where sat on a rickety bench are three decrepit looking old dears all dressed in black and looking utterly forlorn.

"Only got these three old bags left," says shifty. "'Ad a good run on 'em today. Flogged off ten of the buggers."

I am aghast. "You cannot sell people it's against the law!"

He is incredulous. "Is it? Why?"

"Because it is akin to slavery which has been abolished for years."

"Not round here it ain't," says Shifty menacingly. "Case you ain't noticed half the scum round here work all day for a loaf of stale bread which ain't much better than being a slave anyway. Besides, the old bags want to be sold."

"Why?"

"Cause anyone who buys 'em has ta feed 'em. It's in their sale of goods contract."

"Why would anyone buy an old woman just to feed her. I reason that they are well past their prime and would be as much use as a three-legged horse in a steeple chase."

"These old bags are handpicked, mate. They may be a bit slow but they can clean, cook, wash and keep you warm at night."

"I'd rather cuddle up to a dead dog then a sack of old rubbish" puts in Head.

Shifty shoves his grubby hands onto his hips and fixes us with a mean stare. "If you ain't buying why don't ya just piss off?"

I flash my warrant card. "Why don't we just arrest you?"

He is off like a shot and disappears into the jostling crowds.

I go over to the poor little old hags. "Ladies, you are free to go home. You shall not be sold this day."

I am contemptuously glared up at by all three and the ugliest one, the one with a wart on her nose, spits out, "We ain't got no 'omes you bleedin' moron! But we might 'ave 'ad if you 'adn't stuck ya beak in. Why don't ya clear off an' do something useful like drown ya self."

One of the others join in, "Now, now, Ethel. Don't get nasty, the copper was just doin' 'is duty." She gives me a toothless smile. "Why don't I come 'ome wiv ya me duck. A big man like you needs a good woman ta keep 'im warm."

"I have one already thank you all the same."

"Well 'ave two. Think on it; a woman each side of ya in ya bed is just what's needed when the cold old winter sets in. It'd be 'eaven for ya."

A vision of one arm around my lovely Betty and the other around a bag of bones while we lay in bed listening to the rain pattering on the window isn't my idea of heaven. However, I realise

I may have lost these old women any chance of getting food to eat this day. Call me a big softy but I reach into my pocket, extract a hand full of loose change and press it into the old girl's scrawny hand.

"Thanks, Mister. I knew ya was a gent'." She turns to her friends. "Come on girls there's enough here ta get pissed as parrots."

Head and I watch them hobble off and then continue towards the Neck Breakers just as spots of rain pepper down onto our bowlers, the wind picks up and it goes as dark as pitch.

"It's going to pelt down," says Head turning up his coat collar.

"We'll be in the pub in a few minutes," says I noting how quickly everyone is running for cover. A crack of thunder hastens our pace, but we are still a couple of hundred yards from the pub when the clouds open up and dump half an ocean down onto us. We run like hell and make it inside the pub with the wind and rain sweeping in behind us.

"Phew," puffs Head taking off his bowler and shaking off the rain. "Talk about torrential."

Unbuttoning our coats, we shake off most of the excess rain.

"Bloody marvellous," grates I. "One more minute and we'd have made it home and dry."

Crossing over to the bar I note the place is packed as obviously everyone's rushed in for shelter. Sailors, dockers and general labourers mix with prostitutes, ne'er-do-wells and urchins. No one appears to register our arrival.

The same bald headed heavily tattooed hulk of a landlord from the last time we were in here is behind the bar laughing and joking with half a dozen dockers and doesn't notice us until we lean across the bar.

"Not more coppers," he groans fixing us with scathing eyes. "I thought I'd seen the last of your lot for the day. I told that hairy copper all I knew first thing this morning."

"Well you'll just have to tell us as well," demands I, while aware it has gone deathly quiet and we are being seriously eyeballed. "But firstly, we'll have a pint of best bitter each if you'd be so kind."

He pulls two pints and then bangs them down onto the bar. "On the house. I'll just go get the girl in to serve, sort out a few things and then I'll be back."

I catch him winking at the dockers just before he disappears out back and know that Head and I are about to be in deep shit. One of the dockers glares into my eyes while two more go and stand menacingly on my left side. Head and I are now sandwiched between the dockers.

A big ugly sod with a flat snout and bull neck on my right side, sneers, "I can smell pig, Bill, can you?"

"I can," says Bill from my left side. "A right stink it is too, Joe."

"I reckon we should take that stink outside and let the rain wash it off. Don't you, Bill?"

"I do, Joe. That and a good scrubbing with yard brooms ought a sort 'em out."

Recently I have been immersed in reading books about the American Wild West and realise that Head and I are being intimidated just like cowboys in a saloon and if we are to be viewed as real men, we can't back down from our aggressors but must challenge them and prove our masculinity. Or we could just take out our revolvers and shoot a few of the buggers, but that might be going too far. The best form of defence is attack and I nudge Head in the ribs with an elbow, grab hold of my short truncheon from beneath my coat while trusting that Head has done the same and give Joe the first taste of my hard weapon.

Women scream, men curse and fists start to fly in our direction, only Head and I are past masters at cracking skulls as back to back we rain blows on flat capped skulls with furious ferocity and precision and the dockers fall back in defeat. Unfortunately, just like in all the best books, everyone else decides to stampede from their seats and join in the affray as all hell breaks out. I receive a punch to the jaw that rocks my head just as an urchin sinks his teeth into my left calf. Head's bowler flies over me as he yells out the F and C words. The sailor who just punched me comes forward again for another go and receives a nose jab that stops him in his tracks. I crack the urchin on his scabby head with my truncheon and knock him senseless. An upper cut to my guts from Bill takes my breath away but not so much to prevent me from giving him such a crack on his nut he falls back onto a tart and a sailor, so all three become a tangled mess on the wooden floor. I feel another urchin slip up under my coat while I'm trying to fend off some screaming claws-out prostitute and am unable to prevent the urchin from sinking his teeth into my right buttock. Another urchin suddenly runs along the bar taking the opportunity to snatch flat caps and bonnets before running straight into a beer pump and flying off the bar where a ham fist from a huge trollop thumps straight into his ugly little mug.

"Duck!" screams Head, and I do just as an urchin flies over me and the bar, smashing into the display of spirit bottles and glasses on the far side, before jumping up and running off with a bottle of scotch.

Then I take a bad one, an uppercut to the chin that cracks my jaw and jars my teeth together. I am going down as blows from all over rain down on me and I know that Head isn't faring any better. As I fall I hear the sound of whistles, at last the cavalry have arrived with truncheons drawn and skulls to crack. Then the world goes black.

"How do you feel, sir?" says a voice as my eyes, well one eye, flicks open and hazily focuses on the welcoming sight of a plod's helmet.

"As if I've been hit by a tram," groans I, running an exploratory hand around a face that is sore and lumpy.

"You're lucky we turned up when we did," says the plod. "Or, I fear you and the Sergeant would now be dead."

"I thought I was dead," Head's voice sounds coming from my left.

Pushing myself upright on the chair I've obviously been placed on by the plods, I turn a stiff neck to meet Head's sorrowful gaze. He looks a right sod. His face looks like a herd of cattle have run over it. His ripped coat collar's hanging down on one side, his shirt and waistcoat have been ripped open to expose his hairy chest, one eye is as black as tar and his nose appears swollen to epic proportions and is encrusted with blood around the nostrils. Other than that, he doesn't actually look dead, but may not be far from it. My half closed right eye starts to focus and I see there's half a dozen plods standing guard over a dozen or so sailors, dockers and a couple of prostitutes who all appear to have been well battered and are still groaning, while miserably rubbing their cracked skulls. The landlord is leaning against the bar on the customers' side while chatting amiably to a Sergeant who's downing a glass of scotch. I rise shakily to my feet.

The plod grabs my arm to steady me. "You alright, sir?"

"Thank you, Officer," groans I, aware that I ache everywhere while my bum feels as if a wild cat had a go at it and I know that on later inspection I will discover teeth marks to go with the ones in my calf. I lay a restraining hand on Head's shoulder and then limp over to the bar.

"Ah... Detective," smiles the landlord straightening up. "How are you feeling?"

I raise my eyebrows. "What happened to you?"

He stabs a finger at his chest. "Me? I was out back seeing to the drayman I'm afraid and didn't realise what was going on until I came back in to find Sergeant Blackmore and his men sorting out the trouble makers.

"Sergeant Blackmore at your service, sir," says he saluting.

"On behalf on myself and my Sergeant I thank you for our rescue," says I.

His eyes fail to meet my steady gaze as he says, "You are welcome, sir."

I note his thick bushy ginger sideburns and caterpillar eyebrows and the fact that his face is burnt weather brown like a sailor. The landlord cuts into my thoughts.

"I expect you and your Sergeant could do with a drop of scotch, Inspector?"

"We would welcome one."

Two more tumblers are half filled, Blackmore's is topped up and the landlord raises his glass for a toast. "To the finest police force in the world."

"I'll drink to that," says Blackmore and I join him just as Head hobbles over and takes up his glass.

"To painkillers." Half smiling, he chucks the scotch down in one go.

The landlord goes to refill my glass but I put a hand over it. "Thank you, landlord, but no, we have work to do."

"I don't think, sir, if I may be so bold," says Blackmore. "You and Sergeant Head are in no fit state to do anything more than go home and nurse your wounds."

"Perhaps, Sergeant. Only needs must."

"What about this lot?" says Blackmore waving towards the battered customers. "Shall I charge them with affray and assaulting Police Officers, or what?"

"I'd let them go, Sergeant. I think the cracks on their heads have been punishment enough."

He appears surprised. "If you say so, sir. I'll give them all a verbal warning and send them packing." He turns away and goes over to his men.

"Now, tell me what happened last night when the pair of French sailors were in here?" I ask the landlord while staring intently into his unwavering eyes.

He shrugs. "There's not much to tell, Inspector. They came in about ten already two sheets to the wind. One spoke fairly good English, the other none. They drank red wine by the bottle and were quickly accosted by a couple of prostitutes because they seemed to have plenty of cash on them. A few of the locals took offence to them cosying up to English prostitutes and a fight quickly ensued. The Frenchmen got a hiding before I could calm everything down. I then advised them to leave for their own safety, which they did. That would have been about eleven. I didn't know about their having been murdered until that hairy copper and his entourage turned up early this morning and got me out of bed."

"According to my Chief's notes, the Frenchmen were spending money like water. They frequented several pubs drinking only the best wines and smoking expensive cigars. They treated anyone and everyone to drinks in an apparent attempt to win favour, but when their bodies were searched they did not have a single penny or a franc between them."

"As I said to your Chief, Inspector, their murders were obviously money motivated."

"Do you receive wine and brandy from the Sea Voyager?"

He nods. "I do. All perfectly legal, duty payed."

Head suddenly says, "Excuse me, sir I have to visit the gents."

"Very well," says I and watch him hobble off as if he's messed his pants. He has a hand between his legs as if to hold his bits in place and I realise he must have taken a bashing in the unmentionable area.

"Anything else?" says the landlord.

"Not right now," smiles I, fixing him with a 'you're full of crap' look.

There's a mocking sneer in his eyes as he says, "Well, you know where to find me."

"Indeed," says I before limping over to Blackmore who's finished bollocking the locals who begin filing out of the place, which I notice for the first time has been pretty well wrecked.

"Can you show me where the bodies were found, Sergeant?"

"Of course, sir. If you'll follow me."

"I'll just nip to the gents first." I limp off out back to the toilet which is the usual small brick building that you can smell from a mile away. I go in to find Head with his back to me and standing in front of the trough with his trousers and drawers around his knees while inspecting his private area. He cranes his neck around.

"It's you, sir."

"It is. How are you, Sergeant?"

Pulling up his trousers he turns to face me. "My bloody roundies are twice their normal size. Some bastard kicked me so hard I thought they'd shot out of my mouth and had gone forever. Luckily they're still attached but how the hell am I going to get them back to normal?"

"You could try the hot and cold method," suggests I.

He appears somewhat perplexed. "Hot and cold method?"

"Yes, it will get the swelling down more quickly. It works for me when I've had a swollen hand through punching criminals in the cells. All you do is fill two enamel bowls with water. One with water as hot as you can bear, and the other with as cold as you can get it, adding ice if available. Then you dunk your roundies in the hot one, hold them there for as long as you can bear and then transfer them into the ice cold one. You keep repeating that procedure for as long as you can. You'll find they'll soon shrink back to normal."

"I still don't get you."

"Dunk them in hot and then cold. Hot-cold-hot-cold until the swelling subsides."

"Sounds bloody evil!"

"It is. But it works."

"The thing is, they'll tighten up in defence the second I bob down to swing them in the water and I'll have to completely sit down in the bowl to ensure they're covered enough to do any good. The water will spill out all over the carpet and God knows what Chloe will think about it all. I mean how many men come home from work, strip off and start dangling their bits in enamel bowls?"

"Not many," muses I. "But is it any different from taking a tin bath?"

"I suppose not," he groans. "God knows what Chloe will say when she sees them."

"She'll be fine. Now, do you want to me to relieve you of your duties so you can go home?"

"Relief would be good as I couldn't pee just now despite being desperate. What if that kick has killed my love life?"

"Fear not, Sergeant. I'm certain you will soon recover. I think you should take a cab and go home."

He shakes his head. "I'll soldier on, sir. Thanks anyway, but I want to catch up with whoever kicked me and give him a taste of his own medicine. I'm pretty sure I know what he looks like."

I take a quick leak and we go back into the bar and set off with Blackmore to view the scene of the murders. The rain has ceased, the sun is out but there's still a lot of water around. Blackmore leads us to a narrow stinking alley flanked on both sides by brick warehouses where the rain-washed, but still just visible, chalked figures of where the two sailors met their fate lay sketched on the ground. Sounds of the busy docks just yards away assault our ears with the clanging of chains, squealing of pulleys, clanging of cranes and shouts and cries of the dockers. Head and I peruse the scene but there is little to really see. It tells us nothing.

"No witnesses?" I ask Blackmore.

"None. Well, no one's come forward as yet."

We chat for a while and then I allow him to get on. Head and I head towards the quay but just before we exit the alley a ball of horse dollop smacks into my back and I spin around to find my urchin informant standing hands on hips before me.

"What ya, boss," grins he. "Took a bit of a pastin' I see."

"Do me a favour," grates I. "Next time you want to gain my attention just give me a psst or something."

"Where will I get one of them?"

I shake my head in frustration. "Just call out, oi or something. What have you got for me?"

"Heard them sailors was done in by coppers," he pauses to look all around him, in truth he is running a terrible risk talking to us, it could get him killed. "Word is them toads..."

"What bloody toads?" grates I.

"Them French men are nicknamed toads. Didn't ya know?"

"Frogs! They're known as frogs not toads."

"Whatever. Anyway, them frogs hopped onto the cart and hid themselves up, so I 'm told."

"What bloody cart? What are you on about?"

Coming near enough so I can smell his smelly unwashed body he whispers, "They stowed away on that ship that come over and then when the landlord from the Neck Breakers pulled up with his cart and got it loaded with illegal booze the frogs slipped under the tarpaulin and went with it back to the pub. Then they got discovered as the booze was bein' unloaded and taken down into the cellar. Now here's the rub. Them toads, I mean frogs, were coppers in disguise from somewhere called Leharve and were out

227

to get the smugglers on the orders of someone called Mary Ann Twinnet."

"You mean Mary Antoinette. It couldn't have been her because she had her head separated from her shoulders years ago."

"It was her name that my snout reckons he heard mentioned when the landlord was arguin' wiv them frogs."

Head says, "I think the name might be an operation name, sir. Operation Mary Antoinette."

"Brilliant!" says I. "Of course it is. What else?"

"The landlord then pulls out a wad of notes and waves 'em in the frogs' kissers. They shake their heads at first and start arguing, but after a pistol is shoved up ones' arse they change their minds, take the money and piss off."

Head is aghast, "They inserted a pistol in one of the Frenchman's rear end?"

"Nah, not literally, they just poked it in his rear end through his trousers."

"Thank heaven for that," sighs I. "Where was your 'snout' when all this was going on?"

"He'd sneaked into the cellar like he does most nights through the trap door out back, he's got a key to the lock see, anyway he goes in as usual to nick the odd bottle which he sells to his mates, but before he can get out the trap door opens, and the landlord comes down the steps like I've already said. So, me snout, I'd tell ya his name, but I have to keep it a secret…"

"What is it?" cuts in I.

"It's Bert. But don't tell no one. Anyway, Bert hides up behind a big barrel just as there's a lot of shouting comin' from out by the cart. Next thing the frogs are marched down the cellar by a couple of the landlord's thugs helped by a uniformed copper…"

"Whose name is Sergeant Blackmore," puts in I.

"'Ow did ya know that?"

"An educated guess," says I.

He appears frustrated. "That was my best bit. I was looking forward ta tellin' ya about that bastard Blackmore."

"You don't care for him then?" grins Head who seems to have temporarily forgotten his pain and misery.

"'Ee's a bastard 'e is. Thinks he's a bloody king he does sailin' around in his bloody great yacht when all the time he ain't nuffin' but a crook and a brute. Beats the shit out of us kids he does, just for the hell of it."

So, does everyone else I muse to myself. "What time did all this happen?"

"'Bout eight. Them frogs then go out on the piss, but then they're found with their heads caved in. Now no one saw Blackmore an' his men do for the frogs but they was seen comin' out this very alley 'bout eleven, an' when Bert an' his mates went to see what had been goin' on they see the bodies."

"And instead of reporting it they fleeced them and then ran off."

He gives a careless shrug. "Thing is, governor. Who the bleedin' 'ell would they have reported it to?"

"He's got a point there," puts in Head.

"Indeed, he has," agrees I. "Did the urchins who went through the sailors' pockets find much?"

"Nah," he shakes his head. "Bit of loose change is all. Reckon Blackmore had took anything worth 'aving."

"Any idea why Blackmore and his men killed the Frenchmen?"

He shakes his head. "All I know is they were heard mouthin' off in French while they was in the Dead Eagle that they was goin' to do the English coppers and all their smugglin' mates 'cause, they had enough on 'em ta see 'em go to the nick for years."

"Who in the Eagle knows enough French to translate into English?"

"That would be the Bustle from Brussels, Sophie March, more commonly known as bon marche," puts in Head.

"Good and cheap."

Head's eyes go all sparkly, "She certainly is."

"I think we shall move on, Sergeant."

"What about that lot for a tale" enthuses my informant. "Worth a few bob I reckon."

"It certainly is," agrees I. He has practically solved the case for me providing it all checks out.

"Don't forget I gotta pay Bert, Sophie an' several others just ta keep stomp or else we'll all get our necks bruck."

"No, you won't get them bruck, you'll get them broken."

"Whatever, bruck or broken the ends the same, bleedin' gonna be lookin' behind ya forever while your feet point forwards."

"You are very cynical for one so young," says I fishing out a ten shilling note and handing it over which he snatches, holds up and peruses through the sun's rays.

"Cor, lovely," he grins.

"Perhaps you might treat yourself to a bath," comments I, he really does smell like a bog.

He shakes his head. "I got to fit in, guv, an' I won't fit in if I smell like a bar of soap."

I fish out another two shillings in coins and hand them over. "The note is your bonus, these are your wages for the next two weeks."

A tear appears in each of his sharp little eyes. "Me muvver's a lot better since she's been on the cocaine medicine an' me sibs 'ave got fatter. An' it's thanks to you governor."

I am so touched I can feel tears welling up. "You're welcome, um… what's your name?"

"It's Andy."

"Andy, thank you. Now, get yourself off and be careful."

Grinning he sticks two fingers up at me and then disappears down an eight-inch gap between a pair of warehouses.

"Onwards and upwards, Sergeant," says I as we hobble towards the quay. "We shall talk to the skipper of the Sea Voyager and see if he has anything to add to his statement from what little Clump gleaned from him this morning."

"What did the skipper have to say, sir?"

"According to Clump's notes, nothing at all as he didn't speak a word of English other than 'ello, goodbye and roast beef."

"Doesn't sound very promising," says Head grimacing.

"Still giving you gyp, Sergeant?"

"My roundies feel like someone's torturing them with a flaming torch, they're burning that much."

"That's the feeling coming back, Sergeant, which is good news."

"Well I'd hate to have the bad news," groans he clutching his groin.

We continue in silence and ignore the tormenting urchins and the ribald comments from the dockers and sailors we pass. 'Oi, mate, shit ya self 'ave ya?' 'Wus up, coppers 'ad a good kickin' 'ave ya?'

It's the docker who shouts out, "Ow's ya nuts, copper?' that sends Head into a rage as despite his agony he leaps across several feet to deliver a cracking head-butt that fells the mouthy lout down onto his back, legs akimbo. Momentarily the world slows down as everyone winces knowing what is coming next, and it is truly evil as Head's toecap connects unmercifully with the ruffian's roundies.

Stepping back Head glares down at the lout, who's rolling around in agony while clutching at his crotch, and Head says, "Revenge is sweet. How's your nuts? Taste, alright do they?"

"I'll get ya for this," the lout manages to gasp out.

A chorus of 'Get 'em!' comes from the lout's colleagues as they clench fists and make to start another punch up. I am definitely not in the mood and neither is Head as we draw our revolvers.

"One step closer and we fire," warns I.

"You wouldn't dare!" growls a burly docker.

I shoot his flat cap off, which is a hell-of-a shot and its lucky half his thick skull didn't go with it.

"Disperse or the next one will spill blood," warns I.

"Bastard!" yells Burly. "You could've bleedin' killed me. I felt the bullet part me bleedin' hair."

"I am an expert shot. If I had wanted to kill you, you would be dead. Now, piss off back to your work before my Sergeant and I arrest the lot of you."

Mumbling and grumbling they back right off. Head and I continue across the quay and then limp and hobble alongside the quay while looking at the names on the various ships moored for unloading and/or loading while keeping out of the way of the dockers. After a while we reach a rusting old steam ship that is painted above the Plimsoll line in a garish mustard colour and is called La Mer Voyage. Sat out on stools a pair of aged, wax moustached sailors wearing berets and striped jumpers are swigging wine from the bottle and smoking clay pipes.

"This is it, Sergeant," says I appreciating that we can step up onto a short set of wooden steps straight into an open rusty door. "Bonjour," greets I.

"Bonjour," returns they, removing their pipes.

"Je parlour le capitaine?" says I.

They both grin, "Anglais?"

"Qui"

They laugh, "La police?"

"Qui,"

They laugh even louder.

"What's so funny, sir?" says Head.

"No idea," says I. "I'm sure I pronounced my French quite well."

"Parlez avec la capitaine?" says the one with the shortest moustache

"Qui."

At last he rises slowly to his feet, stretches up, yawns, farts and scratches his bum before gesturing us to follow him. We cautiously negotiate the four steps and follow the sailor inside the ship and down a long corridor until we come to an open door where inside sits a tan faced grey haired man with a hook nose by a small round table in front of a cabin bunk. On the table sits a bottle of cognac, a single glass and a cigar smoking in an ashtray.

The sailor speaks so fast to his captain I cannot understand a word of it. The captain turns his head towards us and laughs.

"Entrez, Messieurs," says he.

We go in and I introduce us in my best French.

The captain laughs again. "I speak good English, gentlemen." He gestures with his hand to two folded up chairs stacked in a corner of his small cabin. "Bring up a seat and join me. You can hang your hats and coats on those hooks on the wall"

We do just that and I ask, "I was under the opinion you did not speak English?"

"Please excuse my little lie to your superior, Inspector, but, you see he arrived with that, Sergeant…"

"Blackmore." I cut in.

"Oui. The man is bad, and I would say nothing in front of him. Plus, he speaks excellent French, so I feign ignorance to keep on his side. But you, I know I can trust. Your chief said to Blackmore, 'I will put my two finest detectives onto this case,' and I note the anger in Blackmore's eyes. You have come here for the truth. I will tell you the truth and then you must act accordingly. Comprendre?"

"Qui. I am all ears, Captain."

Standing up he goes to a small cupboard on the wall and takes out two more glasses. "But first we shall drink together and get to know each other a little."

And so we do until we have become old friends having emptied two bottles of cognac and sampled six different bottles of wine, by which time we are all pie-eyed and incapable of speaking any language other than slurred double Dutch.

"What's happening?" asks I of Head goodness knows how many hours later as I struggle to lift my head up from where it seems to be stuck to the table.

"We dropped off," he groans, the palm of his hand covering his forehead as if it's holding his brains in. "My skull's thumping like its being hit with a mallet."

"My tongue feels as if someone's wiped their arse with it."

"Perhaps they did," he groans some more. "I think, sir, we were so far gone anyone could have done anything to us and we wouldn't have cared a pig."

"Fig, Sergeant, the word is fig."

"Does it matter?"

I shake my head which sets it thumping like mad. "God, I shall never drink again. What time is it?"

"God knows." Staggering to his feet he stumbles over to the porthole and wobbling crazily bangs his head against the glass. "It's dark out there. And either my vision's impaired or the dock has moved away from the ship."

"Let me see," says I, rising shakily to my feet. I stumble onto Head and he sort of collapses on his bum and sets to rocking back and forth. "We're moving. Bloody hell the ship has set sail."

"I feel sea sick," says he.

"I fear, Sergeant we have been kidnapped and are being transported to somewhere in the colonies."

The door opens and the captain steps in, immediately he sets a bucket down in front of Head who quickly has a go at filling it up.

"You have awoken at last," laughs the captain. "I wonder if you will sleep for ever."

I fall back against the porthole, "What is happening? We seem to be moving."

"Just to a quiet area on the quay. We are loaded and ready to go but still we are impounded until you have solved the case."

"What time is it?"

"Ten of the clock."

"We must go! Betty will be worried sick," with that I drop to my knees and join Head at the bucket.

"I will get you both a coffee," sighs the captain and leaves the cabin.

Half an hour later and feeling a bit more human, Head and I say au revoir to the captain and his crew and make our way across the quay towards the streets. The area is quiet, but we can still hear the noise of ships being loaded and unloaded further up the quay. Gas lamps shine their shadowy light onto the rough pavements as we walk down an eerily quiet alleyway flanked by decaying slums until a short skinny figure comes swaying towards us. It is an urchin, in one hand he holds what appears to be a near empty bottle of scotch in the other is a cigar.

"Oi, got a light," he slurs and then collapses giggling onto the floor.

"He's out of his head," says Head. "Drunk as a Lord."

"And no guesses where he stole the booze from," grates I. "Grab his feet, Sergeant, we can't leave him here, we'll convey him to somewhere safer."

I take the bottle and cigar from the raggedy child's bony hands and set them down on the pavement and then lift him up beneath his armpits, which smell like a fermented bowl of vomit, while Head grabs him by his bare cheesy feet. He is a pathetic little creature, very thin and undernourished, but at least, for a while, he is deliriously happy.

"There's a light fanning out of that open doorway up ahead," says I. "Let us take him there."

The boy feels weightless as we carry him along, he has stopped giggling and starts snoring like a wart hog.

"He reeks of booze," says Head.

"So, do we," I remind him.

Suddenly our way is blocked by the unmistakable dark silhouettes of uniformed policemen swinging truncheons, six in all, and I realise we are walking straight into a trap. I glance behind us, and there is the unmistakable outline of the landlord from the Neck Breakers Arms who's flanked on either side by a pair of broad-shouldered hard nuts carrying what looks like iron bars. We are about to be slaughtered. We set the boy down against the wall and reach for our revolvers, but mine feels light, light as if it has no bullets in it.

"We have been shafted," hisses I. "That bastard captain has set us up."

"We're done for, Gerald. Do you mind me calling you by your first name?"

"Not in the least, Richard. How shall we play this?"

"We could charge the lot behind us, there's less of them, we might break through and make it back to the docks."

"Are you in a fit state to run for it?"

"Not with my swollen nuts I'm not, Gerald. They're not as bad as they were but running will only make them worse."

"Then we have no option but to stand and fight. Who knows, perhaps we may even fight our way out."

The landlord's voice bellows out, "You pair of twats couldn't leave it, could you? Now, either you join us, or you'll find yourself waking up dead while being dumped so far out to sea you'll eventually wash up on a beach in Honolulu."

"Why there?" shouts back Head. "Where is Honolulu anyway?"

"How the hell should I know? Join us or die."

"Go shag a goat," snarls Head.

"Get 'em boys," orders the landlord.

"Kill the fuckers!" screams a squealy voice as suddenly piling out from everywhere like a load of stampeding giant rats dozens of urchins appear and start throwing everything under the moon at the plods and the landlord's men. Bottles fly, stones fly, bits of wood, balls of dollop, dead cats and heaven knows what else. It is akin to Henry V's archers loosing off hundreds of arrows at the French at the battle of Agincourt. Blackmore, the landlord and their men can do nothing but cover their heads and crouch down just as we have to. Stuff bounces off my bowler like giant hail stones. I hear Head curse, using that C word again as if it's the only word in his vocabulary. Even so, as I take a daring peep through splayed fingers I can see by the extra amount of crap raining down on Blackmore and his crew, Head and I are not the main targets.

"Come on Richard," yells I. "Let's do the bastards."

We are up, truncheons drawn, and risking being hit by missiles we go for the hard nuts first, cracking skulls, hands and arms that try but fail to protect themselves.

"I'll 'ave the bastard," screams an urchin who promptly cracks the landlord over the head with what looks like a wooden leg, and as it snaps in splintered half, I see it is.

The landlord is up on his feet and adopting a fighting pose, he swings punches all around him while seemingly unable to make them count, probably due to the fact his face and eyes are covered in horse and God knows what other shit, so he can't see a thing.

Another urchin wearing a plod's helmet, that's down over his eyes, so he can't see where he's going, careers into the landlord's legs where he receives a punch on his helmet and returns that punch right between the landlord's legs, which is my queue to give the landlord a crack on his skull so hard it would have felled an ox, but not this time. The landlord roars like a demented lion and comes in for the kill, only to be stopped dead when a six-foot-long metal pole wielded by two girl urchins connects to the side of his head. This time he drops like a stone where half a dozen urchins dive on top of him and start stealing anything they can from him, while trying to tear his clothes off and punching him senseless. A set of keys are thrown up into the air which I grab before anyone else can and slip into my coat pocket.

By now two of Blackmore's men have managed to escape and flee from the alley while the other four have backed up against a wall, while managing to keep the urchins at bay despite being bombarded with bricks and the odd bucket of pure. Blackmore is being dragged along the filthy cobbles towards the docks by four of the older urchins while a girl is maniacally bashing him on the head with his own helmet. It is obvious the man is completely out for the count. Head and I have brained the hard men so effectively they have yielded and sit with their hands behind their heads pleading for mercy.

Whistles blow and Clump himself storms on to the scene in front of what looks like half the plods in London. Urchins scream out, 'Scatter!" And they do, melting so quickly into the shadows you wonder if they were ever there in the first place. Order is quickly restored.

"Well, well, Inspector," beams Clump. "It looks like we got here just in time."

"To be honest, sir, if it wasn't for the urchins I fear you would have been here too late."

"Inspector I meant I arrived in time to stop those urchins from killing everyone, except, obviously you and Sergeant Head. Tell me, are you in league with those urchins?"

"Not that I know of, sir."

"Good, we cannot be seen to endorse the actions of these little monsters even if they have, this day, saved the lives of my two best detectives. Right, gentlemen, let us herd our captives back to the Yard and charge them. Where's that bastard Blackmore."

"Last seen being dragged off by urchins, sir," says Head.

"That's him done for then," smiles Clump. "Still it will save us from having to hang the swine."

"Indeed," says I. "How did you get here, sir?"

"By horse and cart."

"I mean how did you know to come here when you did?"

"A French sailor turned up at the Yard an hour ago saying his captain begs us to send men immediately to save you two. We would have been here earlier but as no one spoke a word of French we had to get a translator in."

"I don't understand. The captain set us up. Why would he then try to save us?"

Clump puts an arm around my shoulders. "Let us conflab as we head back to the Yard."

Five minutes later we are sat in the back of a police waggon with four plods heading back to the Yard. It is dark except for a lantern swinging mid-centre from the roof and very uncomfortable sitting on the hard-wooden seats, but it is welcoming all the same.

Clump lights up a cigar which quickly fills the waggon with smoke and cuts visibility down to zero before the smoke is sucked out through the tiny barred portholes in the sides of the waggon.

"This sailor told us that Blackmore turned up at the Sea Voyager knowing that the captain was entertaining you two. Blackmore told the captain he was coming aboard to 'arrest' you two on suspicion of murdering the French sailors. Which was a load of crap and the captain knew as much and subsequently refused to hand you over. Blackmore walked away but hung around the docks with the landlord and their men waiting for you to come out into the open. The captain sent one of his crew to warn 'the hairy policeman', that you two were in peril of your lives. And of course, we responded as quickly as we could."

"It still doesn't make sense, sir," says I. "The captain must have removed the bullets from our revolvers when we were asleep, effectively leaving us unarmed to meet our fate. Why would he do that and then try to save us?"

"Because he suddenly realised what a dangerous situation he found himself in. He could have been implicated in your murders had Blackmore succeeded in killing you both. While you were getting sloshed on duty, I was working over time to sort this mess out. Think of it, Inspector. Why would anyone murder those French detectives over smuggled booze? The French couldn't give a rat's arse, whether or not the Customs get their revenue, it's not their problem. There is no way those detectives where here undercover just to sort out English smugglers. They would have simply left the task to us. No, it had to be for a much more serious reason."

"It also went through my mind sir that no one would risk the gallows by murdering policemen over mere contraband goods. It had to be for a much more serious reason, but so far I have not managed to unearth a thing other than confirm that Blackmore and the landlord where in cahoots in a smuggling racket."

Clump smugly blows a smoke ring in my face. "But I have. Where did you get this cahoots word from?"

"It's an American phrase."

"Oh, colonial hey? Anyway, I contacted the French Embassy who promptly sent an official around and we had a long conversation. I must say, Inspector, what he told me infuriated me. One because they did not liaison with us as to what they were about and two because the nature of Blackmore's crimes where sick beyond belief. Blackmore has been smuggling urchins over to France on his yacht and selling them into a life of slavery."

"Why would anyone want to buy skinny smelly urchins, sir?" cuts in Head. "They're no good for much except for thieving and causing trouble."

"Ah…" ahs Clump pointing his cigar at Head. "Blackmore was cherry picking the best. Those without rickets, free of T.B. free of anything in fact. He chose the best looking, the fittest and those who were double orphans. He would then promise them a new life abroad, conjuring up a utopian ideal of family life where they would live happily ever after. Once in his clutches they were taken away to a secret location where they were fattened up, spruced up and indoctrinated into believing they were on a mission to make childless couples in foreign lands blissfully happy by becoming their adopted children."

"Which sounds wonderful," says I. "But?"

"But indeed, Inspector. Once in France the children were spirited away never to be seen again. However, the French authorities received a tip off a few weeks ago that a unique 'sale' was to be held at a warehouse close to the port of Le Harve and they raided it. Up for sale were several English and French urchins who had been transformed into children. The potential buyers were from all over; Eastern Europe, North Africa, Spain, Turkey, The Isle of White, all over. Several of these buyers were arrested, but Blackmore had already set sail back to England. These children were being sold as sex slaves to wealthy disgusting persons who prefer their meat underdeveloped. Once they were bored with them they sold them on again, or worse, did away with them and then purchased new slaves. The French authorities were determined to smash the child smugglers, and after questioning the English children they sent two of their best men over on the Sea Voyager disguised as crew to put Blackmore out of business, arrest him and take him back to France for trial. Obviously, something went wrong, and the two detectives were consequently murdered."

"I can fill you in on that, sir," says I. I tell him all that Andy had told me and then recall as much as I can remember of my conversation with the captain. "The captain knew that the landlord of the Neck Breakers had a hold over Blackmore and was blackmailing him into ensuring the booze smuggling operation went without interference from our authorities."

"You scratch my balls and I'll scratch yours," muses Clump.

"Exactly. I believe the captain told me all he knew and was truthful. But he still failed to warn us that he feared for our lives and he still emptied the bullets from our revolvers."

"You will have to go and question him about that tomorrow, Inspector. For now, I suggest we drop you both off at home as your women must be frantic worrying where you are."

"Thank you, sir."

"Sergeant," says Clump ruefully. "I noticed you were walking very strangely. Obviously, you have received an injury of some kind. Do you require medical assistance?"

"I shall be fine, sir, once I've applied the hot-cold method to the injured parts."

Clump shakes his head, "Waste of time, Sergeant. Your best bet is to rub butter over them, so they don't rub against your undergarments thus exacerbating the condition. Refrain from carnal pleasures for a week or two and all will be well."

"Thank you, sir. I shall bear it in mind."

"You do that," smiles he, tossing the stump of his cigar out the porthole and then banging on the front of the waggon. "Driver," he yells out. "Do a detour to Sergeant Head's home and then the Inspector's. Do you know where to go?"

"Yes, sir," comes the yelled reply.

Ten minutes later, Head is dropped off and shortly afterwards I am limping around the back of my home intent on entering as quietly as possible so as not to disturb Betty. Silently I unlock the back door, creep through the kitchen into the hall, kick off my shoes and creep up the stairs.

"Is that you, Detective Inspector?" sounds Betty's voice from our bedroom.

"Are you expecting anyone else?" returns I, amazed that she heard me creeping about. I enter the bedroom as light from a table lamp flickers into life and I see my beloved blow out a match.

"Where on earth have you been, Detective Inspector," she scolds. "I've been worried sick."

"Embroiled in a murder inquiry and chasing smugglers."

She gets out of bed, comes over to me and wraps her arms around me. "You stink of alcohol, Detective Inspector. Obviously, it wasn't all work."

"It's a long story," sighs I.

Betty holds me at arm's length as her eyes fill with concern. "My god what happened? Your face is all battered and bruised."

I hold her close, feeling the warmth of her body through her cotton nightgown and despite the pain in my buttock I feel the comforting rise of a part of me that thankfully is uninjured.

"Nothing wrong down there then, Detective Inspector," she frowns. "Come on let's get you stripped off, washed and into bed for a little gentle exercise."

Dawn breaks, streaming light through a gap in the curtains and caressing the soft velvety skin on Betty's back as she lays naked and face down on the bed. I am about to gently turn Betty over when there's a loud thump on the window. Bloody hell! I curse. Swinging my legs onto the floor I go over to the window and yank the curtains back to confront a splattered load of horse dollop covering half the top pane of glass. Lifting the sash up I stick my head out.

"Mornin', boss," greats Andy grinning up at me. "Look what we brought ya."

Behind Andy stand four urchins around a hand cart, gagged and bound with rope to that cart while laid flat on his back is Blackmore. He has been stripped of his uniform leaving him with nothing to cover his modesty except for a white vest and a pair of wee stained long johns. "Give me five minutes and I'll be down." I close the window.

"What's up, Detective Inspector?" yawns Betty, sitting up.

"The urchins have brought Blackmore to me." says I, pulling on my drawers over the wad of dressing Betty put on to cover the teeth marks in my buttock.

"What, dead?"

"Alive I think."

"You said he'd definitely be fished out from the Thames sometime today."

"Obviously I was wrong."

"Shall I make you some tea and toast, Detective Inspector?"

"No time, my little honey pot."

I dress quickly and forgo a wash and a shave. The quicker I take charge of the situation the less chance of the urchins changing their minds and running off with Blackmore, or worse, killing him before we've had a chance to hang him.

I snog Betty goodbye, fly down the stairs and go out to a rousing cheer from the urchins. I am flabbergasted, as stopping in my tracks I spread my arms in questioning confusion.

"You're our 'ero," beams Andy. "'Cause, of you we get to get this bastard off our backs once an' for all an' get away wiv it."

"I am speechless."

"But ya just spoke," says Andy scratching the nits on his head.

"I did, didn't I? Well lads it is a fine thing you have done this day bringing this monster to justice. He is still alive I trust?"

"Give him one," orders Andy.

One of the urchins promptly jabs Blackmore's crotch with what looks like a knitting needle, which results in Blackmore's body twitching and writhing as much as possible under the restraints of the ropes, while muffled curses hiss through a brown streaked, raggedy gag, which looks and smells suspiciously like it once covered a baby's bottom.

"He's obviously very much alive," smiles I, going to take a closer look at the 'prisoner'. "I see you've shaved off his eyebrows and sideburns."

"We did," grins Andy. "They was 'is pride an' joy."

"Excellent," says I, noting that Blackmore has been quite seriously roughed over. His glaring eyes meet mine, beseeching me to help him. He will get no sympathy from me. "To the Yard," cries I, pointing in the wrong direction.

We set off and attract considerable attention from passers-by, genteel ladies cover their mouths in shock with gloved hands on seeing a man in public just in his underwear. Gentlemen tut and frown, but the lower classes raise hats and cheer. For once it is a victory for the common man. God knows what Clump will say when we eventually wheel the prisoner into the Yard.

At last we come into the front of the renowned Scotland Yard. All manner of transport is parked on the forecourt, from awaiting cabs to upmarket carriages and several police vehicles ready to go at a moment's notice. Horses whinny to each other, stamp impatient hooves or merely stand quietly waiting. We draw everyone's attention, cab drivers and members of the public stare at us, but it is the plods and detectives milling around that suddenly lift their helmets or hats to set up a raucous cheer. Windows open, heads are stuck out and it seems as if everyone wants to join in. Obviously, news has travelled fast, and Sergeant Blackmore has become the most vilified policeman ever to draw breath because of what he has been up to.

Clump himself with the glitteringly uniformed Chief Constable Sir Roland Block, come down the steps to meet us as we come to a halt with our prisoner.

"This is a dreadful spectacle, Inspector," spits Block. "How dare you turn up at this esteemed establishment with these filthy urchins in tow and a member of uniform paraded with such derision. We shall be a laughing stock because of this. And you yourself! How dare you turn up dishevelled, hatless, unshaven and wearing odd shoes?"

"Draw ya neck in copper," spits Andy. "We'd done this any other way an' you'd a covered it up as usual." He points at Blackmore. "That bastards been selling kids inta slavery 'e 'as an' deserves the rope. Think ya self lucky we didn't castrate the bastard an' then pin 'is slabs on ya front door."

"What are slabs?" Block asks Clump.

"What are slabs?" Clump asks me.

"Butchers slang for testicles, sir," says I, wondering where the hell they're coming from while glancing down I notice that I am indeed wearing odd shoes, one brown the other black.

"You two," yells Block to a pair of passing plods. "Untie that man from that cart and take him inside, now!" He turns his venom onto Andy. "You and your filthy entourage had better run back to your flea pits before I have you slung in the cells."

"Smile," grins Andy as a bright flash captures everyone's attention.

Neither I, Clump or Block had noticed the press had suddenly appeared like vultures from nowhere.

"Inside, now," orders Block stabbing a finger at me.

"I'll catch up with you later," I whisper to Andy and follow Block and Clump up the stairs as the pair of plods overtake us while dragging a semi-comatose Blackmore along with them. Daring to look back I see Andy and his 'boys' are already surrounded by the press and rattling out their stories while no doubt demanding a fee for it.

Three minutes later I am stood to attention in Clump's office while being stared at by Block.

"You have gone too far this time. Detective Inspector Potty," growls Block.

"It's Potter, sir," offers Clump.

"What is?"

"He is," returns Clump pointing at me.

"Potts, Potter, Potty, who the hell cares! I shall have you drummed out of the force Potty and rest assured that you shall never ever wear the Queen's uniform again other than that of a toilet attendant. Do I make myself clear?"

"You do indeed, sir," says I. "Does this mean my pension is fucked?"

"Well and truly," he smirks. "You will be suspended on half pay during the time it will take me to go through the correct procedures. But do not get too comfortable. I intend to prioritise and ensure you are done with by the end of the week, which is tomorrow. Now get out of my sight."

"It has been good serving under you, Chief," says I to Clump. "Will you shake my hand?"

"Of course, I will, Detective Inspector," says he. Reaching out a hand he gives me a crushing handshake, and then steps back formally and I turn and walk away. All seems lost.

Once outside I fend off the press, for now, and head back with Andy and his friends who are taking it in turns to ride on the hand cart. Andy and I reiterate all we know regarding Blackmore and the landlord. Then Andy comes out with a revelation I hadn't thought of.

"Bert finally escaped from the cellar when 'e 'eard the commotion goin' on later when ya got roughed up. 'E'd been locked in as the key wouldn't undo the lock from inside an' 'e 'ad no way out except through the bar. Anyway, to avoid the scrap he hides under a big ol' tart's dress who was sat in a corner keepin' out of it, said it didn't 'alf whiff under there, anyway, when it all went quiet 'e peeps out an' sees ya an' the Sergeant sat out for the count an' that Blackmore take out ya pistols and empty out the bullets before puttin' 'em back."

"He put the bullets back in again?"

"Nah. 'E puts the pistols back in ya 'olsters but wiv no bullets in 'em."

"Of course, he did," says I, realising that when I took my revolver out to confront the dockers I vaguely remember it felt light. But there was one bullet in the chamber because I fired it.

"Tell me Andy, will Bert and this Sophie March testify at Blackmore's trial if they are needed?"

"They will. I'll see to it. Tell me, will we be gettin' a reward for 'elpin' catch them bastards."

"I doubt it," muses I. "But don't worry I'll see you and the others do well out of it. Trust me."

"Never thought I'd ever trust a bleedin' copper, copper, but I trust ya."

We finally part at the end of my road and as I near my house I am surprised to see Sergeant Head hobbling along beside Chloe. In truth he had gone completely out of my thoughts.

"We were just coming to see you, sir," says he as we meet and shake hands. I give Chloe a peck on the cheek and she blushes, which seems odd considering all the men she must have been with in the past. I realise the young woman is returning to the innocence she must have once had before she was forced into prostitution.

"Wonderful," smiles I. "Let's go in and have a cuppa. Betty will be over the moon to see you both."

Betty is indeed more than pleased to welcome the visitors in. She loves having company and quickly whisks Chloe upstairs to see the new set of underwear she's been saving for when I get my promotion. I haven't the heart to tell her promotion isn't going to happen while being thrown off the force is almost a certainty.

Once alone with Head we go into the kitchen where I put the kettle on and we sit at the table to chat. "How did Chloe take it when you told her about your...um...?"

"Giant swollen nuts! Nothing until I dropped me drawers. Then she fainted."

"How are they now?"

"Halved in size and shrinking by the hour. But I didn't go in to work, sir, I felt like I'd lost a fight with a grizzly bear first thing. How do you feel?"

"Not too bad," says I, and go on to tell him all that has happened since we parted last night. When I say all, I exclude Betty practicing her healing powers on my manhood despite it having escaped any injury, but like she always says; 'A satisfied man is a well man and a happy man.'

"You're telling me that shit bag Block is going to get you thrown off the force just for turning up in the manner you did. Has he no idea what we went through yesterday? The suffering, the degradation, the near-death experience of being hammered by too much booze, which we only drank to ease our pain."

"That is not entirely true, Sergeant. Let us be honest, we would have still drunk ourselves stupid regardless. It was free, it was good, and we had a laugh, we just didn't know when to stop."

"True," sighs he. "What happens now?"

I lean closer to him and offer him a choice of making a mint or ending up in prison if we're caught. He decides not to take me up on my offer as it is too risky. We shake on it and I know I can rely on him to say nothing to no one, not even Chloe.

Betty and Chloe join us, Betty gets out a fruit cake she'd made while I was out which is quickly demolished with a pot of tea before we retire to the parlour for a sherry or two.

By mid-afternoon, Head and Chloe set off home while I finally take a shave and spruce myself up. After dinner and once night has fallen I don casual clothes, a brown woollen suit, tieless white shirt, working boots and a flat cap. I slip a short jemmy bar in my belt.

"You look like a labourer, Detective Inspector," comments Betty running scurrilous eyes over my attire. "What are you up to?"

"Surveillance work at the docks, my little nosey Parker. I have to make sure the Sea Voyager doesn't up anchor and slip out of the dock."

"I don't believe you, Detective Inspector. You are up to no good, I can see it in your eyes."

It is hopeless lying to her and I tell her what I intend doing and why. She is horrified and tries to talk me out of it, even threatening to shut up shop if I even attempt to defy her. But my mind is made up. "I came close to being killed twice last night, Betty. And what shall my reward from the force be? Drummed out with no pension for our old age."

"Mr Clump will never allow that to happen, Detective Inspector," she implores.

"It is beyond his control. I have no choice but to do this."

"Do it then," she snaps. "Only you'll be doing it without my blessing." With that she storms upstairs and slams the bedroom door.

Our first fight in years I ponder sadly as I step outside into the cool air. Luckily there's a good covering of thick clouds over the moon, a perfect night for going on the rob. I set off towards the docks keeping my head down and avoiding the eyes of anyone I pass. Close on an hour later I am at the back of the Neck Breakers Arms and far enough back from the street not to be seen by anyone passing by. The pub is in darkness and I am confident that no one is inside. On the back door there's a police notice that informs the pub is closed until further notice and entry is forbidden under pain of arrest. Taking the set of keys out from my pocket I open the back door, go in and lock it behind me. There is no going back. I either get away with it or get caught.

It seems pitch black inside at first, but once my eyes have adjusted I can find my way around without too much of a problem, helped by street lamps shining in through the open curtains. Negotiating the long kitchen table and chairs I make my way through to behind the bar, go up to the till and jemmy it open. To my horror it shoots out with a crashing sound and a loud ting that echoes around a bar that feels decidedly spooky. The till is empty?

The stairs creak and crack as I make my way upstairs and into what is obviously the main living area, negotiating a suite, table and chairs I search around for a safe, nothing. I pull up a rug hoping to find a safe inserted in the floor, nothing. Bedroom one and two, nothing. At last I am in the master bedroom, and there it is standing by a double bed, a simple key safe that I am confident I have a key to. It fits perfectly, and I open the safe to find a stack of papers, several official looking envelopes, a jewellery box and a wad of notes. Taking the box over to the window I open it to find a fist full of cheap jewellery, my inner ear tells me to leave it, returning the box to the safe I shove the wad of notes in my pocket, close and lock the door. Success, brilliant. Making my way back downstairs I head into the kitchen and step on something that screeches out the most ear shattering high pitched noise I've ever heard before. The shadowy shape flies across the room, leaps up on the draining board and then slams into the window. A bloody cat! Bastard thing nearly gave me a heart attack. I am about to unlock the door when the handle on the door is suddenly rattled and through the kitchen window the unmistakable silhouette of a plod's helmet and shoulders are clearly seen. I freeze and crouch right down.

"Did you hear that, Bob?" a voice booms.

"There's a bloody cat in there, Jack."

"Poor sod's been shut up in there. We ought to let it out."

"Do what? Let it out? How you gonna do that, Jack? Break in?"

"No. But we could see if we can force open a window so it can escape."

"It's a bloody cat mate, it'll survive on mice for months and there must be hundreds about the place. Forget it, let's see if the front door's alright and then go for a pint at the Dead Eagle"

"Think of the shit, Bob. If it's left in there for weeks, it'll be shitting all over the place."

"Nah, they bury it, cats do."

"How's it going to do that, mate? Dig up the bleeding floor boards?"

By now I am becoming pretty pissed off with this dopey pair. Why don't they just clear off so I can go home?

"I'm going to try the window," says Jack with finality.

"Hang on," says Bob. "Let me see if I can pick the lock."

To my horror, I hear the sound of metal scraping around metal and within a minute the door starts to open. I quickly tiptoe into the bar and crouch down underneath the counter.

"There you go little pussy, freedom" I hear Jacks voice carry followed by the door closing.

Thank God for that, they've gone. I crawl out of my hiding place and stand up only to crack my head, but somehow manage not to cry out.

"What was that?" says Bob.

"Sounded like something banging. Just a door upstairs I reckon. We probably caused a draught when we came in."

"We best have a look around," says Bob.

'Do not look around,' I hiss to myself. 'Just piss off.'

"I'll take upstairs, Bob, you take downstairs."

"Shall we find a couple of candles to light or turn on the gas lights?"

"No, best to not attract attention, we shouldn't be in here unless we've got a good reason and letting out a cat wouldn't be seen as a good reason. We'd get into trouble for it."

I hear Jack creaking up the stairs and Bob creeping into the bar area where he comes to a halt barely inches from where I'm hiding. He's so close I can smell his crotch. He looks around while muttering to himself, then I hear the clink of a glass, a cork pop and realise he's helping himself to a drink. A couple of gulps and the glass taps down on the counter and he moves off. I hear Jack creaking about upstairs and venturing out I take a peep over the bar to see Bob's shadowy shape disappear into the snug. I am out and tiptoe into the kitchen cracking my knee on the corner of a cupboard and have to cover my mouth to deaden the swear words. 'Fuck that hurt.' I reach for the door handle just as it starts to open and the unmistakable sound of an urchin's voice hisses, "Bloody 'ell! It's open lads."

The door is slowly opened allowing me time to slide under the table.

"Nick an' Sam, You, get upstairs an' see what ya can nick. Willy, you come wiv me. Jim, you an' Dick get down the cellar and get fillin' them sacks up wiv booze. Don't take no barrels just bottles of spirits."

"I don't like spirits, Joe, I only like beer."

"It ain't for you ya prat. It's ta sell. Now get to it. Billy an' Benny you stay outside an' keep an eye out. Get to it."

I am trapped and consider my options. Once the urchins clash with the plods it will be bedlam and perhaps I can slip out without being seen. Or I could just make a run for it and trust Billy and Benny will get out of my way. I decide to run for it and am about to crawl out from beneath the table just as the door is flung open and Billy and Benny rush in, shut the door and cry out in hushed voices, "Joe! Joe! There's men comin'."

"Hide," hisses Joe's voice loud enough to carry around the pub but quiet enough not to be heard outside.

Billy and Benny run towards the bar area. Thinking clearly, I realise I must lock the door because if anyone tries it and finds it open their suspicions will be roused. I frantically do so and then slip back beneath the table. What a bloody nightmare. Christ I'm looking at ten years if I get caught. What I don't understand is why there's no commotion going on? There's no way the plods didn't hear the urchins crying out and scuttling for hiding places. Unless the plods are also hiding?

A key is inserted in the lock, the door opens and two pairs of feet enter, one booted, the other wearing shoes. I can also hear the unmistakable sound of a horse and cart coming to a halt close to the outside cellar door and several voices chatting amiably.

The one in the boots steps out the door and spits, "Keep it down you morons." He steps back in, "What now, sir?"

"You supervise the loading and keep those fools as quiet as possible while they do it. Make certain they only take what I have told you to take and nothing more. I shall be looking around the landlord's quarters for something he has of mine."

"Very good, sir," says Boots. Leaving he shuts the door behind him.

Well sometimes Christmas can come at any old time. It certainly came early this year. I am listening to the voice of no other than The Chief Constable, Sir Roland Block.

I hear a match strike followed by the flickering light from a candle as Block's feet head upstairs.

Gingerly I slide out, stand up and follow Block up the stairs as stealthily as possible. He goes straight into the master bedroom and over to the safe, one hand still holding the candle which lights up the entire room. He fishes around in his expensive tweed jacket pocket and takes out a key. Bobbing down he opens the safe and takes out the official looking envelopes and sets them down on top of the safe. The candle is pushed into a candle holder and crouching over, he starts to go through the envelopes. He has no idea I am standing right behind him. And I have no idea where the hell everyone else is until I spy a size eleven plod's boot sticking out from beneath the bed. I spy the wardrobe door is a little ajar and reason Nick and Sam are almost certainly hiding there. I pray no one will sneeze or fart before Block finds what he is looking for.

At last, Block straightens himself up, lets out a short triumphant, "Ah…" and keeping hold of one envelope hastily shoves the rest back into the safe and locks it. Picking up the candle holder he turns around and jolts back in shock.

"Good evening, Chief Constable, Sir Roland Block," says I, pointing my revolver at his heart. "I see you have found whatever it is you were searching for."

"Potty! What the hell are you doing here? This Inn is out of bounds until a thorough search of the premises has been made."

"Which is why you are here is it, sir? Searching for evidence?"

"Of course, why else?"

"How about covering your tracks by removing evidence that will undoubtedly incriminate you? Need I go on?"

His face screws up in fury. "That idiot Clump warned me you were a clever bastard, Potty. How did you know I would be coming here? Even Clump doesn't know."

"Call it intuition," smiles I, pleased to know Clump has nothing to do with all this. "I also know how ruthless the landlord of this place is. There is no way he's going to take the rap on his own, he'll take you down with him if he can."

Block shrugs, "Look here, Potty, this is how it is. The revenue bods are due to go through this place with a fine-tooth comb tomorrow. I am here tonight to make certain they find nothing. The landlord will be exonerated and released from prison, and life, except for a few changes in the way we operate, life will carry on in much the same way as it always has. We hurt no one except for the Treasury"

"Except life won't be the same for me, will it Chef Constable? I am to be thrown on the scrapheap and left to perish while you skip off all la-di-da as if butter wouldn't melt. No chance."

"What do you want, Potty?"

"Well for one you can call me by my proper name, Potter, and for two, I suggest you drop your threat to kick me off the force."

"Is that all?"

"You will also ensure that Blackmore and his associates get their just deserts."

"Blackmore and two other uniform officers will swing. The evidence the French Police have on them is damning in the extreme. There have been several arrests across France already and heads will be rolling off the guillotine before too long. Have no doubt of it, Inspector. Now will you please lower your weapon, it is very unnerving."

I shoulder my revolver. "Did the landlord know about Blackmore's slavery racket?"

He shakes his head. "No. He believed Blackmore was running illegal arms to France which were then sold on to dissidents in tin pot countries. He, like me, would never have condoned such dreadful crimes as slavery."

I believe him and know that condoning isn't anywhere near as bad as being indifferent. Even so. "If Blackmore had been trafficking children from the upper classes he would have been exposed ages ago, Mr Block. The indifference from the upper classes towards the poor and destitute in this country is revolting in the extreme…"

"They are scum, sir. Neither you or I can alter the fact and only natural progression will change the modus operando. Until that happens we soldier on, maintain the status quo, and protect our own. Now, are we done?"

"It seems so."

"Good. I shall carry out your wishes, rest assured of the fact."

With that he takes the candle and goes back down the stairs. I follow, he goes out the back door and I immediately lock and bolt it behind him, just in case he decides to send, whoever is with him, back in to take me out."

I wait in the kitchen until the cart finally goes off and then light the gas lights in the kitchen and shout out, "You can all come out now. Which includes you, Bob and Jack. Get down here in the kitchen, it is party time!"

To the disgust of the plods the urchins raid the pantry and begin to scoff everything in sight. Half a leg of ham is devoured in minutes along with two stale loaves of bread, three pork pies, an apple pie, a dozen current buns and tons of sweets. All this is washed down with copious amounts of cider taken from the bar. It isn't long before they start taking turns to go out back and throw up. During this maniacal tea party, I have the reluctant plods sitting up at the table writing up statements on paper I found in the kitchen dresser. They sign their statements, I hand them a few pounds each and allow them on their merry way, each carrying a bottle of scotch tucked under their tunics. Now I have statements from witnesses confirming that Block is as bent as bent can be, should I ever need them. Finally, I throw the urchins out having 'rewarded' each one with a pound note and they stagger happily off to wherever they stagger to. I am just locking the door when bloody Andy and his crew turn up. "You're too late," says I. "Take my advice and leave the place alone for a few weeks."

"We was goin' in the cellar," protests, Andy. "Bert's here wiv 'is key."

"How many of you?"

"About fifty."

Fifty of the buggers I groan inwardly, I can't possible allow that lot to rampage around the place they'll wreck it. I dig out the wad of notes and to Andy's amazement I count off twenty-five pounds. "Share that lot out amongst you. But promise me not a single one of you will come back here for at least a fortnight."

"How long is that?"

"Three Sundays from now."

"Agreed, thanks gov'."

They melt into the night and I make my way back home, chuffed pink that I have the chief Constable no less in my power and will be reinstated by tomorrow. I haven't got as much money as I had hoped, but I must still have at least a hundred left in my pocket, which I'll share with Sergeant Richard Head, ensuring he'll get only twenty percent as I took all the risks. As I took all the risks perhaps I should only give him ten percent? Maybe even five percent? Should I give him anything? I mean, if I had been caught I'm certain, Richard wouldn't have volunteered to do twenty percent of my jail term. I finally decide not to give Richard a thing. But then he is a good friend and I relent half way home and I decide to give him two percent. Job done.

Lightning Source UK Ltd.
Milton Keynes UK
UKHW010650100822
407113UK00003B/1106